I'm Nothing Without His Love

Lock Down Publications and Ca$h
Presents

I'm Nothing Without His Love

A Novel by *Monet Dragun*

Lock Down Publications
P.O. Box 870494
Mesquite, Tx 75187

Visit our website @
www.lockdownpublications.com

Copyright 2020 Monet Dragun
I'm Nothing Without His Love

First Edition February 2020
Printed in the United States of America

This is a work of fiction. Names, characters, places, and incidents either are products of the author's imagination or are used fictitiously. Any similarity to actual events or locales or persons, living or dead, is entirely coincidental.

Lock Down Publications
Like our page on Facebook: Lock Down Publications @
www.facebook.com/lockdownpublications.ldp
Cover design and layout by: **Dynasty Cover Me**
Book interior design by: **Shawn Walker**
Edited by: **Cassandra Sims**

Stay Connected with Us!

Text **LOCKDOWN** to 22828 to stay up-to-date with new
releases, sneak peaks, contests and more…
Thank you.

Submission Guideline.

Submit the first three chapters of your completed manuscript to ldpsubmissions@gmail.com, subject line: Your book's title. The manuscript must be in a .doc file and sent as an attachment. Document should be in Times New Roman, double spaced and in size 12 font. Also, provide your synopsis and full contact information. If sending multiple submissions, they must each be in a separate email.

Have a story but no way to send it electronically? You can still submit to LDP/Ca$h Presents. Send in the first three chapters, written or typed, of your completed manuscript to:

LDP: Submissions Dept
Po Box 870494
Mesquite, Tx 75187

DO NOT send original manuscript. Must be a duplicate.

Provide your synopsis and a cover letter containing your full contact information.

Thanks for considering LDP and Ca$h Presents.

DEDICATION

I'm blessed to have put out another book. It took a lot of hard work, and all my time, to get it finished. First, I dedicate this book to *me*, and to everyone who appreciates this dedication.

To my best supporters: thank you for being down for my books to the max and for keeping me on my toes. I especially thank you for checking on me during the times I wanted to give up.

To all my Wattpaders: you became super fans after reading my very first book ever, and I love y'all too!

Warning this urban love story is not for the faint of heart. This is what real people go through in the real world. And, I'm here to be the instigator for the emotions these characters portray.

Enjoy,
Monet Dragun

ACKNOWLEDGMENTS

To: my deceased friend, whom I won't name. You were so strong, and it was you who gave me the green light to write this story.

To: little girls, and women of all ages who have been abused, I want you to know *we hear you, and you have a voice*. If my friend could find the courage to tell her truth, I pray this story encourages you to do the same.

PREQUEL

Fall 2002
UNKNOWN

"You won't get away with this. Your family's money won't get you out of this one! I love you, and you know I do! One thing you can't take from me is my unborn child! That's something you'll never be able to have." When I said that, Cain lost it and I watched as the spark flickered in the chamber of the gun... *POW!* Cain's trigger finger went wild.

He shot me in the chest causing smoke to escaped from the chamber. Shot me like a dog in the street, like I was nothing. My eyes traveled down to the hole in my heart as blood ran down my chest like an overflowing river. My body slumped over and I began to gargle up blood, allowing the tears to escape my eyes.

Cain grinned in satisfaction. "I loved you but also hated you at the same time. You were my world."

"Cain, you're going down for this," I whispered right before my eyes closed.

"Oh, Lord, who should I put the blame on this time?" Cain sung to himself, as he wiped the bloody knife on the white cloth and tossed it on my face.

Everything seemed to move in slow motion and the last words I heard were, "Oh my God Cain what have you done!"

That night ended with a gruesome scene. There was no way to rid the pain he would put upon others because of my mistakes. I couldn't absorb what he was doing anymore. I failed her, and now Cain was going to torture her just like he had done me. His eyes couldn't leave my immobile body, however, I wasn't dead yet. As I faded in and out of consciousness, I heard a door slam.

Our entire relationship had been sweet and sour — as he'd stated: One's love, was supposed to last forever. That's how demented Cain was. There was no escaping his wrath.

PROLOGUE

When Innocence is Snatched

Summer 2010
Kamilah Smith

As I rode quietly in the Lincoln Town Car Limo, a wide smile spread across my face as my house came into view. *This was the best birthday ever!* I thought. I was eight years old and mom had surprised me with a trip abroad to visit my grandparents. The trip was awesome because I was showered with love and received tons of gifts. However, after being there a week, I was more than ready to get back home. And as much as leaving London made me sad, getting back to Atlanta made me happier than anything in the world. I missed my dad and I couldn't wait to see him—he was my favorite person in the world and he was my hero.

The limo turned onto the U-shaped cobblestone driveway and pulled up to the double glass doors of our house. Ours was the biggest on the block. It was a real life Barbie Dream House with so many rooms, I could play hide and seek all day and never run out of places to hide.

I was so excited to be back, and I could hardly wait to show off all the stuff grandma and grandpa had bought me. *Bliss is gonna love it,* I thought.

Hearing mom call my name, I quickly turned my head towards her.

"Kamilah, stop daydreaming and come on here," she said, as she hopped out of the long white car.

With hair that hung past her shoulders, and smooth pecan-colored skin, my mom was beautiful. She was always dressed to impress, and she made sure my wardrobe was a reflection of her fashion etiquette. She walked with a model's stride and her backside poked out just like granny's. Daddy said she had a lot of junk in her trunk.

"Stop that before you scuff your Dolce & Gabbana sandals," she said, looking over her shoulder at me, as I skipped on the stoned pathway. "And baby how did you get your dress so wrinkled?" She shook her head in an irritated manner. I shrugged my shoulders and continued towards the steps.

"Kareem, make sure you don't drag my Louis Vuitton luggage, dear."

"Yes, ma'am," the driver said, lifting the luggage higher in the air just to please my mom. She was always bossy that way, and by now Kareem, and everyone else, was used to it.

"Mom?" I called out as we walked through the grand French doors. She turned towards me smiling as she responded with a *yes dear*.

"Is it okay for Bliss to come over? I miss her and I wanna give her the doll granny got for her," I said, twirling in my dress with my head slightly tilted to the side.

Mom laughed and nodded. "Sure honey, but first I want you to get changed. Arline has dinner already for you so I want you in your jammies, hair washed, and ready for bedtime. Then, I'll give Bliss' mom a call to ask her if Bliss can come over for a sleepover."

I jumped in excitement. I kicked off my jelly sandals and ran into her arms. "Yay, thank you, mommy!"

In the middle of my excitement, I heard my dad's deep southern voice, echoing, as he came up from his den. Chatting with his brother, Uncle Cain, they were debating sports like always.

Uncle Cain towered over my dad by a few inches. His build was like The Rock's, and he sported a goatee with a mustache. He was the spitting image of my dad, but the way he looked at me frightened me.

My dad was handsome. He resembled a black version of the movie actor, Orlando Bloom, except he had a beard, and a short fade haircut with waves. You would think he and Uncle Cain were the same person because they looked so much like twins. Even though dad was much nicer than Uncle Cain, I loved them both.

"First of all, I'm not about to argue with you on this. The Falcons are better than the Saints any day! We can make this bet more than once and you'll still lose, Cain. Give it a rest, bro." Before Uncle Cain could combat my dad, I screamed my dad's name so loud, I think I startled him.

"Daddy, I missed you so much!" I squealed in excitement as I ran full force toward him. Dad planted little kisses all over my face causing me to giggle uncontrollably.

"I missed you too, shookums! Did you have a great time with your mom and grandparents? I'm sorry I couldn't go. Dad had a lot to take care of." Flicking dad's bottom lip, I smiled from ear to ear, as I nodded my head up and down.

"We had a great time, Daddy! I got gifts and we visited so many places. My favorite part of the trip was dancing on stage with granny. It was so much fun." I smiled.

"That's good sweetie."

"Asim, she looks just like you, man, just with long curly hair, and dimples like her mom. So adorable," Uncle Cain said.

"Aren't you going to say hi to your uncle?" my dad asked me. When he put me down, I clenched his leg tightly. Don't act shy now, Milah," he said.

"Hi, Uncle Cain. I did that move you showed me," I said, waving a hand at him bashfully. With a funny look on his face, he gave me a crooked smile. Mom seemed to stare at me knowingly as her and dad exchanged casual talk.

"Wow, Cain, you never smile. Look at your niece making you show your soft spot," mom cooed. Uncle Cain shrugged.

"I guess she does Sharon, what can I say?" he replied, with his eyes glued on me.

My heart skipped a beat and I hid behind my dad's leg, peaking at my Uncle Cain. He was beaming with happiness which made me feel funny inside. I wasn't used to seeing him this way because he was always so serious and straightforward.

"Well, now that you talked to your dad, go on upstairs and get ready like mommy told you. I talked to Bliss' mom and she'll be dropping her off soon."

I was so glad when my mom told me to go upstairs because my uncle had been staring at me the entire time, and it was the same giddy look he'd give his girlfriends, and I didn't like it. I did my happy dance and released the grip I had on my dad. I turned and took off running up the stairs as quickly as my little feet would carry me.

***

Soon, me and Bliss were playing with dolls in my playroom. We had already eaten pizza and we were dressed in our jammies. Since it was a sleepover, we hadn't heard much from my parents. I guess they were treating me like a big girl since I was eight years old now. It was summer break, so dad had convinced mom to let us stay up a little past our bedtime to eat junk food, and watch Disney movies all night. Still, something was weighing heavily on my mind, so I decided to ask Bliss about it.

Turning to face her I asked, "When you came in did my Uncle look at you in a funny way?"

She looked at me curiously as we lay on the blanketed pallet my mom had laid out for us. "Um, no not really. What are you talking about? He's mean. He never pays us any mind."

I sighed and poked my lip out. "Well he—" There was a light knock on the door before it squeaked open, causing us to stop talking.

"Hey, sweeties," Uncle Cain said, as he popped his head in. I gulped hard. Uncle Cain always smelled good, so his scent hit our noses quickly. He pushed the door open and entered my bedroom. Even though mom had been against us eating sweets before bed, I noticed his hands were filled with candy.

"Hi, Uncle Cain," I said, as a nervous smile crept across my face.

"Hey, Uncle C," Bliss said, with her mouth stuffed with cheese puffs. He smiled and waved at us, placing his index finger in front of his lips. Bliss turned her attention back to *The Princess and the Frog*. I was about to do the same, but Uncle Cain cleared his throat and gestured me over to him. Eating the last bite of my pizza, I stood up from the fluffy bean bag chair and walked slowly to where he stood.

"Yes?" I asked. Bliss continued to giggle at the movie and paid us no mind. He kneeled to my level and smiled.

"I have a surprise for you," he said. My eyes grew wide with anticipation.

"Really, what is it?" I asked with excitement as I clapped my hands together in glee.

"You have to come with me, okay? And then I'll give it to you."

I frowned with a pouted lip. "But my sleepover," I said swaying back and forth. I looked back at the movie and then at my friend.

"It'll be quick and you're going to love it. I promise. Does Uncle Cain ever disappoint you, my lil' Kamilah?" he asked sweetly.

"No, I guess not." I smiled and he patted my shoulder.

"Okay then, let's go. Bliss she'll be back in a minute." Bliss looked at him, then me, and frowned. He grabbed my hand and led me to the door.

"Bliss, we can rewind the movie when I come back, okay?" She nodded but didn't say a word, and the look on her face showed her disapproval.

I figured she'd be okay once I got back, so I followed my uncle out of my room and to the third floor of the house. The room he took me to was a room my father had never allowed me to go into. I wanted to resist, but he was my uncle. His grip on my wrist grew tighter as we got closer to the room.

Once we were inside, I looked around and saw all the gifts he'd bought me. A huge smile appeared back on my face, and I began to feel at ease.

"Wow! Is all this for me?"

"Yes, baby girl, it's all for you." I ran over to the gifts and grabbed them and proceeded to tear them open. During my excitement, I suddenly realized my uncle's footsteps growing louder behind me but paid it no mind.

"Oh my gosh! You got a doll that looks just like me. This is cool!"

Holding the doll in my hand, I spun around in delight and was met with my uncle's tall frame. The smile he once wore was gone and his laughter had stopped. His expression was stern and serious, evil looking. He had unbuckled his belt and the zipper on his pants was down. He moved toward me, closing the space between us, and allowed his pants to fall to his ankles. I stood frozen in place as I watched him stick his hands inside his underwear before pulling them down. My stomach churned and I was in absolute fear of what I was seeing.

"You know I love you, right? You're uncle's little sweet pea, right?" I couldn't answer. I was frozen, and by now the doll had fallen out of my hand, to the floor. Uncle Cain kicked it to the side.

Next, he picked me up and sat me on top of the table. His hand went under my chin as he raised my face to look at him.

"Uncle Cain, w-what are you doing? Please, put me down. I don't wanna play anymore. I don't wanna be here, I wanna go back to my room," I cried.

He placed his hand over my mouth, squeezing tightly. The look in his eyes was so evil and mean, I wanted to scream but couldn't. I didn't want to be there anymore. All I wanted at the time was to be in my mom and dad's arms.

"You're going to do what Uncle Cain says, okay? Do you hear me?" I shook my head *no*.

"Let me go, Uncle Cain, please." I cried. I tried so hard to push him away, but I wasn't strong enough. I was just a weak little girl.

The man I loved and called Uncle was touching me where no one was supposed to touch me. Mommy had told me not to ever let anyone touch me there because it was bad. Trying to fight and pry his hands away from my pajama pants, he grabbed me around my neck, making me gag.

"Did you fuckin' hear me? You are going to do what I say. Do that again and I'll make it hurt worse." I stopped moving and became still.

His hands grabbed at my pajama pants before going inside them. I nearly screamed but he jerked my head back. My eyes began to water and I opened my mouth to yell for my dad, but no sound escaped my lips— it was as if my voice was gone. And I knew he would hurt me. *Where is mommy and daddy? Why did they let him stay here?*

Then the worst thing that could happen happened… Uncle Cain grabbed my small hand and placed it on his private part.

"Now rub up and down on my penis just like this," he coached as he guided my hand up and down. "Don't stop till I say so, okay Kamilah? You're such a naughty big girl."

No longer able to control them, the tears began to trickle down my cheeks faster and faster. I could feel his private part growing bigger and harder. I didn't understand what was happening. The pit of my stomach felt queasy as I felt this awful pain shoot through me. I cried out louder when I realized my Uncle had stuck one of his fingers inside of me. My body trembled with fear I had never felt before and my pants became hot and wet. The noises he made caused my ears to hurt and it scared me even more.

At the young age of eight my innocence was being taken from me. I was no longer a little girl anymore. I was a big girl, but I didn't wanna be. When he forced me to open my mouth and moved my hand away from his private part, all I could do was stare at the dark corner where a teddy bear lay looking back at me.

"Stick your tongue out and lick it. Lick it just like you do those lollipops you like so much." I began to cry harder as he jerked my face around, trying to pry my jaws apart.

"Do. It," he said through clenched teeth.

I closed my eyes and stuck my tongue out, doing as I'd been told. As my tears continued to fall, I felt lost, unprotected, and hurt. Who was going to believe me when I told? Someone I hoped. With my eyes closed tightly, I allowed my mind to go to a happier time and prayed it would be over soon, as Uncle Cain moaned and groaned.

God, please help me… I'm only eight years old.

CHAPTER 1

The Monologue of Cairo Black

Present Day

What is this thing? Do you know what I'm talking about? Oh, you don't? Let's just have a short conversation about what this thing is. Okay? A young boss like me shouldn't have to struggle at such a young age. You feelin' me?

Yeah? Okay.

Well, I'ma just go 'head and give it to you straight and uncut. For starters, this ain't your average love story 'cause my life won't ever be considered average. Life and love are an equal part of the human race, but trust me . . . the opposite sex can do the type of damage that can never be fixed. But still, it's what keeps us goin'. Hell, in this day and age, women and men don't even know what *love* is really about. What I want you to know is everybody ain't got it easy. Shit, you can be the best person in the world and one person can fuck your whole life up forever. You wanna know, right?

Yes.

Okay, this thing, this thing is called *life*— in other words, a particular type or aspect of people's existence. What is *my* existence? I wish I knew. I wish we could all know that. Wait, before I go on and on about how hard life can be, first, let me introduce myself. My name is Cairo Black, African-American male, nineteen years old. I'm just a country boy from New Orleans, trying to figure out my purpose in this world. My life ain't perfect, far from it. Life can be filled with vitality, vigor, or energy, even mine. Half of the time I'm depressed, and to be completely honest with you, it's hard for me right now. So, let me gon' tell you the story of my life.

My life consisted of bullshit. It was either school, drama, no money, no food, or no clothes to put on our backs. Ya' feel me? The fact that me and my brothers ain't have no father in our lives was the worst part of it all. My mother was the only provider me and my brothers had.

It wasn't easy for her to deal with three male egos in one household, tryna teach us to stay out these streets so the streets wouldn't eat us alive. We had to come to terms in the ghetto, and in a damn hurry. But when the ghetto streets got ahold of my big brother, my mother vowed to put her foot down as mother and *father*. See, things in life don't always go like we plan. Life is a big ass ball, seemingly a cycle of the same anonymous bullshit.

This thing called life is weird for me and that twin brother of mine. You're either well-off, rich, or in the pits. You still there, right?

Yes.

Okay, good.

There's this girl, and shawty bad as fuck. She rich with hella' stacks and grew up with that old-money type shit, ya' feel me? She gorgeous as hell. And believe it or not, I'm her side nigga. But I shoulda listened to my brotha on this one. *Why degrade yourself to be a side piece?* I remember him asking me. Well, anyway, she said me and her would never work out because of our *different* statuses. But, still, she had feelings for me, or so I thought.

But, today, right now? I gotta tell her was'sup. I won't be a woman's secret no mo'. No man or woman should ever feel less-than on account of somebody they care for. That shit gon' stop today, ya' heard me?

Looking at myself in the rearview mirror, I checked myself over, hoping to see what I was meant for in this world. Then, it hit me. I was human like everybody else, and damn, a man got feelings too, ya' dig.

***

I pulled up to her crib, located in the nice part of town. Taking a long deep breath, I coached myself on what I was about to do and say. I knocked and waited for her to open the door. It was amazing. I mean, damn, I was so into shawty. The sound of her footsteps coming down the steps were even beautiful to a nigga. If truth be told though, ever since I'd started playing this wicked game of hide-and-seek with Brianna, it seemed like God had been testing me. I knew it wasn't right and it had to end. For a while, she had been the girl of my dreams, but shit changed when I realized I was being sucked dry.

Hearing her stop at the door, her voice filled my ears. "Who is it?" she called out. Her voice was smooth like silk, but sexy and raspy when it was time to do the thing I loved.

"It's Ro," I replied, using my nickname.

The door flew open and there she stood, looking so good and gotdamn fine. Shawty was five foot three with mocha-brown skin, an oval-shaped face, and sculptured cheek bones. Her eyes were upturned and brown, and she had naturally full lips—not the manmade kind from injections and shit. With a slim hourglass-figure, her C-cup breasts sat high and perky, just the right size for her gun-holster hips and round bubble butt.

Licking my lips, my eyes finally met her gorgeous face. She grinned and wrapped her arms around me. But, Brianna was made of pure venom, just poison wrapped up in a tiny body. When I inhaled her scent, I almost lost it.

Snap out of it Ro! Snap out of it Ro! I chanted in my head as I tried to play it cool. *Act normal*, I coached myself.

"Oh, uh, hey. We need to talk," I said, sounding like a damn schoolboy.

She was the only girl who could make me feel that way, like what the fuck? Her face dropped as she pulled away from me, simply nodding her head in response, as she let me in. Taking a slow breath, I didn't dare glance at her face twice. She twisted her hair around her finger, as the gum she chewed popped multiple times, making me cringe.

Trekking into the crib, I was in awe at the grand entrance of the home, even though I'd been in there more than once. Shaking my head at the elegant furniture, my body floated to the couch, and I sat down.

After she closed and locked the door, she sashayed her short frame over to me. "What is this about? The college thing again? Cairo, come on? Just go with what your heart feels. You don't have to go with your twin," she said, as she sat down next to me.

"Nah, I'm past that. My brotha ain't got nothin' to do with this, a'ight," I said with an aggravated sigh. "Listen, Brianna. We can't do this shit no mo'. Shit, I'm tired of the games and all the sneakin' 'round. I wanna real woman who gon' do anything fa' me, not a woman who feels the need to hide me. Somebody who gon' ride for me. And you clearly *not* that woman, ya' feel me?"

She looked at me and nodded. I knew she didn't care. She didn't care about shit, other than herself. "Okay? And?" she said with a low eye roll.

This hoe think she cocky and poppin'. I looked away from her for a quick second and scoffed a laugh. "Well, I'm not yo' damn secret no mo', ya' feel me?" I said sternly.

Brianna waved me off and crossed one leg over the other. Then, she spoke up with enough sass to make any man lose his cool. "Listen, bro, I know you ain't catch fuckin' feelins and shit. You knew I had a man when you was tryna' holla. I came on yo' dick when I needed it, and when I didn't', I was fuckin' my nigga. So, why are you even here? I obviously don't need you, and besides, I already got what I wanted out of you. So you can dismiss yourself, Cairo. It's just that simple. Period. Point blank. You was just the side piece, lil' boy."

I looked at her like she was stupid. Lie, all she did was lie through her fuckin' teeth. I had stooped down to her level long enough and I was done.

"Oh, so that's the game we playin' now? You think you that bitch, huh? You was all on my dick way before I gave you my attention. Bitch, you was sweatin' my nuts like a fiend. Don't play with me 'cause I'm not gon' kiss yo' ass. Bitch you got me fucked up. I didn't give two fucks about your nigga and neither did you, Brianna. Don't forget how you gobbled on my fuckin' nuts like you hadn't ate in days. I, for damn sure, wasn't sweatin' yo' skinny slut ass! Not to mention, you busted it wide open for me every time you hit me with that late-night text, right? Mane, I'm out. Don't hit my line when you miss this dick down yo' throat."

"Don't worry, I won't, I can get dick anytime," she said, and chuckled sarcastically.

"Hoe shut yo' dick-suckin' ass up. And next time yo' nigga kiss you, ask him how my fuckin' dick taste! Thirsty bitch better ask about me," I mumbled as I stormed off. I flicked her off and left.

Just forget about these hoes and keep ya' mind on ya' money and school. Just that simple. Just let things flow. The right girl will come to you, I thought as I made my way back to my car.

CHAPTER 2

Family

Kamilah Smith

It was finally morning was and I didn't know what to do. It had been a long day of practice but I couldn't do this anymore. I had to run again, and, maybe, when I ran away this time no one would find me. If I could slip away that would be the best for me right now. I had to get from under him somehow. The boy who was in my bed had been a waste of my time. He couldn't even last long and luckily dad and mom had left a little earlier than usual. *Thank God neither of them knocked on my bedroom door to let me know they were leaving.*

"Orlando, get up. You need to bounce, nigga," I said aggressively, while standing by the bed. He turned over and rubbed his eyes like he'd been having the best sleep of his life. I rolled my eyes.

"Now, nigga. I don't have all damn day," I said, shaking him to wake his ass up. He was still sound asleep, so I grabbed the pillow and slapped him hard across his face. Startled, he jumped up out of his sleep.

"Damn, Milah! What the fuck, shawty! Why you do that?" he asked, a dumb look on his face.

I grabbed his gym bag tossing it at him so I could sneak him out of the house and hoped the nosy neighbors wouldn't see him, or worse. *Yo' ass was 'sposed to be gone a long damn time ago,* I thought. "Man, getcho ass up. We fucked but you lucky I let you spend the night. You not special so get your shit and go. I got things to do today and you slowin' me down, so come on chop-chop."

I kept the same stale expression when Orlando stood up with his junk hanging out semi hard. He tried to give me that sexy look that usually got my panties wet but that lame shit wasn't't gonna work this time.

"Come on, babe. Let me do that tight muthafucka again," he said, biting his lip.

"Hell nah. Move out my way. You bust too fast any damn way, nigga. The shit be over the minute you slide it in. It's a damn disgrace to have a big dick and can't even use it right." I laughed.

"Man, fuck you. I had yo' ass screamin' in this bitch though."

"Fake. Now get out. You didn't turn me on one bit."

Before he could say anything else, the sound of my door being unlocked made my heart jump. I tried to grab my shirt and slip it on but the door flew open too fast, and there stood Cain. Now I wished my parents *were* here.

"Uncle," I said nervously.

"Don't *Uncle* me. Lil' nigga, you better put yo' shit on right now and get the fuck out before you end up missin'. Say anything about being in this house with her and you gon' definitely be cut up in pieces," Cain yelled.

"Okay, sir!" Scrambling to get his things, Orlando bolted past Cain but never took his eyes off me.

"So this is what you do? Have sex with all types of men, huh?" When I heard the tone of his voice, I tried running for the door. "You not leavin'! Sit yo' ass down right now!" he ordered.

I could smell the liquor on his breath even though it was still morning. This wasn't good, and my body turned cold as fear engulfed me.

"Do it and I'll beat the fuck out yo' ass," he said, as he gripped my wrists harshly.

"Okay." I walked over to the bed and sat down. *I should've known this would happen.* Before I could beg my way out of it, his strong fist struck my face repeatedly.

"Cain, please, I'm sorry," I said, trying to guard my face with my hands. It was no use, and at that very moment, I knew I would be there forever and never get out from his reign.

Cairo Black

After dealing with a woman like Brianna, a nigga needed to blow off some steam at the gym before heading home. Feeling frustrated, I sighed and rubbed my hands through my braids.

I pulled into my ma's driveway and turned the car off. I reached in the backseat for my Nike duffle bag, pulled it by the strap, and slung it on my shoulder before hopping out of momma's Honda Civic. I locked the doors with the key remote and jogged up the path to the front door.

It had been a long day, but fortunately, today was the last day of school. Graduation was right around the corner, and hopefully, my baller abilities would help me secure a bright future. Growing up in the hood, choices were limited, you either studied hard to be book-smart or practiced your ass off to perfect whatever talent you possessed in sports. Since my momma was still struggling to provide for us, my brother and

I had started saving up for some of the things we'd missed out on growing up. Besides, he and I had plans of going off to college — we were gonna become successful and make momma proud.

After pulling out my house keys, I let myself in. My nose was met with the delicious smell of southern food being cooked, and I could hear momma humming her favorite song. I was in heaven. My nose followed the smell as I made my way toward the kitchen. Dressed in a long teal and coral-colored sundress, she stood in front of the stove, with a cooking apron tied around her. Her short hair was slicked down and she was completely barefaced, free of any makeup.

Connie Black was her name and she was a hardworking woman who loved to throw down in the kitchen. Being a pure New Orleans native, her cooking skills were second to none when it came to authentic Cajun and Creole foods. All black women in the south loved their kitchen like they loved their kids, and if you messed with either, you were asking for a beatdown.

"Hey, Momma. I'm back," I said, standing in the doorway of the kitchen.

"Hey, Baby. Where you been?" she asked, as she looked over her shoulder in my direction.

"I just had to handle somethin', that's all. Nothin' all that important," I said with a shrug. *Handlin' Brianna wasn't a big deal at all. At least it's not anymore,* I thought.

"Oh, okay. Well some mail came for you and your brother. He's out there playing basketball with some friends," she said, in her thick New Orleanian accent. She lifted the heavy-looking pot lid and peeped inside the boiling pot.

"Thanks, Momma," I said, and gave her a quick peck on her cheek.

I sat my keys on the table by the door and grabbed the white envelopes off the countertop.

"Morris Brown, Morehouse, and A&T Colleges," I said, reading the words in a soft tone.

Quickly shuffling through them one by one, I found a thick, black and purple envelope addressed to me. Choosing the envelope from Morris Brown, the college that had been my top choice, I licked my lips in anticipation. I took a deep breath and tore it open with my index finger. As my heart thumped hard against my chest bone, my eyes followed every line:

Dear Cairo Black,

Congratulations! It is with great pleasure that I inform you of your acceptance to Morris Brown College, Atlanta, GA. You have been given this opportunity in recognition of your academic and sportsmanship achievements. As one of our top three eighty-thousand dollars basketball scholarship winners, we welcome you as a student and team player, all expenses paid.

I yelled out in excitement and jumped up and down like I had lost my damn mind. Hearing the pots and utensils dropping all over the floor, I tried to keep my composure but couldn't.

"Momma, I got the scholarship! I got it, Momma!" I ran over to her and hugged her and then picked her up. I was so overwhelmed with joy, I sounded like a five-year-old who had just gotten his first bike.

"You did?" she repeated, with a smile that matched mine.

I nodded my head up and down like one of those bobblehead dolls. My mom's eyes were filled with happiness, but she didn't seem as surprised as I was. I lowered her to the floor and folded my arms over my broad chest. With my head slightly tilted to one said, I stared at her with a smirk on my face.

"You saw the envelope, didn't you?" I asked. She tried to play it off by hugging me tightly.

"I'm so proud of you, baby. Did you see the envelopes that came for Rome?" she questioned. Her eyes were filled with tears of joy.

I walked over to the other side of the counter and looked through the mail a second time. There was so much mail I couldn't believe it had all come in one day. After tossing several pieces of junk mail—*boom!*—there it was. Another black and purple envelope, except this one had my brother's name on it.

"I hope he got in too," momma said, "that would make my day."

As soon as the words left her mouth, the door opened and Rome walked in beat boxin' and dancin' to the music playin' through his headphones.

"'Sup, fam," he said, walking into the foyer area. He sat his ball and bag down, and a loud *thump* followed when he kicked off his basketball shoes.

"Bruh, I got in," I shouted.

His eyes lit up and he pulled me into a brotherly hug. We pulled away, then it must've dawned on him. And I guess Rome's sudden frown was due to the thought of me leaving him since we were so close. Afterall, we were twins.

"For real?"

I nodded and handed him my letter but hid his behind my back. He browsed the letter in awe unable to contain the grin that crept up on his face.

"Dang is this for real, dawg!"

"Yeah, mane. And peep this, an envelope came for you too." He looked at it and his eyes grew huge with anticipation. I licked my lips anxiously and my brother mirrored my actions, a habit both of us had.

Jokingly, I asked, "You wanna wait and open it or—"

"Hell nah, I ain't waitin', bruh! I'm 'bout to open this joint right now," he said in an animated tone. He smiled nervously. He walked over to the stool and sat down and ripped it open anxiously.

"You coulda waited on me, bruh," he said dramatically.

"My bad," I replied. "Once I had it in my hands I couldn't wait, mane," I admitted.

He ran his finger through the paper and grabbed the thick letter. My heart felt like it was on fire as I waited for him to read its contents. I rubbed my sweaty palms together and crossed my fingers, hoping he'd receive the same news I'd received just minutes prior.

He pulled out the paper and I watched impatiently, as his eyes darted over each sentence from start to finish.

"Lord, Son, read the thang already," my mom said, on pins and needles.

"What it say, bruh?" I probed in a tone louder than intended.

"Well, it's saying my grades were exceptional but—" Rome said as his voice deepened and trailed off. He looked so heartbroken. He shook his head and his body slumped with defeat.

"What?" I said, my voice eager. His tone was giving me the chills. He looked up at me and his eyes were watery which told me everything I needed to know.

"I didn't get in. I know I worked hard enough to keep my grades tight. Man, why didn't it just pay off? God!"

My heart almost broke in two, and my mom didn't take the news lightly either. Looking at her, I could see the tears being held back.

"Oh, Son, I'm so sorry," momma told him.

He turned to us with a big ass grin on his face. "Sike! I got in with a full ride! We made it, man!"

I fanned him off, pissed that he'd played us like that. "Rome, man, you play too damn much. You 'bout to get momma all upset for nothin'. That was petty, bruh."

"Don't play like that, Son. You scared me half to death," my mom said. She pretended to frown but couldn't help from laughing at his humor. "Boy," she said, as she reached out and popped him upside the head playfully, "you oughta be ashamed of yo'self foolin' me that way."

"I'm sorry, Momma. Gimme some love. My bad, bruh." Momma shook her head and rolled her eyes.

"It's cool, fool." I laughed, grabbing my brother in a playful headlock. Then, we embraced one another long and hard. I had the brightest smile on my face.

"We in there, nigga," Rome said, cheesing like a chess cat.

"We in there, boy," I echoed, as we dapped one another then dapped again and again.

I had the brightest smile on my face. I couldn't believe me and my brother were finally gon' be able to make something of ourselves, especially since some of our family ain't get that chance. Plus, the best part was we would be going to the same school.

***

My brother and I walked down to the basketball court, near the park, not too far from the crib. Yeah, we didn't live in the middle class part of town, the neighborhood wasn't that bad for the ghetto but sadly that's because I was used to this hood shit. Anything could happen at any moment, but we wasn't never scared. Even though we were known around here, we still had to be careful.

Niggas could be overzealous and eager to pull the trigger in these streets. They didn't care if you was an A-plus student, jock, mother, or child, a bullet didn't have no name on it, and once that trigger is pulled, ain't no stoppin' it—somebody was bound to get shot or killed. But me and my twin had dreams to fulfill and the hood couldn't take that from us.

I had the ball and Rome pushed open the gate. "You ready to get schooled, bro," he said with a laugh.

"Man, please." I pushed my hat backwards, as he wiped off the bottom of his shoes.

"So? Did you talk to little Miss Prissy Brianna?" he asked, with a raised eyebrow. I nodded as I got in position with my body slightly low. Hiking up my basketball shorts, I checked the ball to him. He bounced it a couple of times, crossed it over, then dribbled it between his legs.

"Did you talk to her, or *talk* to her? And, you know what I mean by *talk*. You didn't talk with ya' little Peter Wacker, did you?" He burst out laughing.

I cut my eyes at him and frowned. "Man, you always playin'. I cut her off completely. Like, for real. I'm gettin' back to the old me. No more playin' games with her ass. She was high school. It's time for me to start focusin' on basketball and college. I ain't meant to be in no relationship 'cause these girls don't want me anyway. As the wise Chris Brown stated, *'these hoes ain't loyal'*, and, that's the end of it."

He looked at me like I was crazy and checked the ball to me again. I checked it back and he tried to do a crossover. I was on him like white on rice. "Bruh, where you think you going?" I laughed.

He smirked, took a step back, and made a three-pointer shot. "Three to zero. And, you know all the girls want you. I'm ya' twin so we look exactly alike. If they don't you, they mean they don't want me. And if that's the case something must be wrong with they eyes 'cause we both fine, bruh."

I laughed and grabbed the ball from him and took it to the hoop.

"And, that's two to three. Plus, you got a point. For the first time ever, you got a point." Rome mocked me and nodded.

We continued to talk trash to one another and continued to play basketball. I was glad to have a brother like him. A twin was good to have, although he wasn't the only brother I had. We had a special bond and we were pretty much one and the same.

Shifting to the side with the ball, Rome dipped backwards and shot a free throw. "Aye, bro, I whooped ya' ass," he said, after the last shot. He popped the collar of his tee shirt, gloating on his victory, but he knew it was a tie.

Before I could debate, our phones buzzed, indicating we had incoming texts.

"Yo', Pootie Fat Coochie James is having a kickback party since this the last day of school before graduation. You tryna roll?" I asked, "'cause I am."

Rome smirked and I knew he was down to pull up on shawty.

"A'ight, let's go home, get fresh, then we'll be out. They finna' know what's brackin'. Shawty just sent the address in a group message," I told him.

He smiled and dapped me up causing me to shift the ball under my arm. "A'ight, first one home gets the ugly bih'," he said and laughed.

I looked at him and shook my head. He was always thinking of simple shit. Laughing, I rubbed my forehead and nodded in agreement.

"And, go," we said in unison. We took off running like cheetahs, making a fast getaway home. I was gon' win this bet.

We were young niggas, and the only thing on our minds was shawtys and pussy.

Kamilah Smith

I was sitting on the edge of my bed, listening to the *My Dear Melancholy* album, by The Weekend. Rummaging through a pile of clothes, I was picking out the things I wanted to take with me when I went off to Morris Brown College. I was extremely excited to be going to a HBCU for dance.

I sighed as I sat in front of the closet swaying my legs back and forth. Just sitting there staring at all of my clothes, I found myself lost, lost in my own world. Everything was so misconstrued in my life.

My phone buzzed a couple of times, causing me to snap out of my short daze, when the vibrations made the phone slide closer to my thigh. I looked at it. A smile crept on my face as I examined the messages. It was a couple of text from my best-friend, Bliss, and a few likes and comments on Instagram. I tapped on the message from Bliss first because I knew she would definitely put me in a better mood, and I needed that right now. I felt so off and weird, but negative thoughts only brought negative issues, so I tried to suppress it.

Bliss: Bitch! r u coming down to the NOLA to Pootie's party? I'll cover for u. u know how ur mom and dad r. Damn I mean ur dad. Sent 7:34 pm

I sighed and sent a message back. Depression was a constant battle within my life, and I didn't know how to justify it.

Me: He'll never find out. u know I'm down.
Let me get ready. Sent 7:36 pm

I got up from my comfortable bed and closed my laptop. My search would have to be placed on hold until tomorrow. Since I'd always been an honor roll student, I deserved a break here and there. My phone buzzed again as I planted my feet on the plush furry carpet and stood up from the king-sized bed. It buzzed over and over again. I tried to ignore Bliss' overwhelming texts, but the phone buzzed repeatedly. Shaking my head, I looked at it and read it:

Bliss: Girl? I know u hate when I ask this but u r 18 now. How long u gon' keep this secret? All this sneaking around is so lame. U can only do this for so long. Feel me? – Sent 7:38 p.m.

I didn't bother responding. I was tired of this too. A bitch was sick and tired of being stuck in this horrible skin. I hated everything about my life. Everyone thought my life was perfect, but it was far from that.

Going to therapist after therapist, I rebelled on each one. I wasn't the one paying for it, so I didn't give a damn. Nothing they said mattered to me anyway, and it damn sure didn't change the fact that Cain was still terrorizing me.

All I knew how to do was get men and have sex, which stemmed from having been exposed to sexual abuse at a young age. And it's what I used to self-medicate to numb the pain I felt on a daily. I wasn't brain washed by Cain he just terrified me in every sense of the word. It was sad. I pitied myself everyday trying to determine self-worth, but there was nothing around me that ever made me truly happy. My happiness had been taken from me on my eighth birthday. Sex and drugs was all I'd ever know. The only person who would find out was my father, I couldn't risk that. There's no telling what would happen.

My father monitored everything I did by forcing me to go into programs, charities, and fundraisers. He wanted me to be boujee and full of myself. I just wanted to have fun, keep being a bad bitch, and do hoe shit from time to time.

As my mind drifted off to how my life was going to pan out, there was a small, rapid knock on my bedroom door. Sighing lowly, I treaded softly over to my bedroom door. The text from Bliss had made me so mad I wanted to scream at whoever was at my door. *Can't I just be left alone,"* I thought, as I reached out to grab the doorknob.

Opening my bedroom door, my eyes landed on a brand-new pair of Versace Medusa Head velvet black loafers. Once my eyes landed those familiar shoes, I instantly regretted opening this door anywhere. My heart collapsed to the pit of my stomach, as he stood on our applewood floor. *Why did I even open the damn door?*

Cain was tall as hell. He stood seven foot one with a strong build. His face was chiseled like he was made out of stone, and his freshly shaved face was groomed with a sharply-trimmed goatee. His eyes were dark green like a snake's and his hair was wavy and short and tapered on the side. You couldn't tell he was biracial, and the man was evil.

His enormous hands rubbed together as the veins on the top of them bulged. My heart skipped once, then twice, and I felt like it would jump out of my chest at any moment.

He had sexually assaulted me more than once, even when my parents were home. This damn place had never been safe for me, ever. But as always, whenever he was in my presence I just wanted to die rather than suffer from the pain. Nothing in this world would've made me happier than never breathing again. If Cain killed me, at least my soul would be at peace.

My small hands shook as I took a step back, and it didn't take long for me to feel eight years old again. I wouldn't allow my eyes to look in his sinister face. My mouth was as dry as the Sahara desert, as I swallowed hard trying desperately to speak. Slowly my eyes traveled up to his exposed, slightly-hairy chest which was visible through his silk Versace shirt. My bottom lip quivered as his hand reached out to me. I jumped back, away from his reach causing his face to flash with anger.

Suddenly, he flew towards me and grabbed me around my neck before squeezing tightly. I gagged at his demented face and his grip became even tighter. I could feel my face growing hotter as my body winced in fear. I tried desperately to move out of his grip, but he was faster than me. I shook as my body stood completely frozen.

From my head to my toes, fear was the only thing running through my body. No one wanted to believe me, no one. They knew what I was I going through but refused to help me.

Like a slithery snake, his tongue ran over his smooth, light-pink lips.

I opened my mouth to speak and began to stutter. "Cain, pl-pl-please. Why did you come in here? Just leave!"

Cain smirked and pushed me further into my bedroom. His deep voice rang out as he spoke. "Honey drop? I used the spare house key, *remember*? Now, I'm here in your bedroom and you're going to give me what I want," he said in a cold whisper. I began to tremble, I thought I had taken all the spare keys and threw them out. *Mom or dad just had to put one around, damn them.* I wanted to scream as he rubbed his hand up and down my arms.

"Cain, you said you would never do this to me again. You promised me if I didn't say anything, the sexual abuse would stop. Please," I said, my voice trembling. He let out an evil, heart-wrenching laugh. I took a few steps backwards which caused me to trip over my own feet. When I had backed into the edge of my bed, there was nowhere else for me to go. "You didn't keep your promise. Now look at you, your parents didn't believe shit your little whore ass said. So now I'm going to punish you. My lil' Milah, you shouldn't believe a man with a crooked smile. I came here for what I want, and what I want is you, my honey drop. Don't. Say. Another—" He shoved his hand into my velvet shorts and my body became stiff. He pulled me closer to him and huskily said in my ear, "—Word, or it'll hurt even worse, Kamilah. Disobey me and you won't be able to walk tomorrow."

Tears poured from my eyes and stained my face. When he pushed inside me I could feel his nails tearing into my skin. Then, everything became nothing more than white noise.

My body ran cold. I prayed it would end. It *had* to end, how much of this could I endure?

CHAPTER 3

When I'm With My Clique

Kamilah Smith

As I lay in my bed, I hated myself for letting that monster do this to me over and over again. Still feeling him inside me, I quickly grabbed my pillow, clutching it as I tried to stop myself from crying. The toilet flushed and the bathroom door, connected to my bedroom, opened up allowing the fresh hot steam to come out with. Cain stepped through while zipping up his pants. The sound of his thick belt rang in my ear as I cringed in fear. The smell of weed brushed across my nose as his footsteps got closer to the edge of my bed as he grabbed my foot yanking my body closer to him. Cain paused as he took a slow drag from the blunt. I could feel his eyes peering down on me as I tried to hush my cries.

"I don't understand why the fuck yo' ass layin' there cryin'. You did this shit to yo' damn self. Now get the fuck up and clean yaself off," he shouted. He threw a wet rag at me like I was an animal, or better yet his slut. Sniffling, I pulled the warm wet rag off my shoulder and sat up slowly.

"Hurry the fuck up. I'm not playin' games with you, Milah," he hollered, as he slapped my thigh hard.

Trying to move quicker, I grew angry. "Shut the fuck up, I'm moving as fast as I can," I said under my breath, thinking he wouldn't hear me. I ran the rag across my chest and that's when he hit me.

SLAP!

"You little whore! Don't you ever fucking disrespect me like I can't hear yo' dumb ass! Don't make me beat the fuck outta you," he yelled, as he punched me repeatedly in the side of my leg and ribs.

I screamed out from the pain. Then he grabbed my jaw tightly and snatched me toward him. My entire body trembled. The look on his face was one I'd never seen before. Cain had never hit me before and I didn't want it to happen again.

"You want to end up fuckin' dead, layin' in a ditch somewhere or floatin' in the damn lake, huh? I can make that shit happen! Nobody won't ever find yo' body. So if you don't wanna be beat to death I suggest you watch your fuckin' tone with me! Do you fucking here me, Kamilah?" Trembling in his hands, I quickly nodded my head up and down.

"Open you fuckin' mouth and talk before I put something in it! And I know you don't want that, do you?" I shook my head again but quickly opened my mouth.

"No. I don't, Cain, I hear you and I promise. It won't happen again." He cut his eyes toward me, but this time I didn't dare make any eye contact with him. I just sat there with my knees cradling my chest. I felt so dirty. I wanted him to hurry and leave so I could scrub the filth of him off me.

Taking sweet time to get dressed, he halted his movement. I slowly looked at him from the corner of my eye as he dug his hand deep inside his pockets to retrieve something.

"Oh, this shit for you. Here," he said, while tossing two bills and a tiny plastic bag at me. The bills floated down on the crinkled bed sheets.

My eyes watered at the sight of the forty dollars and crack rock on my bed. "What am I, huh? A cheap forty dollar slut?" I asked.

He chuckled as if I'd said something funny. "Go finish cleaning yourself up and take a load off. But don't smoke that shit up too fast now. That's your reward, baby girl. And I left the duffle bag with the stuff in it. You already know how much money I'm expectin' back, so don't disappoint me. Listen there will be consequences if I don't get my shit, use that fat ass and titties to get my fuckin' money and sell my drugs. You hear me?" I nodded and replied *yes*. I didn't want him to put his hands on me again.

He proceeded to pull on his shirt, and afterwards, he grabbed his belongings. Before he left, he made sure to plant a dry kiss on my forehead. Chills ran down my spine as his flesh touched mine. I kept my eyes planted on the teddy bear at the end of the bed as Cain made his way out.

The moment I heard the downstairs door slam, I felt a slight weight lifted off my shoulders. My hand shook as it stretched out to grab the money and drugs. I just needed to be in my happy place. I could hear my phone chime as I grabbed me a seat at the edge of my dresser top. Glancing over my shoulder, I could see Bliss' name roll across the screen.

I picked it up and answered her call. I quickly tapped the mute button since hearing her worried voice made my heart ache even more. Grabbing the rolled up bill in my free hand, I snorted the thick powder up my right nostril. I held my nose as I breathed in heavily. Taking in the toxic drug made me feel lightheaded, but it felt so good. Hearing Bliss call out my name, I unmuted the phone and let the coke settle through my entire body.

"Girl. What the fuck? You was supposed to be here already." The tears began to run down my cheeks and the silence over the phone made me weep even louder.

"Are you okay? Is he there again, Milah?"

"He just left. P-please, just come over, Bliss. He did it again and I don't know how much more I can take. I'm using again," I said through agonizing cries.

"Babe, I'm on the way. Just hang tight and I'll be there in less than five."

Rocking back and forth I couldn't say much. All I could do was mumble, "Okay."

Bliss hung her phone up and I threw mine on the bed. I could feel my heart racing as the drugs began to kick in. However, all the drugs in the world couldn't take my pain away.

Cairo Black

I was in my room looking for something to wear to the party when my brother burst through the door. Something must've been really funny because he cracking up while he stared at his phone.

"Man, Rome, I'm tryna' get ready. Whatchu want?" I groaned from inside the closet. My eyes were set on my jean jacket and a pair of jeans.

"Damn, you ain't gotta minute to say hey to yo' bro?" Since me and my brothers all sounded the same, I didn't realize it was him until I turned around. Keith towered over me as he stepped closer to me.

Face wise, Keith looked different than me and my other brothers. His hair was braided going back, and I hadn't seen that hairstyle on him in years. His beard was longer since the last time I'd seen him, and his face had more of a muscular structure to it than usual. He looked like me, except a much older version, but he favored our father the most. My twin and I favored our mother, with a touch of the man who helped birth us.

"Sup' bro? When you get here?" I questioned with excitement, as I gave him a brotherly hug.

"Not too long ago. Business is business, you know. But, who you 'bout to roll up on?"

I laughed at his facial expression, as he tapped on my gear with his index finger. My mom had bought my twin and me a new pair of shoes, so I pulled those out too. Mom still loved it when we dressed alike as if we were still five.

"Well, me and Rome 'bout to go to Pootie's little kickback party," I said with a shrug. When his phone rang, he nodded and turned his gaze toward it before sending it to voicemail—something Keith always did whenever he was spending time with any of us.

"Now you know damn well Pootie don't have no little kickbacks. That hoe 'bout to have the whole block wildin' out. But, cool. Oh yeah, I almost forgot to give you this stack for making it into college, bro." He tossed it at me, and I dropped everything in my hands to catch it.

Looking at it, this time, the money was bigger than usual. It had two or three rubber bands around it just to keep the money intact. "Damn. bro, I can't take this."

"Whatchu mean, man? You and Rome my little brothers, and y'all done worked too damn hard to stop now. Y'all did something me and pops never did. And I refuse for my lil' brothers to go down the same path I did. 'Cause these streets will chew you up and spit you out. No joke. Sometimes, I wish I never did what I did 'cause gettin' locked up changed me. But, I gotta provide for mine the only way I know how, you feel me?

But now that y'all leavin' for school, I gotta' watch over mama double time. I'm glad y'all ain't fall into the same trap I fell into to get that money. Real talk, hustlin' is just as addictive as anything else out here in these streets. As the oldest, I just did what I had to do to provide for us when dad skipped out. But, on the real, I'm proud of both of y'all, man. Word is bond. So, you take that money and put it towards a car or spend it. It don't make me no never mind. Do what you want, it's yours, bruh. I bet you got hella money saved up anyway, don't you?"

Smirking, I nodded my head up and down as Keith dapped me up. Taking one last look at the knot he'd gave me, I stashed the money away with the rest of the money I had. "Thanks bro, I'ma repay you back for all you done." My brother was good to us and I was lucky to have him.

He shook his head. "No need to. You fam, so, that's good enough. And, I put mama some money in her purse just to keep her afloat, you got me? Don't go dry snitchin' either."

I nodded. "So, when you get baby girl, Layla, pregnant? Don't you got enough kids?" He gave me the screw face, and all I could do was laugh. He pulled out a photo of her, just to show how big she was getting.

"Man, it was about a month ago, I'm a family man, I want a whole tribe, bro, but she ain't gone let me keeping getting her pregnant like that." I laughed with him.

He stood up and stretched. "Well, I'ma let you get ready. A nigga tired and I'm tryna get some sleep before ma' start buggin' 'bout Layla. Plus, I gotta be out in them streets later on tonight." He stepped to the door and was about to walk out.

"Bruh, wait a minute." I called after him before he could leave out.

He turned around and looked at me. "'Sup?"

I sighed. "I want you to be safe out there, ya' dig?"

He nodded and gave me the peace sign. I shook my head and proceeded to get ready.

I rolled on some *Old Spice* deodorant and sprayed some *Polo* cologne over my undergarments since a nigga had to smell fresh. Then I pulled on my clothes. After doing that, I tied my bandanna around my head and fixed my braids to hang just right. Looking in the long-length mirror, I turned from side to side. "Damn, I look fresh." I cheesed at my reflection and put my jacket on, along with my gold chains. Standing over my dresser top, I opted to wear my diamond earring.

My brother knocked on my door, making me look off to the side. My face scrunched up as I slid the earring in my ear. Looking at him fully, my jaw dropped, and I flicked him off. "Mane? Why you have to steal my outfit?" I said and burst out laughing. Rome did the same, as he looked me up and down.

He did a pose and ruffled his curls, then reached his hand out while doing the same to my braids. "We twins, we think alike. Turn to the side, be my mirror." I shook my head and put a little money inside my wallet.

"Oh yeah. Keith hit you too, huh? Yep, and remember you get the ugly bih 'cause I beat you. So give me my money and let's roll out." He gave me a face and fanned me off. Grabbing my round, dark-shaded, gold-rimmed sunglasses, I slid them on my face.

He reached into his back pocket and pulled out his wallet. "You cheated, bruh. But here, damn." He pulled out a twenty then shoved it in my hand, causing me to cheese harder. "Thank you kindly."

He shook his head and chuckled a laugh. We walked out of my room together and headed out of the house. Tonight was going to be a great night.

Soon, we'd be over the party life and off to college, taking the HBCU by storm.

***

We pulled up to the party and the place was packed, just like Keith said it would be. The definition of lit was not going to suffice. "Damn. I knew Pootie's family was rich, but gotdamn! I know a lot hunnies gonna be out tonight," I said, rubbing my hands together. Pulling off my sunglasses, I slid them on the end of my jean jacket pocket. The New Orleans weather was perfect this time of night. We found a park and checked ourselves out in the sideview mirrors.

"Shut up," he said, smacking his lips. Rome's tone was bitter. The look on his face said everything, and I could tell he was still pissy about our bet. Rome loved fine bitches, but due to our bet the only bitches he could pull tonight were the *wanna-be-bad* bitches a.k.a. ugly as shit.

Opening our car doors, we got out. "Don't get mad, get glad," I said, slamming the car door behind me. He flicked me off as we walked up to the gates.

We were on the rich side of town, so the security guard looked us up and down before buzzing the gate doors open. Trekking up the steps, I dapped him up and smiled as we made our way to the entrance.

Once inside, the girls began to flock to us, and all eyes were us. The music was bumping, and the vibe was chill, but I wasn't really the dancing type. I kept it simple, tapping my foot to the beat while bobbing my head to the music and what not. Rome, being the showoff he was, hopped on the dance floor and began doing one of the latest dances. Looking across the room, I spotted the most beautiful specimen I'd ever seen, and I knew I had to talk to her. Her hair was long and blonde with brown roots, and her body was on point.

"Aye, bruh. I'll be back," I said, making my way through the crowed dance floor.

He laughed and dapped me up. "Oh, you tryna pull that bih' ova there?" He looked, and before he could say something, I dipped.

"Yeah, Mr. *'I don't need no broad!'*." I heard him shout over the music. I fanned him off and continued making my way through the crowd, over to her. I knew my brother had a point, but she was just too sexy to pass up. No way was I about to let her get pushed up on by some lame. She was dancing with her friend, and they were both sexy as hell. Approaching her, I thought of the corniest line to bag her. "'Sup, my name Ro, mind if I holla atchu. Mm-mm, 'cause you fine as hell, girl. Make me wanna drink yo' bath water."

The girl and her friend turned around and both burst out in a fit of laughter.

"Hold on, I'm just kiddin'. My name is Cairo, but you can call me Ro. And your name is, pretty lady?" I asked, extending my hand. She started to blush as she reached out, allowing me to grab her hand. Therefore, I kissed it.

"Hello, my name is Milah, and this is my best-friend, Bliss."

She smiled and waved at me while holding the red plastic cup. Her friend seemed mad chill, but she didn't say a word as she sipped out of the Solo cup and gave me a head nod.

"Nice to meet both of you. Can I get a dance or somethin', ma?" She bit her lip and looked at her friend, as if asking her friend to let her have this one moment. I knew what that was about and figured her friend didn't trust her to go off with some strange nigga. But, come on? The way the two of them was looking at me, they just had to know me by name. I was the most popular guy in school.

"Yeah, yeah. You can have her number too," her friend, Bliss, said while laughing. She walked off with me and we danced together for the rest of the night. I even got a kiss from her. She was gon' be my next main if she played her cards right. How she got inside my head was beyond my own control.

"Damn girl, you got me feeling some kinda way. What you doin' to me?" I asked, whispering into Milah's ear. Pressing her face against mine, she grinded against me hard. I didn't know what to do. Holding her close to me, she spun around and pecked me on my lips a second time.

Damn, her lips soft. I grabbed on her booty and she definitely didn't try to stop me. I could tell she'd had a few drinks, and maybe even a lil' smoke, so I didn't push too much. The song changed as we danced body-to-body.

The other teens were drinking and dancing, and everybody seemed to be having a good time. The house was lit! But, my attention was focused on Milah and nobody else. I could tell she was one of those girls who seemed to be popular. I had never seen her at school, or maybe I had and just didn't remember. Then again, maybe it was because my mind had always been on Brianna. But that shit was a wrap. Over. Done. Finished. Fuck that bitch, wasn't no more of that shit.

Milah leaned her head in closer towards mine and pressed her lips against my ear. "You gotta girl?" she whispered softly, "'cause I'm not tryna deal with no crazy-ass female poppin' off ov—"

Before she could complete the sentence, all I heard was the sound of po-po shuttin' the party down. I looked up and my brother was coming toward me full speed.

He grabbed my arm once he got close enough. "We gotta go, man. We can't get caught up in here."

I nodded, and quickly slipped a piece of paper in Milah's hand and planted a kiss on her cheek. I always came prepared, so I already had my name number written down.

"Five-0 in here hot! Get y'all shit and bounce. Y'all know damn well a bitch got warrants," Pootie yelled. She was the first one to dip through the moving crowd.

"Gotta go." Milah waved as the lights flashed down on us. Bliss, her friend, pulled her away by her elbow as I watched them go in the opposite direction.

We left the party and made our way home. It was girls like Milah who gave me some type of hope. Girls like Brianna made it hard for perfect girls like Milah and Bliss.

"I saw you and ole' girl. She was dancin' on you heavy, like she wanted to fuck," Rome said, as we cruised down the street. "She was bad too, bruh. Shiit, I was with a damn grizzly bear with onion breath," he added, referring to losing the race.

I laughed hysterically before replying, "Yeah, shawty was all that. I hope I see her again. Hopefully she'll call, 'cause I wanna get to know her better."

CHAPTER 4

Netflix and Chill

Cairo Black

Two weeks after the party, it was finally time for graduation. Here we were preparing for our departure from the nest. Grabbing all my essentials, I threw them into one of my suitcases. Rome was slacking and really getting on my last nerve. So, I called out, "Bro, are you packing now or nah'?" I looked at all the new stuff my momma had bought us for college. She had got us a gang-load of news clothes, shoes, and necessary items. She knew how to spoil us, even when we begged her not to.

Rome finally yelled back as he pimped walked into my room, causing me to shake my head. "Yeah, man. Did ole' girl call or text you? I actually spoke to her after graduation. She a cool jawn. And, you know I should beat yo' ass mane. That big girl from that kickback won't leave my ass alone," he said, running his hand down his face. Then, he pulled out his phone to let me examine the stalker messages she'd been sending him.

I shrugged my shoulders and laughed. "You know big girls need love too." I started laughing harder and slapped my knee to be extra. All Rome could do was give me a stale face.

"But, in all seriousness, she ain't even hit me back after the party or nothin'. I even hit her up and I was left on *read*. Shawty did me so wrong, but it's cool though. I'm a find betta." He gave me that *yeah right* face, and I shrugged.

"Cairo , you got a feel for that girl, don't you? I saw how you was lookin' at her at the party. Plus, you was grabbin' all that booty she had. I gotta admit she was very *bootyful*." I couldn't help but laugh out loud especially since Rome was laughing so damn hard.

"You crazy, man. Really? *Bootyful?* Of all things, you say that? But, for real, I don't think I'ma see her again. I just feel like we from two different worlds. And I won't blow up no female's phone, it just ain't gone happen bruh," I said with my full, unbothered accent. Rome was about to say something when our mama stepped in the doorway.

"I want y'all to get everything packed, so you'll be prepared. Okay? I can't believe you two are leaving the nest. Every time I look at you two, I see babies," she said with a sweet smile.

"Okay, Ma. And we gonna always be your babies," Rome and I said at the exact same time. She giggled and shook her head, trying to shake off the emotion that consumed her.

"My two babies leaving the nest. Say it ain't so," Momma said. She tried to hide her tears, but they were all too visible.

"Ma don't cry nah'. You supposed to be our soldier. You can't sho' no tears. You know we love you, always will. You gonna make us cry and we can't be cryin' like no punks. We gon' come back to visit. You know that momma," Rome said.

I consigned with a smile, and we all joined in on a group hug.

"I know you will, Son. I'm just so happy you two made it. I'm so proud of y'all and your dad would be proud too." She kissed us both on our cheeks and then ruffled my thick curls. "In addition to that, I want y'all to stay away from those lil' hussies too. Y'all know they just after my basketball babies." She pinched our cheeks, causing us both to suck our teeth.

"Ma stop that," I grunted with a laugh.

She pulled away and fixed her outfit. Taking a deep breath, just like that, she snapped back into the Wonder Woman she truly was. "Well, I'm off to work. Y'all be good, ya' hear? And do not mess up my house, I mean it."

We both nodded, and she headed out.

"C'mon bruh, let's get this done, so we can chill," he said.

Rome had brough all his junk in my room so we could pack together. As we continued to pack, my phone chimed a couple of times. Pushing the clothing items around, he passed me my phone.

"Well shit, thanks," I said sarcastically since I had no intentions on answering. I stopped what I was doing and focused my attention on the phone.

Milah: Hey, I'm so sorry I took so long to get back to u. U were on my mind. Do u mind if I come and see ya? - Sent 4:12

The frown on my face quickly turned into a smile. "Man, ole' girl just texted me," I said, showing him the text.

He chuckled and said, "That's what's up. Let her come over. Momma, ain't home and you know Keith don't care. And tell her to bring her cute friend too. It's our last weekend before college so let's live a little." Chuckling, I shot her a quick text message, letting her know she could come by. I sent my address then tossed my phone down.

"I know you ain't over there cheesin'?" Rome said, looking at me side eyed.

"I ain't," I said, and wiped the smile off my face.

He laughed and shook his head before patting me on the back. "Yo' nose so wide open, I can see a path to yo' damn brain. You so damn backwards, bruh. One minute you don't want nobody, the next you walkin' 'round all goo-goo gaga for the girl from the party. I knew you liked her. I'll be back," he said, before walking out of the room.

Did he just call me sprung? No the fuck he didn't. My nose ain't wide open. . . How can it be wide open when I don't even talk to shawty? I sat down on my bed and thought about my brother's words. Was it true or not? Did I really have feelings for this girl after one look? A guy like me was never supposed to feel this way. Ever.

"You is, nose so wide, you can smell da' Georgia peaches!" Keith chimed in, cracking up as he walked past my room.

"Shut up! I don't even know that girl like that!" That was all I could say, 'Cause I didn't know her like that, but I wanted to know her. I toyed with my braids and debated on texting her to tell her not to come. But, I pressed against the thought. There was no harm in talking and being cordial.

My brother strutted back in my room and plopped down on my bed, right next to me. "Sup fam, why you got that look? What you up to?" he questioned. Then, he put his index and middle finger together and pressed them against his temple. Next thing I knew, his other two fingers were against the temple of my forehead. This nigga had his eyes closed and said, "Twin telepathy, twin telepathy."

"What in the entire fuck are you doin', Rome?" I slapped his hand away. "I swear, you can be weird as hell sometimes. How are you my twin anyway?" Next, he began rolling around on my bed, cackling like a hen in a fit of laughter. "Oh, you can't live without me, mane," he said, snapping his fingers.

But, here I was still stuck, shivering slightly. "I'm just confused. You already knew that from your *twin telepathy*, right? Always on a nigga dick man." I asked while typing away at my phone.

He looked at me with a perplexed look etched across his face, then backed away from me while holding up his hands. "Awh Lawd! My twin brother, sus! You comin' out the closet on me!" he yelled dramatically. I just gave him a snarled lip he was just getting on my nerves. Looking around for the closest thing near me, I threw something that was on my bed at his head.

"Shut up with that stupid shit! I ain't on the low down or no shit like that. I'm just confused about Milah. You know. . . the girl who's about to come over."

He nodded. "Of course, I know who she is. I was just playin', bro. For real," he said, chuckling. "Hell yeah, I know shawty a fool. She bad and she seems cool but is she trustworthy? That's what you gotta' think about, bruh."

I nodded as he got up and walked out of my room, pulling up his pants. My phone vibrated and my screen lit up. I looked at it and smiled.

Milah: We just pulled up. - Sent 4:20 pm

Exhaling deeply, I closed my phone and smoothed out the wrinkles in my shirt. It was time for me to give myself a pep talk. Grabbing my phone and sliding it into my back pocket, I got up from my bed and made my way downstairs to open the door. I wondered how this evening was going to play out. I pictured Netflix and chill. But, this wasn't the first time me and Milah had linked up. Rome had suspected something from the way I was acting, but he was about to find out the truth right now.

Kamilah Smith

Me and Bliss pulled up to Cairo's house. It was just across the way from where my house lay dormant. His house was nice and looked to be in a cozy area. My life made his look small. It actually made me smile when I realized how down to earth he was. I was truly sick of boujee Richie Rich folks. Those were the only people I found myself around. It was draining, and to be honest, I hated my life. Absolutely dreaded it.

Bliss turned the car off and turned her focus toward me. "Are you ever gonna to tell him, Milah? How many times you gonna sneak out here to see him on the low? You know your dad, man. If he ever found out, I don't know what would happen. I'm glad I won't have to cover for you no more since we both headed to the same college. If you like this dude, why don't you tell him? You don't like the dude you with now anyway. I hate to see you go through this. It's all your dad's doin'," she said. I kept my attention on the parked car in the driveway. My eyes were burning, holding back tears, as I thought about what Cain had done to me yet again. And now I had to listen to Bliss run her mouth about what I was doing. She was giving me a headache. "We're not dating, B, so chill. I don't even like him like that. Okay? So, stop bringing that up. All we doing is gettin' to know one another." Bliss breathed heavily. This was a conversation we'd had more than once, a conversation I was tired of.

The look on her face unapologetic. "And, how is Ken gonna feel about that, huh? Just tell him how you feel and stop stringing him along. And maybe, he'll stop stringing your heart along too. I know your circumstances, your pain, Milah? I know what he did to you. For God's sake, you're my damn sister and I wish, I just wish I coulda stopped what he was doing to you. You don't have to do this to forget your pain." I huffed and folded my arms.

Ignoring her I said, "I don't have to tell Ken anything. Kenneth made his damn choice. My father made his choice when he forced me and him to be together." Bliss rolled her eyes as she swayed her head back and forth.

"This is not the Kamilah Smith I know. You're strong. I know you are strong so don't let this break you. Fix your open wounds. You can't keep faking like you're someone else for the rest of your life, Milah. You need to break this vicious cycle, sis. It's not healthy for you, Kamilah. You're already on medication and going through therapy. Stop pushing the ones you care for away. You need a clear mindset, and you need to let all the negativity go. Fuck Cain! I hate that bastard for everything he's put you through."

Even though she was right, I tried to block out what she was saying. Biting my lip nervously, I placed my attention out the window. I felt like my body was going to explode internally, and it was breaking me even more.

"This is who I am, Bliss! I can't even be *myself*! I am *Milah* and *Kamilah*! I've been controlled my entire life. When can I say enough is enough? I can't. I'm stuck because no one will save me. This guy? From the first time I laid eyes on him, I felt something— something I've never felt before. He made me feel things no other guy has ever made me feel. Can't you just understand that? Bliss, can you just process that for me? You know me so you know it won't last. I'm fearful of guys who fall in

49

love with me. My past won't let me trust them or love them back. Just allow me to be happy while it lasts."

Bliss kept her mouth shut and looked at me. "So, how many people are you gonna hurt to prove this shit? How long are you going to keep hurting yourself, Milah?"

I shook my head. I didn't want to hear this. But knowing, Bliss, she would keep pushing until she felt she'd gotten it through my thick skull. So I said nothing.

"Kamilah, just listen to yourself? You deserve happiness after everything you've been through. You need to forgive and forget. Remember, you can't keep your pain bottled up."

"Whatever. Either you're coming or leavin'. I'll find my own ride back home," I scoffed and got out of the car.

"Just get out the damn car, you big baby. Just know you can't keep doing this."

I nodded. "I know that."

She smacked her lips and walked over to me on the driver side of the car and gave me a hug. Soon we walked up to the door and knocked. A few moments later, the door open and the most beautiful man stood before me.

"Milah, right? Well, I'm Rome, Ro's brother. Obviously, you can see that since we twins. Don't call his corny ass Ro though 'cause his name is Cairo. He on the couch right over there. Ohh? Who this be? Hey, you sexy thang you. What's your name, ma?"

"Rome let them in," Cairo yelled from a distance. Yo' pickup lines whack anyway! You already tackled me to get the damn door!" he shouted.

I laughed and Bliss stared at Rome smiling. "Pepper spray," she finally responded, "that's my name. And for the record, I like girls and not scrawny, corny niggas like you," she told him.

Rome toppled over in laughter.

I nudged her shoulder and she shrugged. "Don't mind her," I said, "she's easy to crack. Don't believe what she says either. Bliss is strictly dickly. Oh, and it's nice to meet you again, Rome."

Bliss gave me the side eye. Rome nodded with a smile and bit his lip while staring at her. Opening the door wider, we walked in. I looked around and my eyes landed on Cairo.

"Girl, I'ma call you *Blistex*, cause, ma', them lips look too soft." She turned and giggled. But, she had the nerve to talk about me, even though she was completely right. Everything Bliss said about me was right. I wanted to use and abuse guys all because of what one man had done to me all these years.

"See, told you, Rome, I told you she was easy to crack." I laughed and walked over to Cairo. His brother closed the door behind us and followed us inside.

"Hey, the artist formerly named as Cairo," I said playfully. He looked over at me and gave me a smile.

He got up from his sitting position and stretched. Then he leaned in and gave me a hug. His scent was intoxicating, and his strength was tantalizing. I took in his scent for a while longer, as it was sending me into heaven. His hand rubbed my lower back, and at the same time, his soft lips opened to whisper in my ear. "So, did you come over here again to chill, *or Netflix* and chill. I missed you and I wanna know how long we gon' be a secret? I don't wanna be yo' secret, Milah." I laughed and so did he, even though he was serious.

Cairo was right about one thing, and I could tell through his thick rough voice, he meant what he'd said. *He was on to me and he'd figured out I was keeping him a secret.*

"Well, Ro, I'm not what you need right now," I said, snapping myself out of his trance. He still held onto me. I had no intentions on letting him go either. I needed this. "We c-can chill, just chill." I bit my lip. I wanted to do so much with him, plus, why not? I was already what everyone thought of me anyway, a whore. Why not do the only thing I was good at doing? It was also going to be my last time seeing him, so why not go out on a limb?

I was going off to Morris Brown College and never looking back. Bliss said forgive and forget. *But how could I, a young teenager, do that when I had been burned and scarred more than once? I was sure of one thing, my father wasn't sending me off to an Ivy League college— that was never going to happen. I wanted to be enrolled as a faithful black student to an HBCU. Even though I was biracial, It was just time for me to embrace who I was, a beautiful black woman.*

Cairo's deep-accented voice captivated me, snapping me out of my thoughts. "You good? You sho' you just wanna chill, ma'?" he mumbled against my neck. The slight feel of his breath sent chills down my spine. Usually, I was the one in control, but he had this weird hold on me. We hadn't even pulled away from our hug.

"Nah,. we can do more than chill." Bliss was right. I couldn't keep doing this. Using people to make myself feel good. Although it wasn't healthy, people didn't know my story. I needed to live my own life. After this, Cairo was never gonna see me again. And all he'd ever have known would be the *Milah* who had never given him her all.

CHAPTER 5

Think Like a Female?

Cairo Black

My mind was reeling with thoughts as I lay in my bed, with my hands behind my head, just staring at the ceiling. The ceiling was off-white with the annoying sharp dots. My eyes were zoned out as I thought about her. To say I *missed* Milah's touch was an understatement, to say I missed her in general was crazy. That day she came over was tantalizing, it hadn't been the first day either. The feelings that transpired from Milah couldn't be described. The fondness I had about the way she was acting was beyond me. I don't know if it was something I'd done, or if it's just that women like playing dudes—meaning, they simply wanna *fuck and duck.* Then, they choose not to have any kind of contact ever again.

Don't get me wrong, men do the same thing, but I wasn't with that. If I had genuine feelings for a female, I was going to let her know what was up. But, I wasn't going to do that to Milah anyway. We hadn't even had sex. Sure, she had given me some bomb ass head. We were young, and it had been the last week before going off to college. Why not live a little? Milah was a wild soul. I just never thought she'd be the type to cut me off. She did it though. I don't know what I did or what I said, but when she did it, it had cut deep.

I really wanted to go all the way with Milah, just straight thinking like a male. How many times would I continue to allow these females to straight dog walk me? Shaking my head, I wanted to kick myself. The sound of a click rang in my ears. I shifted my eyes to my door as Keith walked in with swagger. He stood silent for a moment as I swung my legs over the edge of my bed.

"What you ova' there gazin' bout?" he asked.

"Man, nothin' really."

Keith's lips twisted to the side as if he didn't believe me. He did a slow bop to my bed and took a seat next to me.

"Kind of walk was that?" I asked, laughing.

"It's the walk with the slow bop, player. You heard me?" he said, in Bruh Man's voice from the ninety's TV show, Martin. I burst out laughing and tried to catch my breath. It was honestly hilarious because that was one of his favorite shows.

"Nah', but what's wrong for real? You look like you got something weighing heavily on ya' mind? Is it 'bout ole' girl? Or school?"

I sighed and nodded truthfully. "Both, to be honest with you. Yeah, she played me, yo'. I don't know what it is with me and these females."

Keith bobbed his head. "Yeah, all she wanted to do was the gawk-gawk double-twist slurp-spit 3000, huh?" That was Keith's version of head. "She just wanted the pipe and that's all." He tried to contain his laugh but I stale-faced him. I was being serious and here he was making corny jokes.

"Shit ain't funny yo'. Keith, we didn't even have sex. I'm not thirsty now."

He put his hands up in defense. "I know, I'm tryna lightin' up the mood. Ya' feel me. But, brother to brother, she played you, man. I don't agree with it at all 'cause you a good dude. It's not you, it's her. Whoever hurt her did her wrong. And I got a feeling she takin' the shit out on every man she come in contact with."

I gave him a look. Truly, I had never thought about it that way. I may be intelligent but when it came to females, I was a dud.

"I know man, I know," I said. I ran my hand down my face and held it there for a moment. I didn't know what to say about the situation. I would have never thought I'd be going through anything like this again. All the girls flocked to me, but I never wanted to use them or anything like that.

The way she did me was so dirty and wrong. But, did I really know her? Not. At. All. Milah was a mysterious girl and that's what I liked most about her. I couldn't read her like I could read other girls, and that's what made her different.

"So, what you gon' do, sit around and mope all day? Get yo' drawers out your ass, brutha. Snap back," Keith said, in a deep baritone and a raised brow.

Removing my hand from my face I opened my eyes to look at him. He had a piqued demeanor on his face.

"Nah', man. I'ma focus on college, that's all. Maybe a good broad will come along the way. I need to forget about this girl, 'cause clearly I won't be seein' her again. I need to worry about myself, my career in basketball, and my personal life. I can't let no lil' girl stop my grind. I almost let Brianna do that shit. Never again."

He nodded in satisfaction as we dapped each other up. "You sure? 'Cause what if this girl come back into ya' life somehow or another? You still gonna feel the same way?" he probed.

I stroked the hairs on my chin and thought for a moment. "There ain't no possibility that's gon' happen, G. Shawty played the game raw, and I know she ain't gon' pop back up. I put that on life."

Keith nodded half-heartedly, but he didn't protest my words. "Aye, you never know. She may be a lil' Ro at heart. Petty as shit."

I squinted my eyes at him and shook my head at the thought. He always knew how to ruin our brotherly moments.

"I'm so done with you, bro. Get out, me and Rome gotta be up early. We goin' over to the campus. We already did our orientation but we gotta check out some of the classes, especially the AP courses. Plus, we wanna check into our dorms. Do you know how hard it's gonna be for ma to let us go? Man, I hate to see her like that."

Keith had a solemn look etched across his face. He knew exactly what I meant since he knew how momma was. "Get up," he told me, tapping me on the arm.

"Come on, let's go get Rome's bony ass up too," he said, with that same somber look on his face. "Y'all come downstairs after you get him."

I scooted off my bed, while Keith stood over me waiting, with his hands stuffed deep in his pockets—I could only wonder what he was up to. Once he was sure I was up on my feet, he made his exit without another word. Letting out an agitated moan, I stretched and jogged out of my room, and went to get Rome.

I knocked on his door tapping a routine beat we'd been doing since we were kids. Seconds later, his tap echoed mine.

Rome opened his door with a goofy grin on his face. "Guess who got rid of biggems-so-big, her-stomach-bigger-than-her-ass, Renee?"

Hearing the name his stupid ass gave her, I couldn't help myself from hollering out hysterically. I laughed so hard, I caught a cramp in my stomach. "Fool, you cold for that!" I wiped a tear from my eye and concentrated on being serious. "But, why?" I asked, trying hard to keep a straight face. "Renee is head ova heels for you. Come on with me though. Keith want us downstairs." Rome nodded in agreement.

"Well, Bliss did me a favor and got that big donut lovin', *Homer Simpson/Peter Griffin* lookin' chick out of my life forrrreeevaaa! Your bet almost got me stuck with a fast ass stalker Renee." I shook my head at his stupid antics, as we walked out of his room and downstairs.

"What she do? Nothin' bad, right?" I asked in a serious tone.

"Nah', nothin' bad, Ro. She just gave her a lifetime supply of Chipotle's gift cards," Rome said, with a cheesy grin. I didn't know what to say after that. "She love food more than d—"

"Whoa, whoa," I said before he complete his sentence. He was worse than me with the pettiness. "Come on, man. Chill on the big girls. I heard they got that good puss."

He held his hand up, signaling me to just stop. "Shut up before you make me throw up."

When we reached the bottom of the staircase Keith and momma were talking.

"You so damn mean, yo'," I said.

"Like you ain't, but what you want from us, Key?" Rome said, calling my brother by his nickname. He rubbed his hand down the side of his face.

Key smiled, and momma pulled out two matching small boxes and handed them to us.

"Your official graduation gift, and for making it into college and out this hellhole."

We looked at them then at one another. We hurriedly opened the boxes. Inside each box was a set of car keys.

"Y'all didn't?" I said.

"Yo', y'all got us whips?" my brother asked.

Mom and Keith nodded. With mom in tow, Keith moved to the glass door and opened it. And, sure enough, there sat two white and black Jeeps.

"Thanks, Ma'," me and brother said, one after the other.

"Don't thank me, thank your brother."

Keith held his hands up in surrender when me and Rome ran to tackle him like we used to do when we were little kids. Mama laughed at our foolishness. Man, life couldn't get any sweeter than this. I couldn't believe it. My family was the best! Too bad Rome and I were leaving them for a while.

Leaving New Orleans was gonna be hard, but not *that* hard. Thinking back on Milah, I thought she was gonna be different. Too bad 'cause ole' girl had missed out on something good.

Kamilah Smith

The next day . . .

I tossed and turned in my bed. My PTSD was acting up terribly, so my therapist gave me a new prescription for my medication. Of course, I didn't take heed to that. I didn't want to take those huge pills to fix my broken soul, to make the horrible days go away. I hated those pills. The side effects were terrible, and they were tearing up my mindset. The thing I had hated the most was the hallucinations. Sometimes when I slept I'd experience night terrors from time to time. One thing I could never escape was my past, my memories, and my mind. None of those things would help me break free from the man who made me a helpless victim.

Now, as I lay sleeping, another one of those terrors began to engulf my mental being. However, this time, my mind couldn't break free from it. It felt way too real than normal.

Beep. Beep. Beep. The sound of the heart monitor clicked in my head. I was unconscious yet wide awake but I couldn't move. As I lay in the hospital bed, I begin to feel as if someone was sitting on my chest

I couldn't talk and my lips felt as if they were glued shut. I watched as my mom screamed for the doctor. "Doctor! Doctor! She's moving, my daughter is moving!" Sharon, my mother screamed, as she watched my finger twitch.

But, I couldn't feel my limbs moving. I wanted so desperately to move my body and run away from this wretched place. Then, the place started to turn black. I could only move as I watched everyone move around me.

I could see a figure appear from the dark. My eyes bulged as I saw his red eyes. The Devil himself. I tried to scream, yell, holler, cry, but there was no use. His cold hands touched my skin and it burned so badly.

His face finally appeared, and it was Cain. I began to relive that night repeatedly. There was no escaping the horror, and I was the young teen he'd taken advantage of. Cain began to growl and grunt as his monstrous pipe drilled into me.

Finally, the tears flowed from my eyes as I stared into his demented eyes. I could feel hot, red blood dripping down from my private as it was being deflowered. Finally, a yelp escaped my lips and I started to cry hysterically.

"Shut up, bitch!" Cain yelled in a deep voice, as he backhanded me. Everything was surreal. The night terror looped over and over until I lost my breath. I couldn't breathe, and my heart began to quicken like never before. Cain was strangling me now.

I couldn't escape the sadistic nightmare. Then, it looped again. But, now, he was gagging me with my own bloodily underwear. As sick as it was, he found pleasure in my gags and cries.

"If you throw up, I'll kill you!" he yelled into my ear. No one was coming to save me, no one ever did, not even the nightmare. I was still forgotten. . .

I gripped my bedsheets, unable to wake up. My sharp nails dug into the thin fabric, ripping straight through them. I was drenched in sweat, my salty tears stained my satin pillow, and my cries echoed throughout my room.

Ken heard my cries and groans from the other room since they had awakened him. He didn't know what was going on in so he knocked before entering.

When he heard me scream, "No!"

He busted in the room and found me tossing and turning in the bed. He ran to my side and woke me up, shaking me with all his might.

I was tearing holes in my sheets and this was a side had he never seen from me. But, he wasn't about to judge me from this. Ken grabbed water from the bedside table and splashed it in my face, sending me gasping for air, as I sat up straight in the bed. His face was astonished as he stared at my terrified face.

"Kamilah, are you okay? Were you having the night terror again?" he questioned, with fear laced in his tone.

"Yes, damnmit. And, no, no, I'm not okay!" I began to sob. He didn't know how to take it all in. I looked so helpless. I rubbed his face, but he looked scared to touch me.

"Kamilah?"

"Please, just hold me. Please?" Ken didn't hesitate. He just pulled me into his arms and let me cry. Ken didn't want to ask what was going on. Because he already knew I was damaged to the point of no repair. Deep down in his soul he wanted to help me. But I wasn't his concern, and neither were my problems. I just didn't want to believe it or think it, I couldn't be a burden on everyone in my life. I know this side of me scared the hell out of him. I just cried as he rocked me back and forth. I didn't want to go back to sleep after that. I had to figure out things for once in my life, coming to terms with what Cain did to me was never easy. So I avoided it in every way possible, but it always came back to haunt me. I just didn't know how to get right. Sometimes, in the darkest part of my mind, I just thought of letting all of this go, but the other half was stronger than that. As he held me in his embrace, I felt something, like, I was actually wanted, but I knew this was all a front. I continued to cry as he rubbed my hair and kissed my face. Suddenly, it was as if a drought had suddenly hit and all the tears stopped. I knew exactly why my tears had stopped, because this wasn't love at all. I wanted to experience love, *real genuine love*. I needed to know what real love felt like. I became lost in my thoughts while staring into the dark corner where a teddy bear lay looking back at me I felt like that poor little defenseless eight year old again. I had to pull myself together and try to love myself. Tomorrow was my big day, but I didn't feel special at all.

***

We had finally arrived on the campus. After doing orientation, interviews, viewing the campus, and signing up for the housing program, I was so ecstatic to finally get here. Looking at my parents, I was relieved. I was relieved to be escaping the very people who hadn't cared enough to keep me out of harm's way.

"Okay, dad. I love you so much. Mommy, I love you too. I'll be good, and I'll see you guys soon." With a huge smile on my face, I lied to both of my parents. Honestly, I was ecstatic not to be seeing them for months. My momma had tears in her eyes and wouldn't let go from her embrace. *How fucking fake, crying 'cause I'm leaving for school but didn't shed a tear when I was raped.*

"Okay. You better be good and get that degree."

I faked a smile as she released the grip she had on my waist. My dad didn't show as much affection as my momma did. I needed my parents but what was the use? They had never believed a damn word I'd said. The fact that my mother thought of me as liar only made my dad think the same thing. I hated them both for it. Each time either of them said *I love you and be safe,* caused me to cringe inside. Not having their love to get me through those horrible days made their words disgusting to me.

"I love you, baby," dad repeated. I wanted to vomit from hearing him say that.

I couldn't hold back my tears of joy but I had to. I was going to be on my own and glad of it.

After they left, I looked out at the huge college. An obnoxious voice rang out, causing people to look around and whisper, even laugh. Me, myself, I looked forward as my eyes beamed with happiness.

"Kamilah, my main, my soul, my sis, my bish," I heard the loud voice yell out. It could only belong to one person.

We opened our arms, like we hadn't seen each other in ages although it had only been the other day.

"Bliss, my hoe, my woe, my patna' in crime, my bitch," I yelled, as we ran into each other arms and hugged like we would never see each other again. This was a daily for us, a bind of friendship that no one could break. She was a friend who withheld all my secrets and I knew she'd take them to the grave.

When we pulled away, Bliss' smile faded and she gasped dramatically.

"Girl, you won't believe who I just saw going into apartment dorm 2914!?" she shouted.

"Who?" I asked curiously. She turned me in the opposite direction and pointed. I focused my eyes in the direction she pointed.

Them, I thought, as they came into view. Getting on my tiptoes, I moved my head around the crowd, and then, I saw them, the *twins.*

Cairo and Rome. Holy fuck.

"Oh, my God! Oh, my Lord, help me!" I began to panic when I spotted them. Bliss looked at me with disappointment etched on her face. She shook her head again and again. She held up a finger and proceeded to wave it back and forth in my face. To top it all off, the look she was giving me spoke the words her mouth didn't.

"Told you to tell him the truth and to just be yourself. But no, no, no, no, not you. Instead of keepin' it real, you chose to dip on him. Fuck all that. I told you so, she shouted in my face. "When you hide shit it always comes back to haunt you, Milah! Now you gon' have to face him anyway. See, karma, bitch."

"Stop! You're drawing attention to us, hoe! He gon' see us." I tried to pull her in the opposite direction of where they stood but she yanked me back.

"Uh, no bitch. It's too late to run now. I'm sorry," she said, as she bit her lip.

I becoming angry and she knew it. I looked behind me and tried to hide. "Bliss, for Christ's sake," I said to myself. What the hell was I going to do to get out of this sticky situation? The bitch began singing *Caught Up* by Usher! But, she was my best and only friend. Who else was going to look after me?

CHAPTER 6

Comes to Light

Kamilah Smith

Cussing under my breath, my hand latched onto Bliss' wrist. She was standing there on the sidewalk, looking like a scared baby Elk that didn't know how to escape from prey just yet. Snatching her down to my level, she let out a small whimper, as I basically dragged her through the crowd. To say we looked stupid was only the half of it.

"Bliss look what you did you little cunt! Shit, gotdamn," I said in a loud whisper, as I maneuvered us through the crowd. I occasionally looked behind us to see where his tall ass was. I spotted him walking through a crowd of people so I took that as my chance to dip and get the hell outta dodge.

Still hauling ass with Bliss still in tow, she tried to yank away from me, but all that did was give me even more leverage when her hand slipped into mine. Grasping her hand even tighter, I almost broke that muthafucka off trying to run.

"Bitch! Ow! You trippin', let me go!" she said dramatically, as we took off running for the hills.

"Shut up, we gotta get to our dorm now!" She looked back and so did I. He wasn't in sight.

"Damn, let my arm go 'cause you can't run from him forever. We *are* on the same campus, dummy," she said, rolling her eyes and trying to catch her breath.

"Shush! How are you out of breath? Didn't your loud-mouth-ass take track? I didn't know he was coming to this school," I said, stomping my feet. We made it to our dorm in victory. But, this was a clear one for me. He was going to see me today, tomorrow, or next week! Hell, this campus was huge, but that didn't mean he wouldn't run into me somewhere. He was on the basketball team and I was on the damn dance team. Pacing the pavement, I tried to think of something to get me out of the bullshit.

Bliss stayed put with a look of disgust on her face. Looking towards her, I waved and ushered her over to me. Her head slumped down in disappointment, but I didn't care at all. She shrugged her slim shoulders and walked behind me, and together, we walked to the dorm room units on side AB.

With our bags already waiting for us at the dorm, she grabbed my shoulder roughly and turned me around with force. "You are just too much, Milah and I've had enough of your bullshit! You're ignorant, you know that. For someone of your caliber, you are such an ass! You play people, especially boys. Because of your father and mother, you do this? I know that's not truly why, but you have no right to do that to others. You rebel and hurt people, and I'm sick of it. You used him, just dipped without a word. Now look how you're caught up. You both go to the same school, and, on top of that, Ken goes here too! Now look what you've done, Milah," she shouted in my face.

I had so many emotions bottled up inside. Bliss was right. "I can't change what I did but Cairo nor Ken can know who I really am! *Milah* is the outgoing and—"

Bliss put her hand up, cutting off. "Stop that lyin'! You've lived a double life almost all your life! It's not your fault yet it is. I'm sick of it. I'm sick of covering for you. You're my best-friend, but, Kamilah, you need to get your shit together, and fast. Ken just fits in your perfect society, perfect circle, and perfect wealth, but you don't love him. You two were put together, by who? Exactly, your father! Just because he thought wealth plus more wealth went together.

Girl, I know it's more to you than meets the eye. You've tried so hard to tell you father the truth, the truth about what happened to you. You never stood up to your father so you created the sassy Milah—the girl who does what she pleases, the girl who gets what she wants and who she wants. Steps over people like gum on a shoe with no remorse. You proclaim to do any and everything to everyone, and I don't wish any bad on you. I hope you learned from this because this is gonna turn damn ugly and it's all your fault." Bliss rolled her eyes as she opened the door.

I had tears in my eyes because she was right. She was always right about me. If Ken was to find out my whole cover would be blown. But, I didn't love him, I never did love him. And, Cairo? He was just another me, but we'd never work since opposites in my society never attracted. I sighed and walked inside the room. Bliss had sat down on the other side of the room pretending to be busy, not paying me any mind.

Looking at her, I said, "Bliss, I'm-I'm," then I just broke down.

"It's okay, but you needed to know, but I'm here for you. If I need to put you in your place, you know I will."

I nodded. "You're right. I needed to be checked."

She got up from her bare mattress and a smile crept on her face, as did mine. We were like sisters. We fought then made up with no problem to the record. Bliss and I stood up at the same time as we met each other halfway, then pulled one another into a hug. There was a slight knock on the door, causing us to pull away. Bliss went to open it.

"Hey, Bliss. Are you coming to the party tonight? First time in college so we gotta turn up," Andre said, as he stood covered in tattoos.

"You already know, Dre. We'll be there. I came to slay, you know this."

I waved at Andre and he waved back. They had their brief conversation and he left. I continued to sit on my bed, thinking things over.

Looking down at my nails, Bliss charmed me with her southern voice. "Maybe, you can fix this? Kenneth, I mean Ken will be leaving after the party. He won't be here for another two weeks so maybe you can fix things with Cairo?"

I looked at her as she swung her arm around my shoulders.

"Yeah? Maybe that'll work. 'Cause now he knows I'm here. I can't hide from him or his loud mouth brother," I said, rolling my eyes.

She sucked her teeth and mushed my head. "Don't do my loud mouth bae. That boy was sculpted from God himself," she boasted, "oh, he's a fine piece of light-skin chocolate!" She bit her lip and held her hand up to the sky dramatically.

"You're crazy but we should get a little rest heifer before the party."

"Okay," she agreed and got all her stuff settled in the dorm.

I, on the other hand was thinking about Cairo.

Cairo Black
6: 40 a.m. earlier that day

Rome had just come out of the bathroom and I was already getting dressed. "Can we get some breakfast on the way? Mom seems a little upset this morning. I know she don't won't us to go but it's not that. It's something deeper."

I looked at Rome and sighed. Frowning my brows together, I spoke up. "How upset did she seem?" My face was etched with curiosity.

He looked at me with a stale face. "After we leave, she's staying home from work, Cairo, and that's not like mom at all. Mama works fuckin' hard so something is off."

I nodded because he was right. Mom worked herself to the bone. She loved her job and never skipped a beat. I rubbed the back of my neck and looked at him. "Yeah, I feel you. We can stop for food on the way since it's early as hell, and besides, we got a long drive. Just be downstairs and ready."

He nodded and left out. I continued to wonder why my mom had decided to stay home. This was another thing I had to worry about. I grabbed my last bag and my Jeep keys, and left out of my room, closing the door behind me. I went to my mom's room but she wasn't in there. Breathing hard a little, the door to the bathroom open and out she came, humming "Yes."

"Hey, Momma? You a'ight?" She pulled away from her photo album and looked up at me with tears in her eyes.

"Come on, Mom, don't do this. It's not like we movin' away for good."

My mama nodded, as I wiped the tear from her eye. "It's not just that. Your father called me today. He said he just wanted to let me know he was doing okay, but I had a feeling there was more to his call. So, I checked my account and all my money was gone, every penny of it. I don't mean to spring this on you, Son—"

I pulled my mother into a hug as she softly cried. "What did Keith say?" I questioned, as my blood began boiling.

"Keith was furious. He stormed out and I haven't seen him since. I want you and Rome to go to school and take advantage of everything it has to offer so you can be better than your parents. I want my sons to be the best, and that's that. Now get on so y'all can get there early."

I didn't give her any back talk. Nodding, I kissed her forehead. "Okay, Mom. I love you."

She smiled and told me she loved me, and I got up and walked towards the door. Looking at her one more time, I blew her a kiss before walking out. Making my way down the hall, I had to figure this out.

"Is mom a'ight, bro?" Rome asked, as we walked out of the house and to our separate rides.

"Yeah. Yeah, she's fine. She just wasn't feeling so good." I knew better than that. I just did. Rome looked at me and nodded. I didn't want to tell him that mom's bank account had been wiped clean and she thought dad had did it. I didn't want to ruin his day like mine had been ruined. Finally, we hopped in our Jeeps and took off down the street, off to make a better life for ourselves. Nothing else could ruin my day now.

***

We pulled up to the college and it was packed. We parked and made our way to the office. Afterwards, I went to check out the Calculus AP class. I walked in to see my teacher standing in front of the class.

"Excuse me, scholars," she said when she noticed me. "You must be Cairo. The office buzzed me and told me you might be stopping by. I'm Ms. Rolan and I'll be your professor this semester.

"Hi, Professor Rolan." I extended my hand.

"Advanced Placement will be best courses for you. They'll earn you more credits per course toward the overall accumulative credits you'll need in order to graduate," the teacher explained.

Yeah, I was smart and all, but this was going to be too much work. I was gonna be overwhelmed with work. Even though this was easy for me, and I had no problem with doing it, I still had to account time for practice. It would boost my GPA and grades but I had other AP classes as well.

"Okay class what is the answer to the equation, The two functions f and g defined by... Ahem, Cairo? Can you answer the question, please? This is only a practice question to be sure this is the course for you."

I looked at Ms. Rolan and nodded. "Sorry, I wasn't paying attention. Can you repeat the question again?"

Everyone looked at me and she nodded. "True or false. The two functions f and g defined by: $f(x) = 3x + 3$ for x real and $g(t) = 3t + 3$ for t real and positive are equal?" she said, explaining the question.

I looked at her and thought for a second, and then it came to me. "False. Two functions are equal if their rules are equal and their domains are the same."

"Correct. I knew this class was for you. See you tomorrow which will be your first full day joining us," she said and turned back to the class she'd been teaching.

I smiled at a few of the hotties and made my exit. I had so much more to do before my first official day.

Mom was still on my mind and I was so conflicted with a lot of stuff in my life. *What if my mom didn't really just stay home from work? What if something else happened?* Then, thoughts of my father started to creep into my mind. My brother walked right beside me down the huge hallways of the college and the twin telepathy must've kicked in. I knew he knew what I was currently thinking, but I'd have to get over it because I didn't have time for any setbacks today.

***

Cursing up a storm, I slung my suitcase across the room. I was being lied to and dogged out left and right. First, my own father stole everything my mother had, then, I had the nerve to find out Kamilah was attending this very school. By no means was I a fuckboy.

Looking at my brother, I said, "Bro, I know you saw her. I may have bad vision, but I know what I damn well saw." Roughly running my hands down my face, I sat back on the bed as my body bounced a little. The bare mattress was covered with plastic but you could clearly hear the coils in the spring.

Rome's voice boomed in anger. "Cairo, you damn sure ain't blind. I saw her ass too, and her little friend would've got away with it if they wasn't meddling with their own stupidity. But, shit, this is crazy. Milah lied to you and you ain't gon' do nothin'? Even her friend lied. One thing I can't be cool with is a lie," he yelled.

I sat up and just looked at him. His face softened and he calmed down. He could see I was in a damaged state because I'd never been through any of this with a female.

My voice trailed off as I stared at the tan, twisted fabric rug. "I don't know what to do. Every time I try, she goes left. I'ma just leave shawty alone." He knew I was lying through my teeth. But, I didn't need a lecture. So, I was thankful when one of the guys burst into our room.

"'Sup, mitches," he yelled, as he flopped down on Rome's bed. Rome and his damn OCD was about to flare up. He had a complex about people on his bed. Plus, he just made the mutha up. It didn't take long for his nose to flare open.

"Malone, you got zero point two seconds to get yo' nasty ass off my bed. You may be my boy and teammate, but you a straight hoe. I don't won't no STD on my bed," Rome shouted, actually causing a smile to creep up on my face.

Malone smacked his teeth and eased onto the floor, mumbling something under his breath. He quickly changed the subject and spoke up about some damn party. Was I in a partying mood? No. But, there was no way Rome was going without his other half, me.

"So, y'all coming or nah?" Malone pressed, while grabbing the fidget spinner that was poking out of my backpack. I began to spin it, just to keep my anger and animosity down. I sighed and stood up, adjusting my hat, as I continued to flick the spinner. As I laid it between my middle and thumb fingers, I thought for a second. Rome had agreed to go so that meant I had to show out with my blood. I nodded and pulled out an outfit that was neatly folded, due to my momma.

Looking towards Rome, I tossed him the spinner before I announced, "I wanna get a little drunk and high. I need to ease my mind."

My brother didn't say a word 'bout it. This was gonna be our very first campus party. I was nowhere near eager to attend but I was gonna turn up. There was no way I was going to act all sour about Milah. *It is what it is*, I told myself. Shit comes to light, and that changes everything.

Malone soon left out of the dorm. Walking over to my side of the room, I got some of my personals to do my business. Rome got ready and went about his business. But, before he exited from the room, he turned around and said, "Ro, don't find—

I cut him off, already knowing what he was about to preach.

"I ain't about to pick up no girls, a'ight? Point blank, period." Rome paused as he let what I said soak in. He nodded, then exited the room. Closing my eyes, I rubbed them, then got ready. Shit was about to be real weird tonight.

***

Soon, we pulled up to this big Frat house that truly looked like something off TV. I hadn't expected it to be so lit already. We weren't even in the house yet and peeps were dancing outside on the grass with red cup in their hands. The ladies and guys were walking across the street talking and what not. I cruised in my Jeep examining the setup. We had decided to drive one Jeep since both of our trucks were so big.

Looking around for somewhere to park, all you could hear was giggling females. A lot of hunnies were walking up with some short ass dresses on, making damn sure it hugged all their curves in the right places.

"Ohh-wee! Finna get me one tonight," Malone said, as his hand slapped down on my shoulder. My twin and I both rolled our eyes.

"This nigga," we said at the same time, as we walked up to the house. He dapped the man at the door. We didn't have to pay to get in 'cause we had them connects. The music blasted from inside of the Frat house. Kendrick Lamar's record could be heard as clear as day.

Entering the house, it felt weird that we would no longer be in our own town going to these types of parties. The feel was so different, much wilder to be honest. All the hooting and hollering, and the usual ladies leading the dude upstairs to have drunk sex with a sock on the doorknob— that kinda stuff never failed at a party 'cause it never got old. The scene of the wallflowers, smokers, the girls who got dragged to the party by their friends. It was a typical college party.

For a while, the party was jumping. The music had switched to some hot southern music. I found myself not really interacting with anyone. I was just laid back, peeping the scene with my drink in my cup.

Taking the cup to my lips, I felt someone tap my broad shoulder. I looked to the left of me and my eyes lowered as I looked at the girl.

"Uh, hey, Ro? Remember me, Bliss?" she said with an uncomfortable tone.

I looked down at the light-brown skinned female. Moving back a little, I scoffed to myself as I kept a lower eye contact on her. How did she know I was the right twin?

"'Sup? You sure you got the right twin?" I pressed, as I looked up for a moment then gave her my full attention.

She sighed and grabbed my hand. Frowning a little, I tried to pull it back but, little mama had a death grip. The music faded to Russ' *Losin' Control*.

Taking another swig of my drink, I finally spoke up. "What you want, man? What," I groaned.

She was taking all the buzz I had from the dark liquor, mixed with Coco-Cola.

She tugged my hand forward. "She wants to talk to you. Be easy on her. Please, just listen to her." I laughed as she pushed me in front of Milah. Why hadn't I figured they would be at the party? She looked up at me and then down at her drink, trying to prepare her speech for me. My eyes stayed right on her, not evening caring how distraught she was looking. I didn't cause any of this, she did.

"What'chu want, girl?" I said, with a slight attitude.

The song remixed through the speakers as she bounced her leg. Placing the plastic cup down, her eyes caught mine again.

"I'm sorry, I really—"

"Tuh. Save it! I don't want to hear any of that bullshit that's about to pour out'cha mouth." She sighed and grabbed my hand. Licking my lips as I looked at her, a shallow breath exited her mouth as she began to speak again.

"You have to understand, there are some things you don't understand about me. I don't know how to just be myself plus stay with you. It's hard for me to just show you the real me, give you all of me."

I laughed a little bit more. How could she want any type of sympathy from me? Just leaving someone with no explanation. Using them like a human being that ain't shit then want to explain?

Pulling my hand from hers, I was going to stand my ground on ole' girl, I'd been through it once, never the fuck again,

"What? That you stuck up and too good for a real hood nigga like me! Is that it? You just used me like I was poor trash with a touch from God!" Before I could even walk away from her, Milah's tiny hands grabbed me and pulled my face to hers. Before I knew what was happening, she'd dived in and planted a deep kiss on my lips.

When she released the lip-lock, she looked in my eyes. "You're not too good for me. You're perfect for me and I'm sorry."

Searching her eyes for the truth, I grabbed her face and continued the kiss she'd started. I don't know what took over me. I couldn't stop kissing her. Her hands pushed at my chest as she gasped slightly, trying to catch her breath.

"You have to go slow with me. I don't know about this. I'm new to this Cairo but I can't keep running away from what I want. And, what I want is you."

I grabbed her ass to shut her up. I used my strength to pull her body towards mine. "Just shut yo' fine ass up and kiss me, a'ight? Just be real with me. Ain't no nigga gon' make me go nowhere. *Not again.*" I pressed my lips into hers and brought her body even closer to mine. Her friend made a noise and moved away. I just kept her close to me while kissing her, not caring what anyone had to say about it. If she was going to be real, then I was too.

I didn't know what she meant when she said *'there were some things I wouldn't like'*. But, for some reason, shawty just had this hold on me. No other girl had me like this. Not even Brianna, but that hoe was a different story. She had showed a new light I just couldn't blow out.

But, Milah, I just kept giving her chances, but how many chances could I give shawty? I knew my brother was gonna have a tantrum. A day ago, I was the same ole' me. I kept telling myself to focus on college and basketball, just forget about this girl, but I couldn't. Something inside just wouldn't let me. I knew it wasn't love because Cairo Black didn't fall in love. *But could I?*

Her lips got away from mine, as she finally opened her crimson brown eyes. "Cairo? Oh God, you gonna have to stop with this," she said, trying to push me off her neck.

"You like it, and I'm a little tipsy. You need to make up with me. You still got yo' explainin' to do about tryna dip on a nigga too."

She sighed, trying to suppress the moan. That's when I let up with a smirk and pulled my lips away from her skin.

"I'ma leave you here to think about that." I slyly laughed at what I did to her. But, she needed to know how it felt to have someone play with your mind. She had the goofiest look on her face. But, it was only going to be for a few days until she got her shit together. 'Cause, I didn't play that bull she was trying to pull. If she was trying to run game on me, I would show her how a real playa' did it.

CHAPTER 7

Playa' From the Himalayas

Cairo Black

I was just getting ready to leave from my dorm room. I had classes to get to at 11 a.m. and it was now 8:34. Even though it was early, it was a good time for a run, just to clear my head. But first, I wanted to go do my post workout for a bit, just to get it over with, while my brother was passed out sleep in his bed.

I finished getting ready, making sure I had my water bottle and other workout essentials. Grabbing my Nike shoes, In plopped down my bed and slipped them on. Afterwards, I sprung up, ready to get pumped.

Hearing a high pitch groan I turned around looking towards Rome. Shockingly, Bliss was lying next to him. Bliss left her best-friend lonely. But, whose fault was that other than hers? To be honest, I wouldn't blame her for wanting to get away from the drama. And, that's what she got for tryna play somebody. But, she wasn't as good at the game as she thought she was. Her ass got busted quick and then she got scared and apologized. That's one thing you didn't do, apologize to someone you intended on using and abusing. I hadn't spoken to Milah since the party, and that had been two days prior.

I wanted her to learn her lesson, to show her she could be herself and didn't have to be some out-of-the-box character to impress me. I smirked, thinking about what I'd done to her at the party that night. Shaking my head at my own antics, I grabbed my phone and earbuds and pulled my Morris Brown hoodie, with the sleeves cut off, over my body. I walked over to my door and made sure I had my keys before making my exit.

With my AirPods in my ears, I turned on my music and began to walk down the hall. I had my head down looking at my phone when I bumped into someone, causing my phone to fall out of my hands. If my phone was cracked all hell was about to break loose. By the way the person slammed into me, it seemed to be on purpose. Why didn't the person that was walking in front of me move out my way? But, I was going to be the bigger man and apologize.

When my phone was in my grasp, I looked at it. Shaking my head, it had a small nick on the edge of it. "Oh shit. My bad." I looked up at the person to see exactly who had bumped into me and rolled my eyes. I sighed deeply. "What you doing here? Stalking me?" I asked, trying not to smirk.

"No. I was coming to get Bliss for dance practice. I didn't know you even stayed in this dorm. Thank you," she said shyly, but yet her voice was laced with a sassy tone. I looked down on her and licked my lips simultaneously. I scooped my hand around her waist still looking down on her with my eyebrow raised. She was staring at my lips, probably reminiscing about the kiss. Licking them one more time, I caught her attention. Her eyes finally left my lips. She blushed.

"What, Cairo?" she asked, trying not to look at me.

Shaking my head with a wide smile on my face, I raised my hand to the side of her face. I pushed her hair back. "Look at me. You want me don't you? You want me *so* bad! You love me, don't you? I'm wearing you down, baby," I said, wiggling my eyebrows and sounding like Steve Urkel.

She burst out laughing which led me to burst out too.

"Shut up, you cornball," she said Milah, tapping her hand lightly against my chest. When her laughter died down she tried not to look at me. Once again, I had her weak at the knees and I hadn't done a thing to her.

"You want me to stop frontin'? But, for real, on a real note, let me go do what I was about to do before we ran into each other." Either it was my accent that made her stare at my lips, or my lips were just that sexy. So, I licked them slower this time. I smiled and showed my straight pearly whites, making my dimples show.

A light gasp escaped her mouth as she finally answered me. But this time with more confidence. "And what on earth makes you think that?" she said, shifting her weight to one side. She popped her hip in the process as her right hand landed on her hip.

Cocking my head to the side with my lips turned to the side, I said, "Well, I'ma about to go for a run. Maybe I'll see ya' around later."

Milah, didn't have anything else to say. Shrugging, she gave me nod. I could tell she felt defeated and unsure of herself. Playing the card just right, she moved around me. She was about to walk back to her dorm room, when I grabbed her softly, spun her around, and kissed her. The kiss was short but good.

When we pulled away, I smirked and told her, "And, that's for tryna' play a nigga." She was leaning forward with her lips still puckered for another kiss. I didn't want to laugh because she was so cute. "I'll think about giving you another one." I laughed with an *aha,* as I jogged backwards and away from her.

"Stop, Ro! I'm sorry. It's just something you won't understand," she said, poking out her bottom lip. Her face was serious this time with a pout. But, she was sure I wouldn't understand. The look she had was of uncertainty. But, she didn't know me at all. I had seen a lot, I knew a lot. I had to grow up and become mature fast. So, of course, *I would understand.*

"What? How will I not understand if you don't talk to me? We can't be cool if we don't got no communication. Pull ya' self together, girl. I know you want me, and you know I want you." She fixed her mouth to say something, but I held my hand up with my eyes closed. "Now, if you will excuse me, I need to get my workout out the way. And fix your face. You look like you just lost ya' best friend." I threw my head back in laughter, waved my two fingers from the side of my head, and jogged off, leaving Milah standing there.

Oh yes, making her pay was going to be fun. Just give it three more days and she'd be crawling, craving, and being humble for a nigga.

***

Getting back from my run, I felt refreshed. I may have been a little on the musty side, but I was just getting pumped up for practice today. I had to be on top of my game. If the New Orleans twins was two of the top five college draft picks, we had to be the best standing on half court. After all my classes in the afternoon, me and my brother had to go to our basketball meeting. There was no way in hell we could be late. We had already met the coach and you could tell when you were in his presence. You had to speak like a man and be all about your business. There was no slacking with coach Belly. That man was an ex-marine, and me and my twin didn't want no trouble.

On the first day, it was a stretch but this was college. There would be easy days and hard days. We had to keep our reputation up and stay on our toes. I couldn't let one girl stray me away from that, even if she *was* fine. I wiped off my hair with my colored washcloth just as I stepped inside my dorm room. Then, I shook my braids a little to make sure no cuco-bugs were in my hair. My brother was sitting on the bed doing some papers.

"'Sup, Bruh." He looked at me and fanned me off. Throwing my head back some, my face frowned up at his stank attitude all. "Hell wrong with'chu?" I said, cocking my eyebrow at him.

He looked up at me as his short braids flopped back. Rome's face looked irritated and wrinkles creased across his forehead. "You, mane! You playin' this game with Milah and shit! I couldn't even get none from Bliss. If the friend sad, that equals no pum-pum from my girl! You fuckin' up, you feel me."

I fanned him off like he once did me, not even trying to hear what he was saying. "Mane buzz the fuck off! I'm just messin' with her. I'ma get that, don't worry."

Rome smacked his lips. "Yeah, right. You playing with her is messin' up my flow. You know how fine Blistex is? Huh?" Rome said dramatically, as he flopped his arms in the air.

"Mane quit all that. Yo' punk ass will get some pussy soon enough. I'll talk to Bliss. A'ight?" I questioned, as I rubbed some hair products in my hair to freshen my long Braids up. I looked at him from the side, as he mimicked me. I flicked him off.

"Yeah, for real, punk. If I don't get some of Bliss all hell gon' break lose!" His full accent came out, as I acted as if I was scared. Then, I scoffed a laugh.

"Oh, I'm so scared of my look-alike. Is you done or are you finished, nigga?"

Rome straight-faced me with his lip turned up. "Yeah, whateva. I'll beat yo' ass. Hurry up, so we can head off to class. I ain't tryna' be late 'cause you stupid," he said, being all demanding.

I shook my head and finished putting the product in my hair. After doing all that, I pulled on my basic black outfit with Jordan's and jacket, soon heading out of the dorm room. I locked the door behind me since Rome had left before me.

Meeting up with him at the end of the hall, we went on to walking to our class. We could hear counting on the field, and I looked over to see Milah and her friend practicing.

"I ain't know they was really on the dance team," I smirked, as we walked by.

"They sho' know what they doin' too." Rome and I both shook our heads as we went to the classes. Nothing but Calculus and Advanced placement English, like, come on, we did this in high school so why we gotta do it again? I sat and thought about what to do next, until a familiar voice caught my attention. I looked at my brother and he looked at me while pointing to the door. My whole faced dropped when I saw *her.* I couldn't believe she was coming to this college. Her ass was supposed to be out of my life for good, but no, she just had to bring her boujee ass back into my life. I had to get my girl before this bitch started WWIII in the damn college.

"Aye, she bringin' her ass over here. God be with us 'cause I don't wanna have to choke a hoe today. Lawd, please. Bless me from not using my slap-a-hoe-card today," Rome said, with his hands in a prayer-like position.

She walked up the stairs to where we were and smirked at me. Opening the door to the room, she entered and wiggled from side to side to pull her dress down. It only stopped at her ass, so she couldn't pull it down that much further.

"Hello, Cairo. How are you doin'? You know I've missed you, baby boy, and I know you missed me too," she said, as she tried to run her hand down cheek.

Slapping her hand away, I scrunched up my face and waved her off. I didn't give a damn what she was saying, therefore, it went in one ear, and out the other.

"Girl, gon' 'bout yo' bi'ness. I don' want your dried-up ass. You been dismissed."

She laughed and moved her hand down to my chest, making me do the shimmy just to get her off me.

"Baby, you know you miss me. I'll see you around."

I shook my head and focused on the lesson. The teacher turned around, giving her a look. Brianna stood there for a minute with her gaze on me. Then, she swirled around to go to her seat.

My brother tapped my shoulder, noticing me trying to get myself together.

"If her and Milah meet all hell gon' break lose," Rome said, speaking the honest God truth.

"I know, shit. Man, she fuckin' up err'thang," I groaned as I sank down in my seat, tapping my pencil against the desktop. I couldn't believe this shit. One door had opened and another door had closed. She just had to come back into my life to 'cause hell.

Kamilah Smith

Julia Michaels' song *Issues* blasted through the Sony speakers. "And hit it ladies!" The ladies were messing up on steps three, all the way to damn seven. Spinning around, I waved my hand back and forth, signaling them to stop and listen. I pinched the bridge of my nose in frustration that they couldn't grasp the advanced techniques.

"Okay, ladies. Step three to seven. Y'all not grasping these sharp hits. This is how it goes again. You step out with your left foot, snap your right fingers, then *pop, pop, pop* your hips left to right, jump slap both knees, three in the back do jump splits, then two in the front, up and down *pop* your booty, sexy *pop* head up! Make sure to flip and whip that hair. Sway down to the beat, dip and kick out leg, pop the booty a little. Then, last step: bring arms up, make it sensational and sensual! Arch the back and curve down to the floor. Okay? Got it, hit it! Bliss play that song again," I told her, as practiced with our dance team.

She nodded and played the track again. "Do you think the moves are too sexual?" Bliss questioned quickly, as we watched the ladies do the steps again. It was much better and cleaner this time.

I sighed and did one of the moves again, just to keep the ladies on track. "I don't know. She's the one who came up with them," I said pointing to the new girl, Brianna. So, really, she should be the one directing this shit."

"I ain't feelin' her too much. She got the girls doing stripper shit. She too stuck up for me," Bliss said, as she and I placed our hands on our popped-out hips. She gave me the side lips, I huffed. Brianna looked in our direction, as if she was reading our lips.

While she danced, she stomped her foot like a two-year-old having a tantrum. "Y'all just can't dance, shit!" Brianna hollered, as she stomped both feet repeatedly then angrily clicked the music off. She rolled her eyes and I stuck my tongue out at her. Bliss and I moved out the way and on the sideline.

"Yeah, yeah. But, I get a bad vibe from that bitch. She a New Orleans chick too, right? How she gonna be from our city and act like that? She act too stank and she always giving us the side eye like we the bitches. Is she cockeyed or something? Better check her damn eyes?"

I couldn't help but laugh. "Girl, stop! You so mean. Got my damn stomach hurting." I laughed so hard I rolled over while holding my stomach. Bliss shrugged in a nonchalant matter. "I know and I don't care. I'm a mean ass bad bitch who will make yo' ass cry. So, what that mean? It mean, don't start shit *she* sure as hell can't finish."

I shook my head at her pettiness, but of course, she had a valid point. "Love you, Bliss, but what's up with you and Rome? Are you two a thing now?" I looked Bliss up and down. She bit her lip and rocked back and forth before twerking wildly.

"Girl, you should really make up with Cairo, because Lord knows they both fine. They truly blessed from the God above."

I nodded, agreeing with her. "Yeah, you right. Cairo kissed me today and I almost collapsed. He is just— Oh, my Jesus!" I fell back on the thick grass dramatically. Bliss burst out into laughter.

"You need to get him before that Brianna girl gets her hands on him. I'm like snoopy bitch, I know hoe-traits when I see 'em. You know the *word* gets around fast."

I looked at her and sighed long and hard.

"Stop sighing and just go get yo' man. 'Cause I don't want to see you suspended for pulling a bitch's weave out." She was so right and realizing Ken would be here in about two weeks was all the more reason I had to get my shit together. Quick, fast, and bullshit free.

CHAPTER 8

Be My Baybeh

Cairo Black

Rome and I walked from basketball practice with our bags in tow. I was still a little shocked over the fact that Brianna was bringing her sneaky ass to this college. *The bitch didn't give a shit as to why I was going here, now she just happened to be attending the same fucking college.*

With deep lines embedding in his forehead, Rome's lip twisted to one side as his facial expression resembled Ice Cube's mean mug. His eyes to became squinted as he stared me down. "Stop thinking about her rat ass," he said, snapping me out of my thoughts.

"Get out of my head, man. Ugh."

He shrugged and elbowed me.

"What?" I asked as he caught my attention again.

"There go ya' girl," he said, cheesing.

I rolled my eyes and threw my head back. "For the last damn time, she is not my girl. Not yet anyway, damn."

He pressed his lips to the side and laughed. I didn't say much because there wasn't much to say at all. "Yeah, *yet*." Rome continued to mock me and it was truly pissing me off. All I wanted was a break and it shouldn't have been this hard to achieve.

The girls noticed us and waved. In my head I didn't even want to walk remotely close to Milah. Just the vibe from her would have me in a different state of mind. Even though I didn't want to be next to her. For some reason I just could stay away from Milah. So I sucked up my pride as we walked over to where they were. And, damn, she looked so delicious in her shorts and sports bra. It was a shame that a specimen like her could be so cunning.

"Hey, Milah," I said nicely. She looked at me and blushed, like I had never said anything to her before in life. But, something took over me when she talked to my brother. Something I didn't want to happen. The way she moved and acted. Her posture made me think for a bit, made me want to get my act together, stop being such a tough breed ass nigga, and just step to the side. Pull her with me, just to tell her what was truly up. Looking straight at her, I was about to speak up when she did it first.

"Hey. Uh, can we talk?"

I nodded with and mumbled, "Fa'sho." I looked over at Rome and Bliss eye-fucking one another. Shaking my head, I began to walk across the football field with Milah, away from everyone for a little bit of private conversation.

"So, was'sup?" I asked with a questionable tone. Milah did her infamous soft sigh, as she twirled her fingers in that silky hair of hers. Her finger twirled endlessly around in habit as we walked. Then she pulled me to stop. She pulled her shorts down a little, but that wasn't going to stop them from rising. Here I was standing in front of her staring in those hazel eyes. She kept her gaze down avoiding any eye contact with me. *Was that a nervous tidbit as well?* I thought to myself. I couldn't help but lick my lips, just trying to figure her out.

Milah took a moment to speak before her gaze finally raised to mine. Then, she began to talk in a calm manor. "I don't want to play this game anymore, okay? I really am sorry for what I did. It was ratchet and real petty. Y-you just don't know what's going on with me. Okay?" Milah said with complete honesty. Her body language was telling me everything I needed to know, but her gaze quickly looked down at her feet.

"Well? Why don't you tell me? I'm a good listener, believe it or not. For real, I'm here for you so tell me what's up."

She shook her head and her head slowly rose to look at me. "You wouldn't understand me. But, I like you. I don't want to chase you off or make you think I'm crazy, 'cause I'm not. I don't wanna allow you to think I'm playing with your emotions. It's just my family and me. They wouldn't approve of us. They barely approve of me," Milah raved but whispered the last part.

I raised an eyebrow at her. "I'm not thinking anything like that. But, what are you getting at? I'm not good enough for you?" She stopped me quick and fast.

"Really, it's nothing like that, okay? Really, it's just my father. He is just-he is a wealthy person and he faithfully believes in that status bullshit, you know? He would call us something I can't stand for him to say, alright? He wants me to be in a wealthy relationship so I can keep my family's old money growing. But, the truth is, I like you. I really do. The things you do are things no other guy has done."

Milah got cut off by the devil herself, Brianna. She came up switching like there was no tomorrow. She came up strong and stood right beside me. She almost got chin-checked, on some real shit.

Then, the dragon had the nerve to speak. "Baby? What are you doing over here with her?" she asked, her tone full of hatred. She grabbed my arm and caressed it, running her sharp nails up and down my skin. She stood in front of Kamilah not hiding her evident attitude.

I snatched my arm from her grip, causing her to look at me sideways. My entire body flipped as my face turned up in a disgusted expression. "*Baby?* Bitch? Girl, if you don't," I started, about to go from zero to one hundred.

Milah pulled me into her with a firm grip and crashed those rose-petal soft lips into mine and kissed me just to spite the devil. I guess she really got into it, and so did I, 'cause she was sucking the hell outta my soul.

Brianna was stuck with her mouth open. Milah pushed me back, made me stumble, and then placed her hand on her hip. "For one, girl, he is not your baby. Two, step on away from *my* man, Brianna. You may be captain, but I won't be saving a hoe today. Shoo fly, don't bother me."

I was still stunned at how she kissed the hell out of me. Who gave a damn about how Brianna felt? 'Cause I sure as hell didn't care.

"Girl, if you want to keep your position, I'd suggest you watch your tone with me," Brianna stated, obviously trying to get under Milah's skin. Milah laughed. I had to step in fast before a cat fight got started out here on the field.

"Brianna, I was never ya' baby and you know that shit. You hear me? You was just a suck, fuck, and duck. We was never together, so stop making it seem like we was in a fuckin' relationship. I been cut you off, I meant that. I told you you'd come crawlin' straight back to me. So, step off, I don't want yo' ass. Go back to your boyfriend, whatever his name is, Vince or some shit," I said snapped. I was done with her and I'd never be a side nigga ever again.

"Whatever. You'll be back when you find out her shit is whack."

Milah rolled her eyes. "Hoe, I'm classy. I don't buss my punani open for every dude I meet. I'm not walking around campus showing all my ass, Heffa. Come on Ro Ro, baby." She pulled me away. I smiled.

"Really? *Ro Ro*? You just gon' act like we didn't have a thing? Like you don't know me?" I chuckled when Brianna continued to plead her case helplessly.

Milah, on the other hand, smiled a huge smile with a look of triumph on her face. "What? I had to make it real and you are my baby, cutie," she said with in uppity voice. I looked at her sideways, as her soft face started to blush again.

"You don't need to blush 'round me. But, if you fuckin with some-body else you need to tell me now. I ain't finna be strung along, and I'm not 'bout to be nobody side piece. I'm ya' only nigga, got it?" Her face looked shocked at my tone, but she nodded. If she truly understood where I was coming from we wouldn't be having any problems.

"I don't have a boyfriend. I want to be with you, I promise," Milah said, with honesty in her tone. Licking my lips, I ran my hand down my face and nodded without another word.

We made it back to where Bliss and my brother, and I swear, Bliss gave her a look I really didn't understand. I tried to put it together but the pieces just weren't connecting. Bliss mouthed something to her. But hell, I couldn't catch it 'cause she'd did it so fast. It was even weirder that Milah's attitude changed so quickly in response.

"Come on now, Milah. We have to finish this routine. Plus, we gotta do this damn work for math class." By the sound of Bliss' stern tone, it seemed she had an attitude with Milah for no reason.

"Okay, damn, Bliss."

Bliss rolled her eyes so hard it's a wonder they didn't get stuck. "Now, Kamilah," she said, even more demanding.

Milah looked at her like she'd lost her damn mind, like she had grown two heads. The look on her face was one I couldn't tolerate. "Get yo' thong out yo' ass, I'm coming."

Rome, being the clown he was, took the opportunity to get a good peep at Bliss' backside. She knew exactly what he was doing though and hit him playfully before she took off running.

"You hidin' something from me?"

Milah shook her head from side to side. "There's just a lot I have to tell you, but can we hang out lata' at my dorm?"

"Please? I swear, I don't want no one but you."

I thought the invitation over for a second and when she stepped closer to me, I ran my hand down the side of my face. I was lost in the sauce so I pulled her into a hug.

"I'll be over there," I finally said, " and wear somethin' you think I might like," I added. "'Cause, girl, these shorts you got on now," I said, grabbing a hand full of her plump ass, "got a nigga ready to say, 'I do'. Ya' heard. She slapped my chest and swatted my hand away.

"Stop that, the hell wrong with you?" she said giggling.

"Mm-hm, whatever. You like it, you like it." She rolled her eyes and pulled away from me.

"You and all these quotes from songs, TV shows, and movies are gonna be the death of me." I wiggled my eyebrows, causing her to giggle again. "Girl, you know that ain't yo' real laugh. You probably sound like a horse when you laughing. You can't fake me out." She gasped dramatically and placed her hand across her chest. She tried to hit me again but I caught her hand. Her mouth flew open as if she was shocked by my fast reaction. I licked my lips and jerked her forward into my chest.

"Keep tryin' to hit on me and you gon' get yourself in trouble, you feel me?"

She looked away, then back at me with a smirk on her face. "Okay," she said softly. Seeing the other two in my peripheral vision, I let her go when Bliss walked up breathing hard.

"Having fun?" I asked jokingly. Bliss flicked me off.

When Rome walked up to stand next me, he had taken his shirt off and thrown it across his shoulder. "She got a nice right uppercut I swear!" he said, breaking out into laughter. I began to laugh myself as he wiggled his jaw.

"Mm-hm. Milah, you ready?" Bliss asked.

Milah gave her a nonchalant shrug and looked back at me before kissing my cheek and walking off with her friend.

"Yeah, I'll see you later, Ro." She winked at me causing Rome to give me a questionable glance. I didn't try to go there with him at all.

"I saw that shit! Yeah, my bro finna get that."

I fanned him off since I wasn't trying to make something out of nothing.

"I had already had that, but still, I got a bad feeling she keeping something really important from me. And I don't like it."

He moved his eyebrows so one looked higher than the other. "You think?" he questioned.

I nodded with confidence. "Yeah, and I think it got to do with another guy. I just got that feeling, brosky."

Kamilah Smith

Who she think she is yelling at me? I thought.

"Again, why you lying to him like that? You're stupid. You're gonna get caught and I'm not going to help clean up the mess this time," Bliss stated, while pulling off her Hampton tank top, throwing it in the hamper.

"Bliss, you don't have to talk down on me. I'm—"

Bliss raised her hand to cut me off. Then she gave me that damn look, and not the good one either.

"To hell with that! You are playing damn cat and mouse and it's all a game. Ken will be here in how many more days and you haven't ended it yet? Come the fuck on, what are you holding on for? I bet you he sleeping around on you or probably got a girlfriend."

I sat down on my bed and laughed to myself. "Did I say something funny?" she said, placing her hands on her hips.

"No, but we aren't *really* in a relationship. We do see other people. We just haven't ended things."

She gave me a face and fanned me off, completely dismissing what I'd just said. "You know what? Fuck that, fuck you, and fuck *it*! I'm damn tired of this conversation with you. I'm going to see my man, you are filled with too much despair to listen. You can figure this out on your own. I'm through with it. When Cairo finds out, I'll be praying for you. And, that bitch Brianna is sneaky. I've got a bad ass feeling about her, but hey! You don't wanna get a grip on the shit so it's on you. I think her little boyfriend is closer to us than we both know. And you know Ken is gonna on the basketball team, oh, my lord. You fuck up everything, Kamilah," she boasted, then stormed out after she'd changed clothes. She slammed the door on her way out.

Bliss was right about everything she'd said to me. She knew me like the back of her hand. She could always tell when I was lying and when I was up to no good. Ain't that some shit!

She was right. I was gonna lose him. I didn't want that to happen. Cairo was everything, and his twin was too. I had to fix this some type of way. I got up from where I was sitting, walked over to my dresser, and looked at myself in the mirror. Staring at my reflection, I tried to figure everything out, including who I truly was.

To tell him or not to tell him? That was the question now invading my mental peace. A tear slipped down my eye as I pulled myself away from the mirror. I couldn't stand to look at myself any longer. A folded piece of paper on the dresser caught my attention. I opened it and read it aloud:

Kamilah, I watched you fix your hair. Then, you put your panties on while standing in front of the mirror, Kamilah. Then your lipstick, Kamilah.

I can't keep doing this. I flopped down on my bed and cried myself to sleep. Everything going on had resulted from my wrong doings, but I just couldn't own up to them.

***

A few hours later, there were a knock on my door. I didn't feel like getting up at all. Grabbing my Kimono robe off my bed post, I pulled it on and tied it up. The draft in the dorm was breezy. It was ninety degrees outside but sixty degrees in the room. The best naps were the shortest ones. I got up feeling too groggy to move. Rubbing the dry sleep out of my eyes, I stretched and went over to the door. It was now dark outside and I couldn't believe I'd slept that long. In all actuality, I needed the sleep since I'd been overworking myself.

I opened the door to Cairo standing in the doorway. His body was glistening in a white wife beater, white Gucci shorts with the matching socks, and flip flops. All I could do was think, *how the hell?* The shorts were loose, and I could tell he didn't have a thing on underneath them. Lawd give me the willpower not to fall into temptation.

"Well, are you going to let me in? I can't be no third wheel," he said, looking up toward the night sky.

I nodded and opened the door wider. "Yeah, yeah come in." He walked past me, and his cologne hit my nose. My knees buckled and I almost pounced on the boy.

"What were you doin'?" he asked, sitting on my bed. "It's still warm."

"Well, Snoopy, I was sleeping," I said, sitting next to him and grabbing my Mac laptop.

"So, *Netflix?*" I smiled and nodded. We sat back on my bed, and I swear I was getting so hot, I had to move over a bit, a little farther from him.

He noticed and snickered. "Aye, you too far away. Sit on my lap. Why the hell you moving so far away?"

I shook my head. I couldn't even grasp the words to say anything. So, I just sucked it up and sat in his lap, and that's when I felt *it*. I jumped a little and tried to keep my cool.

"Cairo?" I said nervously.

He gripped my hips and kissed the back of my neck. "We need to stop playing and make things happen, shawty." He nibbled on my neck, causing my words to get caught in my throat. To say I was new to this was a real understatement.

"I have to tell you s-something for real. It's important," I said, struggling to get it out.

"Can't it wait? I need you, girl. Come on, baby."

I just kept it to myself and everything slipped out of my mind. Cairo grabbed me softly. He began to kiss all on my cleavage. He turned me backwards and smacked my behind one good time. I spun around facing him. He grabbed my hand and moved it down to his package, and he was truly blessed.

"I know you feel it but do what you know what to do, baby?" He lay back on his hands and looked at my behind.

"Cairo? Just listen for a second."

He sent a nice stinging slap to my ass. Then, he rubbed it softly as he leaned up to whisper in my ear. "Don't talk back. You know you want it, Milah. I ain't come here to fuck. I came to make love. So, let Ro Jr. out."

I was hesitant. I licked over my lips. "Cairo, I'm not about to have sex with you. Aren't you listening to me? I can't do this. I'm not ready for all this. I'm scared. This is all new to me."

He frowned and spun me around. "Then we won't do that if you're not ready. I can take no for an answer. Just tease a nig then." His tongue trailed down the back of my neck as he moved closer to me. Therefore, I started to twerk on him. He leaned up and slid his hands in my shorts before proceeding to pull them off.

"You playing, and I like that. I just want you to be my baby. I just need to see that ass moving in those panties of yours. And now I gotta' show you that *Cairo Black* don't play."

My mouth gaped open as he went to work. My hand found its way in his shorts somehow. *I hope Bliss don't start no bullshit, and keep her mouth shut till I'm able to tell him the bitter truth,* I thought. And then his full head of hair found my black queen, Kamilah. Bad dreams, Kamilah.

CHAPTER 9

You Don't Own Me

Cairo Black

The owl hooted outside of her window. I was still in her dorm room and things had turned up a bit. We were doing things that escalated so good from Netflix and chill. It was turning out real good. Yeah, she was ready. But, there were other things I could do to her that didn't have to result in me using my good hood pipe on Milah. My lips touched her skin. She would shiver at each kiss that landed on her flesh. Her hand caressed the back of my neck, and I kissed her neck. But, I had to stop. Something in me wanted to wear her fine ass out but I couldn't, and I knew that. What she'd said earlier was weighing heavily on my mind.

"Wait, Milah." I rose off her and placed both of my hands at each side of her head.

She breathed heavily, trying to catch her breath before she spoke. "Yes?" she answered while looking into my eyes, making me want to kiss her down.

"What were you trying to tell me?" I knew my sexual thoughts were taking over my brain but I couldn't get past it. "What did you have to say?"

She sighed, then lifted up a little bit. "Well, I mean, I don't want to kill our vibe, honestly."

I eyed her and she sighed once more, a clear sign that she was holding some heavy shit back. "Tell me, man? Really, if we gon' go far with this, I want us to be honest with each other."

She bit her lip and nodded. "Well, uh about my father he put me and this guy together when we were young, but I broke up with him. My father is from Cairo, Egypt and he has beliefs from his culture. My mother, on the other hand, is mixed with African American and British. The guy was never my type, and I couldn't be with someone I didn't like or love. So, I ended it and my father doesn't know."

I raised an eyebrow at her. *Was she telling half the truth?* "Is that all? Really? C'mon mane, I can see right through you. I can believe the *arranged* dating shit. But, tell me the whole truth. Are you still with him or are you pullin' my damn leg, Milah?"

She quickly shook her head no. "It's the truth. I'm not with him. We're seeing other people. Well, I'm not seeing anyone yet. I want you, Ro, and I really mean that. But, for the sake of my father, he and the guy still act like we're still together. But, listen, we don't kiss or anything like that. The terms of the relationship are completely platonic. It's just to keep my father happy. And, my mother is hard to crack too. She-she wouldn't approve of you either. I'm sorry I'm laying this all on you, this fast."

I sat up and looked at her. I pulled her legs on top of mine. "What do ya' mean she won't approve of me? I'm not tryin' to marry you! And why, 'cause I'm not rich, or is it 'cause I'm from da' hood?" I asked, getting a little bit on the angry side.

Milah nodded truthfully, while dropping her head in shame. But, I couldn't blame her. I was hood, born and raised in the gutta. But, I was doing something with my life. "So what, you sneak around?"

She looked up at me. Her eyes were dilated as she nodded her head in confirmation. "I don't want to talk about that, okay?" She dropped her head once more, sniffling as she continued to pick at her nails. I felt bad. I climbed back on top of her and kissed her deeply and then all over her body.

"Hey, look at me. I wasn't tryna hurt your feelings. This new to me too, shawty."

"Cairo? I don't want to hurt y-you either," she said in tears.

I drowned her out and continued planting soft kisses on her body. I wanted to know the truth and that's what I had gotten. I insisted on knowing so I got what I wanted. I could trust her, right? I had to try at least. Trust was something I needed to work out on. Her manicured nails clawed at my shirt as I kissed and nipped at her neck. Her body squirmed and wiggled to my every touch and her back arched under me. She was driving me wild.

I slipped my hands under her cotton crop tank and her body spasmed. Milah shook at the feel of my cold hands, as they cupped her perky warm breasts. I held them in my hands, rubbing them softly. Her silk pearls had soon turned into hard pebbles. Her back slowly arched again, as I continued to massage her nice breasts. I heightened her pleasure by sucking on her perfect neckline. I could hear her moans getting a little out of hand and I hadn't even done anything to her. It was turning me on so damn much.

I just hoped she wasn't telling me a bold face lie. But, who would lie about an arranged relationship like that? Right now, I just had to have her right now. I was trying to get the whole conversation out of my head. I pulled her thick, flat-ironed, short-blond hair to the side of her face and planted kisses from her lips to her neck, and then to her flat, perfect-toned stomach. She was so sensitive. She bucked like a wild bull from the sensation of my wet and soft kisses.

"Tell me how you want it," I asked in a gentle whisper. My eyes were locked in on her beautiful face.

Her chest heaved up and down as she looked down at me, our eyes connected on one another, building the tension even more. "I-I don't even know where to start. I'm scared."

I smirked and nipped at her thin black panties. Her small hands landed on mine as she pushed them down, giving me the big hint to pull them off. A wide smile came across my lips. I licked my tongue across my lips as I stared at the black thong she had on. I took in the sight of her. Like I'd said before, I wasn't tryna fuck her, I was tryin' to show her who the real deal actually was and who she belonged to now.

I wanted to treat Milah in a different light. I never had a true, real, and loving relationship. But, with her, I felt something different. I didn't know what it was, but it's like she blinded me from all the hoes and distractions. If she was playing with my heart, I couldn't see it. It's like I was blinded by her exotic beauty, personality, smarts, and body. And she was right here under me, caving into the soft touch of my fingers, the feel of my wet tongue, and the power grip I had around her thick, curvy waist.

Placing my hands under her knees, I maneuvered her carefully, so that her soft plump booty rested on the edge of the seat. I slipped my fingers underneath the worn elastic of her panties, strung across the points of her hips. As she lifted her hips giving me all access, I slipped them down to her ankles. I slowly kissed her thighs and softly drew her knees apart. Then, I pressed my thumb against her throbbing, watery ardor. I was eye level with her glistening pearl, and it was exactly how I imagined it. The smoothness, the lips, the perfect pink hole. And then when I was about to slip my finger in, my other hand went under her thigh and cupped her thick booty and entered her. She was so tight, I was driving her crazy.

"Oh, my gosh wait, Cairo," was all she could manage to say. And the rest of this night was history. My mouth fell agape as my wet lips attached to her swollen pearl.

Her head fell back and her mouth fell open, making love sounds. "Ro-Ro-Cairo. . ."

I lifted from between her legs and looked her deep in her eyes.

"Girl, you been eatin' pineapples or strawberries? Huh? Which one, 'cause you tastin' good as hell right na'." Milah's eyes closed again, as my tongue swirled around her pearl, "You ain't gon' answer me, baby?"

She moaned once again as I was doing my little work on her womanhood. There was a soft knock on the door but it didn't break my concentration. My hold got tighter on her thighs as she tried to inch up.

"Ro, l-let me up, please." I hummed against her and she started wilding out. "Oh, my God, Ro! Slow down p-please!"

I laughed against her. She shivered against my trembling voice and her back arched. Someone knocked again, much harder this time. I rolled my eyes and removed my index finger. Milah jerked forward. I chuckled at her reaction and got up from my position on the floor. I ran my thumb across my lips, wiping her juices away.

"W-where you going?" she grumbled in her sexual state.

I shook my head and trucked towards the door, first checking my manhood. I was good. I unlocked her door and opened it. Some dark skin nigga stood there with an ATL high school basketball duffle bag. I looked him up and down wondering why the hell was he here and interrupting my moment with my sweet, fruity juicy treat over there.

"Sup', mane? Who you here for? If you looking for Bliss, she taken and ain't here.

He looked me up and down like I had done him. He tried to look in the room but I pushed him back with my forearm, "Gon', bruh? Who you here for?"

"Man, I'm here to see Kamilah. Is she here?" He was rich and proper. *I know this ain't that nigga she was talm' 'bout.* Well, had to be because if he was rich like she said this had to be the dude she was arranged with.

"Well, she ain't here at the moment so bounce that ass on somewhere." I slammed the door in his face and turned to Milah.

"Was that the nigga?" I questioned her.

She sat up with a bewildered face, up on her elbows and looked at me confused. "Who?"

I looked at her like she was crazy. Then, I laughed as I rubbed my chin, looking at her with squinted eyes. "Yo' don't play with me and shit. Playin' coy. Who the fuck was that dark skin ass nigga lookin' for? Was it that nigga you was tellin' me about?" I asked with my strong accent.

"Cairo, I don't know. I didn't even hear his voice. You got me gone over here, baby."

I shook my head. Maybe I was tripping, maybe. "You bet not be lyin' to me. I swear fo' God, girl."

She looked at me and waved her hand at me.

"You think I'm playin', huh?" I laughed and darted towards her, immediately grabbing a hold of her legs. Holding her down, I dived in.

"Okay, Cairo!" My eyes met hers and I smirked. "You know my other name." She grabbed my head and I knew I had her where I wanted her.

"Daddy!" was all that poured out of her mouth. I looked straight at Milah and devoured her core.

"Mm-hm, that's what I like to hear." And that's what I heard for the rest of the night.

***

I lay in the bed with Milah as she snuggled in my arms. I thought about how vulnerable she'd been. She was sleeping hard since I had put her to bed. She loved every bit of the pleasure that dripped from my tongue. I knew she'd never had that done to her before, and I could tell. The way her body reacted had let me know. My phone buzzed against the mattress causing my eyes to shift downward. I looked to the left as I outstretched my arm and picked it up. I had no messages which caused me to frown because it had to be Milah's phone instead.

I picked it up and pushed her power button. Her screen popped open and there were a few messages from Bliss(two), Simone(five), Trish(two), and Ken(seven). Those seven messages caught my eye. But, I didn't want to be nosey or pry through her phone. It was his name that rang a bell. So, I decided just to look. Sliding her phone to the left, it unlocked. I looked at Milah and she didn't move. Hearing breathing was soothing, but my lip turned up, and I hoped I wouldn't find something I didn't want to see.

I sighed and pressed her messages on her iPhone 7 Plus. I went to his message and clicked on his contact photo. When I saw his face, I instantly began to boil. So, I read the text message.

Ken: Listen, I had made it to the school early. My scholarship finally came through. Sorry, but hear it is, out in the open. I don't mean to drop this on you. But, I found the perfect person for me. I know we supposed to be in an arranged relationship and we keep playing like we're together. For both our parents' sake. I don't know, if I can anymore. the truth is, Milah, I like men. I'm gay. And, again, I'm sorry, but I'll continue to fake this relationship, so you won't have to deal with your father. I love the man I'm with. Sent- 6:12 pm

I had to put the phone down. I couldn't believe it. I looked over at Milah and she was still out cold. Looking back at the phone, I pressed the home button on the center of the phone but then decided to go back into her messages again. I had to mark the message as unread. I sat her phone down and let out a long deep breath. Milah shifted on my chest, and I couldn't help but still think about what dude had just said. How was Milah going to talk herself out of this one? Would she even tell me? Would she lie? How would she even be with me? All these questions swarmed in my brain like flies. So, I decided to close my eyes and get some sleep. Stretching my arm out, I twisted the switch to turn off the bedside lamp. I was internally tired.

CHAPTER 10

The Pressure

KAMILAH SMITH

Snoring loudly, I was in a deep dream as I was floating like a crane in the sky. Everything was so peaceful here, until I felt a strong and big hand smack my ass. I shot up and moved some of my hair out of my face. I looked around and it was basically morning according to the sunshine coming through the blinds. I lifted the small blanket only to see I was half naked. A smile came across my lips as I looked over at Cairo. He was lying on his stomach with one arm still on me and the other halfway off the bed. I leaned over and kissed his neck and back but he didn't budge. I thought he was playing. I was sure someone's hand had smacked me across my bottom.

I moved his arm and it caused him to groan just a little bit. I maneuvered over him as he shifted to get comfortable on the bed. I looked from him toward phone with its lighted screen. I picked it up and pressed the power button. I saw a had a lot of damn messages flooded on my home screen. Half of them were from Bliss but one name stood out from all the rest. What was the need for so many texts?

I looked down at Cairo and bit my lip, debating on whether or not I should read the messages. He could pop his head up at any given moment. Taking a deep, long silent breath, I spun over to Bliss' side of the room and took a seat on her bed. Cairo continued sleeping peacefully, growling like a grizzly bear. Maybe it had been in my head and no one had really smacked my ass to begin with. Rolling my eyes as I looked from Cairo to my phone, the sight of big paragraphs sent my heart raging. My eyes went from left to right as I read. Something inside of me broke inside. I couldn't believe he was here and throwing this on me now. How would my dad respond to when, or if, he found out?

Running my hand through my tangled hair, I tried to process the fact that Ken was gay and had the nerve to keep it from me. No wonder we hadn't done any intimate things together. It kind of killed me that at any moment he could stop our façade and my world could come crashing down. I went through all his texts and it was crazy. Text after texts, my heart caved more into my chest.

Ken: I'm sorry for dropping the bomb on u. Talk to me, please Kamilah?
Sent- 6:25 pm

Ken: The guy at ur dorm was cute, mama. Perfect for u I hope ur happy.
I'll do whatever u need to keep ur pops off ur back. Just hit me back. Sent- 6:26
pm

Ken: Honestly... I think u need to tell ur dad the truth. I'm going to come
out sooner than later... Seriously. No more hiding for us. Sent-6:27 pm

I sighed and tossed my phone onto Bliss' bed. I flopped back and
kicked my legs in the air like a galloping pony. I covered my face with
my hands, trying to let the unnecessary tears fall. As I lay there, I tried
hard to regulate my breath. I stared up at the ceiling. My vision was so
blurry, I couldn't focus. I felt the bed dip by my head and I didn't dare
move because I knew it was Cairo stirring awake. I didn't want him to
see me down like this.

"What's the matter?" Cairo questioned. I didn't say a peep. I just
stayed as I was. He laid on top of me and moved my hands, but I kept
my eyes closed, "C'mon? Is it 'bout ole' boy?"

My eyes popped open and I looked at him with an angry expression. "How did you know? You were snooping in my phone."

He rolled his eyes and pecked my lips. "I'm ya' man. I have the
right too. And it was bogus how he did you like this. Y'all like friends,
right? So why would he keep you in the dark like that? And what if
someone finds out 'bout that. They'll start shaming you. What will happen to your credibility and reputation?"

I looked at him and had to admit, he was right. If anyone found out
about this, I don't know what would happen. I was one of the star dancers on the team for the college and that would just ruin everything. I got
myself into this now I had no idea on how to get out of it. I was surprised
Cairo had taken it so well.

"I don't know what to do. I have to fake like me and him are still
together but he wants to come out. How are you taking this so well?"
He shrugged, and I squinted my eyes at him. "It's because he's gay, isn't
it? You can't fool me?"

He shrugged again. "I mean, I guess? He still acting like yo' boyfriend and I gotta act like I'm just yo' friend. I have to be cool with this.
He's gay, I know that. I know he won't be touching you. I mean, it ain't

98

cool but at least I'm the one who will be hittin' it every night whenever you let me."

I slapped his chest as he broke out laughing. "But, nah, for real. I'll be cool with this for na', but don't let this shit get outta hand, Milah. For real yo', I ain't playin' with you."

I smiled and wrapped my legs around him. "I won't, Ro." He hummed an okay, and I pecked his lips. Cairo, deepened the kiss.

He quickly got a satisfied moan out of me. "Mmm, don't start nothing this morning. We got classes to get too. Plus, practice."

I made a sad face and he shook his head. "One more kiss then."

I bit at his bottom lip as we started to make out. He made me feel like I was on cloud nine. While we were making out, he slipped his hands underneath me, making me smile and giggle into the kiss. All of a sudden, we both heard *Hey There* by Dej Loaf outside of my dorm room. The door unlocked, welcoming Bliss into the room. She walked in but stopped dead in her tracks, as Cairo and I lifted ourselves from *her* bed.

"Ah hell, now I have to burn my sheets! I loved those too." She shook her head and Cairo's brother followed behind her.

"Ohh! My brother done killed the punani!"

I rolled my eyes and pushed Cairo off me and sat up straight. "Shush, we were not having sex," I said, fanning him off. He did it back to me but with so much sassy attitude, trying to match mine. "You so Sus for that, Rome," I said causing Cairo to burst out laughing, and Bliss did too.

Rome side-eyed Bliss, then his own brother. "Girl, I'll punch you right in your downward sloping nose."

I flicked him off and went over to my side of the room to put on some clothes, though they couldn't see anything since Cairo was covering me up like a second skin.

"Bruh, you know that donkey-kong looking ass bih' stopped by our dorm looking for you." Rome was so blunt, he didn't even care.

"Who?" Cairo said back to his brother, clearly confused.

"Bro! Plastic surgery ass, musty-armpit-breath ass, Brianna. She stopped by talm' bout and I quote: 'where is my man at, Rome?' He betta be here and he bet' not be with that sag-pussy-ass trick.' No offense Milah, but ya' girl, Blistex, handled her ass."

Bliss slapped the back of his head, making him cut his eyes at her. "The hell girl? Told you 'bout puttin' them paws on me." He slapped her ass and she rolled her eyes, completely ignoring his entire existence.

"Yes girl, this bih' thought she was—"

Rome completely cut her off by hugging her from behind. Her entire expression changed.

"Keep playin', you know the deal."

I just chuckled while I pulled on my sweatshirt.

"Whatever, Milah, we'll talk about it on the way to practice. Since jackass and jackass-lite wanna be all in our Kool-Aid. But, we all got to get going. Classes starting soon," Bliss announced.

We all nodded. Looking over at Cairo he was biting on his entire bottom lip as he eyed me up and down. I pecked his lips and caressed his cheek. "I'll see you later on, okay?" He nodded and planted a tender kiss on my forehead.

"Sure thing, Shawty."

I damn near caved under the touch of his voice. He walked out of my room. I closed the door on his way out. I turned my back towards the door and slid down to the floor is pure dramatic fashion, blowing out an exhausted breath.

"Girl, he got ya' ass sprung that fast? You is open like some ripe ass Georgia Peaches."

I bit my lip, but I instantly thought about the news Ken had hit me up with. My reality hit me like a ten-ton boulder.

"I have something to tell you and be serious about it."

Bliss began frowning her eyebrows at me then nodded as she took a seat on my bed.

"So, how should I say this? Okay, I'ma be real and quick on this one. Ken is gay."

Her mouth fell open, just like mine had done.

"No!" was all she could say. I nodded in agreement. "No, way! No fucking way! Thick beard, big muscles, deep voice, Ken is gay? I thought I'd heard it all!" Bliss was in shock.

"What am I supposed to do, Bliss? I'm in deep this time, like six feet under deep."

She came over to me and brought me into a hug. "I'm glad you told Cairo the truth. I'm proud of you, Kamilah. You're progressing. You *did* tell him everything, right?" I looked up at her with a not-really look on my face. She sighed.

"Damn, Milah. Why?"

I shrugged. "I couldn't muster up the strength. It would've been too much for a person to take in in one day. I couldn't put on my big girl thong and tell him." She shook her head in disappointment. She held me as a tear slipped down my cheek.

"It'll be okay. I promise. You just gotta tell him. Once you do, you'll be fine and everything will be settled. You hear me? You deserve to be loved, Milah. You do."

I'd heard what she'd said, I just wished it was true.

***

As we made it to dance practice, I could see Cairo and his brother training as the football players were practicing on the dewy grass field. They looked so good running the track. Bliss elbowed me, and I smiled at her. "Girl, Brianna is over there talking to Kenneth."

I looked in the direction she was looking in and shrugged. "She don't know the half and I'm not even worried." She gave me my props and we continued to finish the routine. Brianna stared at me The whole time, so I decided to say something. "What's your deal? Why the hell you keep staring at me? I don't give a damn just 'cause you the captain. This is not high school, boo-boo-kitty-lookin'-ass hoe. I am not the one."

She smirked at me and waved me off. "Girl, don't even go there, okay. You should get your man 'cause he don't want your rag tag hoe—"

I grabbed her by her weave and she was stunned by my actions. "Listen hear, bitch! I'm not the one to be played with. Touch my man and all hell gon' break loose, okay!" I pulled her hair tighter in my fist prompting her to nod her head up and down at a rapid pace. "Good. And if you talk to Cairo or Rome, you better be prepared to catch hell from me and my girl, Bliss. Now, treat us with respect or it's gon' be some more problems between us." I let her go and all the girls standing on looking laughed. "Oh, and if you want to keep your damn spot as captain, get yo' shit together 'cause your steps be a little off, homey. You can't kick me off the team so don't even think it." I flipped my natural blonde hair and we went on our merry way.

"You handled that really well. But, I think you need to talk to Ken. He needs to explain to you why he didn't tell you sooner. And you need to do it before he causes problems."

I nodded in agreement. "I'll talk to him soon enough. Right now, I have to gain the courage to tell Cairo about the rest of my past. It's going to be hard, but I'd rather tell him before anyone else does." I bit on my lip in frustration. I didn't know how on earth I was going to tell him the rest. I was far from perfect. I, Kamilah Smith, was flawed all over.

CHAPTER 11

Baby, Come My Way

Cairo Black

I cracked my knuckles as I eyed the tall muthafucka. Rome saw the look I had plastered on my face and knew it wasn't good. His hand gripped my bicep, pulling my arm back.

"You are not about to go over there and talk to that nicca, Ro. I see that damn look in your eye," Rome said. I nodded and lightly pulled my arm from his grip and walked over to ole' boy, Ken.

"Aye, bro? You Ken right?"

He nodded as his eyes trailed up and down my face. Ken stood with a hard look on his face as we stood toe to toe.

"Yeah, mane. I'ma need to talk to you, homie." My brother's eyes were wide. I had many reasons for not telling him Ken was gay.

"What about?" he said, putting his bag over his shoulder. Ken stood tall, breathing like a bull.

"My girl, Milah." His whole faced changed, and I knew some shit was going to be said. I just had to put my pettiness to the side and be a man about it. Ken was the type of dude who wasn't a man at all. He wanted to pussy up and go the short route instead of the long one. I hated so-called men like him, absolutely despised them. Not because they were homosexuals, but because they would hide who they truly were. He had hidden behind Milah *and* his daddy's money.

I was born and raised in the ghetto hood, had to get dirt on my knees to prove myself to some of these people out here. Looking at Ken, I knew he wasn't that type. He was the snooty type who got everything he wanted. Me? I had to earn everything to my name. Just looking at him now, I knew he was a true fake who wanted attention. With my eyes directly on him, I tried hard to keep my cool. However, the shit he was saying was really pissing me off. "My girl, Milah? You know who I'm talking about, don't act dumb," I said, letting him know what was up, for Milah's sake. I didn't want this to get dragged into the ground because of their families, but it wasn't my choice. It was Milah's. Her father trapped her, plus he controlled her life. And it wasn't right. Ken looked at me and I looked at him. He was trying to look all tough and shit, knowing damn well he be snapping his fingers, popping his lips, and screaming shit like, '*Yasss, Boo, you killin' tha' game.*'

Shaking the thought out of my head, I tried to focus on the norm. But, like I said, I was trying to be non-petty about the matter. "You're going out with Milah? How? That's my girl, so I think you should step yo' country ass away from her," he said, twisting his face to the side. They knew how to play their secret good as hell. I started laughing and my brother looked at me like I was crazy.

"Listen, bro, I'm trying to be cool about this shit. I know the whole damn ordeal between y'all, ya' feel me? So, I think you need to come correct with ya' tone."

He scoffed and took off his duffle bag. The boy was trying to get buck with me as he inched closer to me. "Man, you don't know shit, a'ight? And, speaking of Milah, she ain't even yo' girl. She been my girlfriend for a long damn time and that'll never change, homey. So, I think you need to step off. Like I said, you don't know shit about me and her."

My brother stepped in front of me, pushing me back. He knew I was getting more heated by the second. "Come on, Cairo. Don't do nothin' stupid. We got our scholarships on the line and we just gettin' our feet in the door here."

I sighed and was about to speak up, when Ken spoke up, saying some more smart shit. "Yeah, don't do no dumb shit. Listen to yo' bro before you get hurt, yo'."

My brother pushed me back once more. I wasn't about to let this nigga step to me like that. "Man, I think you should shut up with all that! You ain't 'bout that life, kid. What I can give to yo' ass will put you in check! I'll knock yo' ass clean the fuck out!"

He laughed and I knew this shit was 'bout to get ugly as fuck.

"Ro don't stoop to his level," Rome yelled, pushing me away.

"What's going on here?" I heard Milah say, as she walked up on us unexpectedly. I fixed the wrinkles my brother's grip had caused in shirt.

"Nothing at all, shawty," Ken said, putting his arm around her shoulder. Ken gave me a look, but I could see the heat fumes escaping Milah's body. On the inside, I was heated. I knew I was going to have a big problem with this.

She looked at him and then at me. "You sure?" she asked, looking more so at Ken. He kissed the side of her face, and she gave him fakest smile ever.

"Yeah, we good. Uh, what ya' name is? The artist formerly named as Cairo, right?" Ken had jokes.

I rubbed the side of my face and I swear, if my brother wasn't holding me back, I would have socked him in the mouth. Dude was really trying my entire soul.

"Stop, Ken. His name is Cairo, okay? That wasn't even necessary. We need to talk anyway," I said. "In private," I added.

Ken turned his attention solely on Milah and, at the same time, he backed away from her slowly and asked, "Why? You finally gonna be a woman and tell ya' pops was'sup? Or are you going to keep being a pussy about the matter at hand? Huh? Scared someone gon' *touch* you again?" Ken blurted out in front of the crowd that had started forming.

Milah's face nearly dropped to the ground and so did Bliss'. All I could do was stand there looking dumbfounded, wondering what the hell dude was yapping about.

"I ain't about to be with yo' ass forever! You not even on shit, look at you?" Ken said, laughing in her face like she was trash. Some of the students gasped while others snickered.

"Why would you say something like that?" she said, with tears in her eyes. "You don't even know what the fuck you're talkin' about, Ken."

He laughed in her face once more and it took everything out of me not to fuck him up. "So, you fuckin' around with this hoodrat?" Ken said, changing the subject.

Milah just stood there as her tears soaked her face. "You wanna cry now? Huh? You the one who can't speak up for ya' self! Daddy's little girl too damn scared to step up and say something."

I had to stop this because it was clearly getting out of hand.

"I ain't tell a gotdamn thing, that's complete bullshit and you know it. Ken. So, why are you doing this to me?" Milah said, trying not to make a scene.

I managed to step around my brother and push Ken. "Keep talkin' to her like you crazy yo'!"

A smile crept on his face, and Brianna strutted over to him like a damn peacock. It was like he had set the whole shit up.

"Baby, you okay? Why you over here by this wanna-be?"

Milah stood there defenseless. I couldn't help but want to hold her.

"Brianna, get your trickin' ass away from over here. He don't want you, so why you tryna make Cairo feel some way. Get you nasty-mouth ass on somewhere," Rome said, stepping in.

"Rome shut the fuck up! You——-"

He cut her off and shut her down real quick. "Bitch, you a hoe! Tell him how you got a boyfriend and ya' nasty ass got a STD from his hoe ass. Yeah, what you gotta say now, you nasty, crusty, funk-mouth trick! If his ass want you, it's disgusting, well not that disgusting because he"

I cut him off, made him look at Milah. "Take ya' asses on somewhere," I said to both of them while I tried to comfort her.

"Cairo, are you intimidated by a man like Ken?" I laughed in her face. Brianna had no idea how much of a bitch he really was.

"Bitch, he ain't no man. So, get out my face with all that."

Milah looked down to avoid my face and I couldn't believe she had let Brianna and nigga cut her down like that.

"Ain't no more to see here. Get the fuck on," Rome and Bliss said.

The crowd began to whisper as they began to disburse. Some looked at Milah, others looked at Brianna and Ken with disgust. The rest just walked away laughing. I looked down at Milah as Bliss tried to soothe her. She rubbed her hand up and down Milah's shoulders..

"Cairo, I think I'll take her back to our dorm," Bliss confessed. She was tried to talk to her but I don't think Milah was hearing it.

"Milah? What was he talking about? Are you okay?" I asked with concern laced in my tone.

She finally looked at me and gave me a small smile. I grabbed her hand and ran my thumb over her knuckles. "I'ma be fine, I promise. C'mon, Bliss," Milah said as she pulled her hand out of mine I wanted to ask but I just let it go. They walked away as Rome and I stared at them. We were completely shook at the situation.

"What type of shit is this? This shit is circus-like," he said, picking up his bag. I just shook my head.

"What do you think he meant by 'you gon' let him touch you again?' Do you think——"

I signaled him to stop. "Just leave it alone, bro, for real. I'm praying it ain't that."

He nodded and we walked to our dorm. I had to talk to my brother, Key. This was just out of control.

Kamilah Smith

It was later and my day had been crap with all the commotion that went on. I sat doing my college work but I couldn't focus. I couldn't believe he'd said that. I couldn't believe he'd put my business out there like that. Writing with my pen, I couldn't find the means to finish my work. I could feel all my emotions running back to me like a full-on train.

"Milah, you okay?" Bliss said from across the room.

I felt my eyes watering, but I wouldn't let myself cry again. "Y-yeah, I'm fine." I lied. The pen dropped out of my hand as I looked down at the lined paper.

"No, you're not. I'm going to call Cairo. Y'all need to talk this out." I shrugged and Bliss stood up. I thought she'd been joking about making me talk it out with him. I followed her every movement with my eyes. She grabbed her phone, unlocking it to make the call. She wanted someone to come to my rescue and I knew who too.

Looking up at her, the droplet size tears rolled down my cheeks. I spun around in my rolling chair and faced her. "I'm okay, really."

Bliss shushed me. She knew me all too well. "You are not! Have you taken your medication lately? That boy brought up your past, hit you straight below the belt, Milah. He had no right to do that. He hit you low and you didn't say anything. You need to tell Cairo what happened to you. Why you do guys like this only to continue have Ken run all of them away?" Bliss bolstered as she threw her hands in the air.

I shot up from my seat with tears in my eyes. I didn't want to hear anything she had to say. "Shut up, shut up! I'm tired of you telling me this, okay? This was never my damn fault. My life has been fucked up for nineteen damn years! I never asked to be born. If it wasn't because of my race, my lifestyle, my family, the money, and this damn fake-ass relationship I was put into, I'd be fucking normal! It's the men I've trusted who hurt me, so you don't you ever say I brought this on my fuckin' self," I yelled as I pushed her out of anger.

Bliss' face was filled with so much hurt, you could see her body shaking. She stood there with her phone in her hand. Hearing a muffled voice, my heart gravitated to my stomach when his voice registered in my brain. I never knew she had called him in the first place. Me and Bliss didn't know anyone was on the phone. I gripped my hair as fresh tears replaced my dry ones.

"No, no, no," I whispered, as she began to plead with me.

"Hello? Aye, I'm coming over there now," Cairo said through the phone.

I pinched the bridge of my nose, paced the floor, how could she let me do that. I couldn't believe she let him hear all that. Her mouth hung agape before she offered an apology. "I'm sorry, Milah. Please forgive—"

Raising my arm up with my hand at a standstill, Bliss' mouth closed suddenly. Shaking my head, I raised my hands and covered my face. I felt so overwhelmed. As every passing minute went by, all I could do was lie on my stomach and sob. A stern knock on the door caused my sobs to become harder.

"She's lying on her bed, Cairo," Bliss said upon opening the door.

I buried my face in my hands and closed my eyes tighter.

"Baby, you good? We need to talk, like now," Cairo said softly, but seriously. The usual playfulness was gone from his voice. He wanted answers, and I knew he deserved them.

With no choice but to face him, I opened my bloodshot eyes to little bright dots floating aimlessly. I adjusted my vision and lifted my head from the pillow to speak. "Cairo," I began, as I took a quick glimpse over at Bliss, "this was not how I wanted to tell you about my troubled childhood. "I'm okay. Don't worry," I stressed. Bliss began to bounce back and forth ready for a fight, and I flinched at her.

"If you feeling froggy, jump! You already pushed me and I shoulda slapped you then," Bliss said, holding her hands up in battle mode. I was about to hop off the bed and tackle her but Cairo pulled me back.

"Both of y'all chill out," he said calmly.

I rolled my eyes and brought my knees to my chest.

"Say it, what's the matter? I heard what you said while I was on the phone. Tell me what's up?" Cairo insisted. It seemed as though he was looking into my soul. I turned my head so I wouldn't have to meet his gaze.

"Nothing! Okay." My voice trembled.

Cairo continued to stare at me as he lowered himself right on the bed next to me. I was so full of anxiety, my hands shook uncontrollably, revealing my nervousness.

"You're shaking like a leaf, man." He grabbed my hands and kisses them. "What's going on?" he probed. His sincerity was evident in his tone, and I could tell his concern was genuine. Noticing my procrastination to answer, he pulled me into his chest and held me close, and tight. Like a baby needing coddling, he rocked me from side to side gently.

That's when I broke down and let the water fall like an erupted dam. With all the courage I could muster, I set my secrets free. "The reason I'm so fucked up is all because of him. He molested me when I was little, okay? I didn't want to tell you this way or this soon. But Bliss, Ken, and everyone else was pressuring me to tell you. They didn't go through it, I did! Everyone makes me feel as though I'm some kind of monster when I'm not. He is, he's the monster, Cairo!"

His mouth formed an O-shape, but several minutes passed before he responded. "I'm sorry that happened to you, Milah. Has he stopped? It's not still going on, is it?"

I looked up as I hugged my knees closer to my chest. My eyes looked to Bliss, pleading with her to help me explain. She nodded and answered, "Y-yes."

His fists balled up as he pulled me into his chest again. This time tighter, allowing my tears to soak his shirt. "Wh-who was it? Who did this to you? Why did they break you?"

When he asked that, a lump grew in my throat and I pictured his face. His God-awful face, the sinister face he sported, the flames that came with him when he walked.

I mumbled, "A family member." All my words came out shaky. I was shook and I couldn't believe I had to talk about this again. I had vowed to never tell my story again, especially after no one believed me the first time.

"A family member? But, who? Baby tell me. Let it all out. Let all the pain go."

I sighed and used the back of my hand to wipe my tears.

Bliss cleared her throat as she wiped her own tears from her cheeks. "I'ma go see Rome. I just can't hear this again. I'll let you two be alone." I nodded and she left.

When she was out of the room, I looked at Cairo.

"So, baby, you can trust me. What happened, how old were you when it happened?"

I avoided looking at him when he asked that. I felt sick to my stomach. Scratching my arm, I looked at everything else but him. I couldn't stand to look in his dear eyes.

"I was six when it first happened. I didn't know it wasn't right, but I had a feeling it was wrong for him to sneak into my room when he'd come over to visit. He'd say things like, *'just touch it or you're of age. It's right. You are my little girl now.'* But, I knew in my young heart it just wasn't right." A tear slipped down my face and I tried to hold it in. But, I couldn't hold back the pain anymore.

"What did your father do? I know he did something. Did you tell him?" I laughed a little thinking about what he'd said the day I'd told him.

"He said his brother would *never* do anything like that. He believed him over me so it went on for years. H-he took—"

Cairo stopped me and all I could do was cry louder and harder.

"He took your innocence, didn't he?" Cairo asked, with certainty in his tone. I nodded. He rocked me back and forth in his arms.

"I never had the chance to give it to the love of my life so that's the reason I do guys the way I do. I'd rather lead them on than genuinely give them the time of day. I don't give them sex or anything like that. I just move on to the next guy, and repeat the cycle over and over. It's a void that can never be filled again and it's the only way I know to guard my heart and mind."

Cairo kissed my shoulder. I felt his tears falling on my forehead. "I'm sorry, so damn sorry that ever had to happen to you. A father who wouldn't even help his daughter is no father at all. I wish I would have known you then. I would have never—"

Raising my finger to his lips, I stopped him from talking. Then, I ran my four fingers down his cheek, smoothing away the tears I never meant to cause.

I raised my lips to his cheek and kissed him lightly before I whispered in his ear, "That was one of the best nights of my life, Ro. You made me feel loved. Made me feel beautiful, like a young woman should feel. We didn't have sex but it was special to me. Even though I'm not pure, I want you to think of me that way. Cairo can you? Can you just hold me for a moment?"

He nodded with big brown glossy eyes and did just that. "You can tell me everything, alright. I mean everything, baby. No more secrets. Promise me that. Okay?" I slightly nodded. Cairo was the second boy I'd told. I made the mistake of telling Ken. I thought he was, at best, my friend, but that was all a lie. He was never like this with me. But he would pay for what he'd done to me. Oh, he would pay.

"Don't you ever let your crown fall, just let it tilt some. But, don't ever let it fall. Shawty you're something special. I see you out there on that field dancing. You're going places, Kamilah. Your name means something real. You're a pure Egyptian queen in my eyes, my black queen. And I'm going to do everything in my rushing power to give you all my love. I'm not going nowhere, even if you try and push me away. I'ma be here till the end."

His words made me break and cry. Maybe God brought him to me for many reasons. Like I once wrote in my diary:

What good is a jewel that ain't still precious? How could you run off on me? How could you run off on us? You feel like God inside that gold. I found you laying down with Samson and his full head of hair. Found my black queen, Kamilah.

Bad dreams, Kamilah.

CHAPTER 12

Love on the Brain

Kamilah Smith

Several months had passed. It was now February fourteenth. We had been in school for a solid six months, and, finally, everything was going well. Bliss had been proud of me since I'd told him the truth. I had no more secrets except the ones I was withholding from my scandalous father. How could I tell him that he doesn't run me anymore? What can I say? Cairo was everything I needed. And today was Valentine's Day. I didn't expect him to do anything special for me, and I hadn't bothered to ask for anything after what I'd recently told him. He stayed by my side when I'd cry at night. Plus I hadn't spoken to Ken and that was a good thing since what he'd done was toxic. I had nothing to say to his fruitcake ass. I would've been wrong to put him on blast and tell all his business like he'd done me. But who was I to do that? I had my own baggage and pride.

Ken had cut me deeply. He reopened wounds that left them fresh to the touch. They would never heal. I would never do that to anyone, I really wouldn't. What did I do to him? *He was never like this before*, I thought. We were friends and the way he'd turned on me was cold as fuck. Don't get me wrong, I wish he hadn't done it. He only did it because of Cairo, I had told myself. The crazy thing was he didn't like me as a girlfriend, so why would he stoop so low?

I swear, I had a feeling that bitch Brianna had some type of influence on him. He could keep being a down-low brother all he wanted. I would always know what he truly was. *A fraud.*

"I'm leaving Milah but if I see Ken just know I'ma check his ass," Bliss said.

I gave her a small hug from the position I was in. She waved at Cairo and he did the same. Then, she grabbed her bag and went on her way. I was kind of staring off into space when I heard Cairo call me a few times.

"You good over there, Shawty?" I looked over at Cairo and nodded with a grin on my face. "You sure?" he asked again.

"Yes, I'm sure. Just doing this work. Isn't the Pythagorean theorem $a^2 + b^2 = c^2$?" I asked, trying to redirect his train of thought.

"Yeah, some shit like that. I'on fuck with math unless it got something to do with my paper. Now, I'ma ask you again, are you okay?" I sighed and finished my last problem, and then I sat up and closed my book. He got up from the other side of the room and walked over to the bed. He got in and sat down, allowing his back to rest against the headboard. He grabbed my legs and put them in his lap and rubbed them softly.

"You know you can't keep thinking about that, right? It ain't good, ma'."

I nodded, knowing he was right. "I know. It's just hard to let it go. It's like a plague I can't get rid of. I've had counseling but who could ever forget that? Ya' know?"

He slightly nodded and continued to rub my legs. "You want me to put your mind to rest?" He smirked. I rolled my eyes and slapped his hand. "Like, ow! What you pop me for?" he asked, playfully sticking out his bottom lip.

"Because, you always thinking about sex," I said, folding my arms over my chest. He rubbed his hand and looked up at me with a straight face.

"Nah, that's a lie. I don't think about sex. We haven't even had sex. Why you lyin' on me like that? Well, it was that one time, but that wasn't really sex if you ask me. I made you cry out with my tongue so it was more like some foreplay type shit. And, shit, that was a month and some weeks ago. Head don't count as sex, shawty." My mouth fell open. "Close ya' mouth, you know I ain't lyin'."

I twisted my lips to one side and he looked at me curiously.

"A day ago you said if I didn't stop playing, you was gon' bend me over after practice and tear dat ass up," I said, attempting to mock his bad-boy New Orleans accent.

"Lies! Foul on the play! Fuckin' interception! You was backing yo' ass up on me playin' and shit, plus you had the damn audacity to be playin' with my dingaling by twerkin' on me! Stop ya' lyin', Kamilah." He laughed out loud.

I snickered and he cut his eyes at me. "Well, listen. We gotta finish our work, sir."

He shrugged and diverted his attention in my direction. "Why? We don't have classes tomorrow. Besides, I finished my work, therefore, you acting like you don't have your own work to finish." I stuck my tongue out at him. "Plus, it's Valentine's Day, and I got you somethin' special." He rubbed the back of his neck and got quiet for a moment. "You what?" I questioned him in disbelief.

He blew out a soft breath and rubbed my leg. Then, he inhaled and exhaled a longer breath. "Well, I know we ain't like "datin'," he said using his middle and index finger to initiate quotes, "but, I got you something special, like I said. You been mopin' 'round and I hate to see you sad. So, I made some calls and made somethings shake for you," he said with a smile.

"Something like what?" I probed.

He tapped my legs for me to move them. I moved them so he could stand to his feet. He went to his closet, reached inside, and pulled out a giant bag. I covered my mouth as a smile crept on my face. He handed it to me, and I felt like a child on Christmas Day. It had been awhile since anyone had done something nice and unexpected for me. I was loving the moment.

"I bought you this with the money my brother gave me before I left N'awlins. You know college kids be broke as fuck, and I don't got money like that. Plus, I ain't get my credit card yet. So, I spent the money on someone real special, you."

I glanced over at him almost wanting to cry. "You got all this for me? You shouldn't have." I looked at all the candy, drinks, teddy bears, and more. "Really, you shouldn't have." Cairo nodded and smiled before he bent down to kiss me. I looked at the gift— it was so beautiful. He was truly the best.

He grabbed the bag and dug deep into it. When he pulled his hand out, it held a velvet box. He opened it and slid a ring on my finger. "Yes, I should've. You deserve it."

At a loss for words, all I could do was stare at it with my mouth wide open. He took his place on the bed beside me and kissed my hand. I got up and walked over to the door, making sure the room secure. Once I'd made my way back to him, I tackled him backwards on the bed and moved the huge personalized duffle bag to the side.

I flipped my hair over my shoulder and focused my attention back on Cairo. He bit his bottom lip and it turned me on like it always did. "But, I didn't get you anything. I didn't know we were going to do this." He waved his hand letting me know it was all about me. He grabbed me around my waist as his eyes traveled up my body to my almond eyes.

"You don't have to get me anything, Milah. As long as you're happy, that's good enough for me. You deserved it, so hush all that. I don't need nothin' materialistic. All I need and want is you." Smiling at him I sucked in my bottom lip at the sight of him. I pulled away and took off the big Morris Brown sweatshirt I had on. He frowned his eyes at me, at what I was doing.

"I wanna give you a little gift," I said while smiling. He shook his head and I pushed him back into position onto his bed.

"Nah, you don't have to do this, baby. I wanna take things slow."

I spun around and began to grind on his lower half. I could hear him take in a deep breath. "Aye, stop playin'," he said softly, almost like he didn't want me to hear him. I sat in his lap and started grinding on him harder. He couldn't help but put his hands on my waist.

"Yo', for real, Milah. You gone wake him up—"

I turned around and kissed him deeply, just to stop him from talking. "I'm gon' what?" I started kissing on his neck as his hands fell onto my ass, putting a death grip on it.

"You gon' get fucked up if you don't stop what you doing right now."

I kissed his jawline, then his neck. I went up to his ear and nibbled on it. "I want you to do that," I whispered deeply into his ear. His body pumped upward underneath me, and I smirked against his skin. His lips attacked to my neck. This was going to be a great Valentine's day. But, was I truly ready? I was so anxious to feel what Cairo could give me. But, I was so into him words couldn't explain it. He was my King.

He flipped me over, making me giggle as his lips kissed mine and then my nose. He then trailed his plump lips down my skin. My heart began to speed up as his cool hands touched my hot skin. His fingertips traced down the thin fabric of my cut-off spandex top. His thumb pushed back the material as his skin brushed across my nipple, making me moan softly.

"That's what I love to hear, baby." He held my body as *So Anxious* played through my TV:

Nine o' clock, home alone, paging you. Wishing you'd come over, my place, after while, let me know. We can just keep talking 'bout the last time, you were here. What we did (no sleep till morning), only bubble baths and back rubs. Hit me back, girl I hope, you hurry 'cause-.

Cairo Black

I got on top of her and kissed her neck, making Milah squirm under my touch. "Is this what you want? Really, I won't do this if—"

She gasped as my lips kissed on her stomach. It made me smile at how sensitive her skin was whenever I touched her. "Yes, I want it, Cairo. You the only person I want to give myself to," Milah breathed out.

I looked up at her once those chilling, sexy words came out of her mouth. I kissed up her body slowly as I came up to her lips. "I promise, Milah, I'll make it feel like your first time. Baby, you are pure to me. I won't do anything you don't want me to do, Milah." My words took her back a little as I kissed her just to keep her quiet. "I promise I'll never let no man hurt you like that again." I planted a wet kiss on her collar bone, one of the many sensitive spots on her body. She shook as I ran my hands up her body to her hands. Gripping them, I raised her hands above her head.

A knock ticked on the door. "Bro I need my text books. Open up, I forgot my keys." I heard my brother yelling from the other side of the door. I groaned, which caused Milah to sigh in frustration. Letting her hands go, she reached out and grabbed at my shirt as I got up from the bed. Grabbing his books, I noticed a loose sock on the floor and grabbed that too. I made sure to put that sock on the door outside of the doorknob so we wouldn't be interrupted again, I opened the door and partially flung his books at him.

Rome looked at me with an angered look. "Damn, bro, that was rude! Damn," he said, catching them at once. Giving him a look, I tied the sock onto the doorknob. "Wait! Oh, yo', she must be in there." I gave him a face, and he quickly shut up.

"Gon,' Rome, dang."

He laughed. "A'ight, you tryna get you some nookie, I see you. Okay, let me shut up. I'm sorry." Rome flicked the hanging sock then reached into his pocket and threw a condom packet at me. "Better strap up. Make sure you play with his dingaling, Milah—"

I slammed the door in his face but I could still hear him singing it. Shaking my head, I pinched the bridge of my nose.

"He is so crazy," Milah said, with a giggle. I rolled my eyes. She watche, as I pulled my shirt over my head. I made my way closer to the bed and tossed my hat on the pile of clothes. She looked at me with lust as I began to take off my shorts. Her eyes grew big like she'd never seen it before.

"It's like you grow every day or something." I chuckled and ran my hand down my face and I licked my lips.

"Don't do that face! Gawd, you gettin' me wet. Come here already."

I chuckled again and took my grill out my mouth before she stopped me. I looked at her, stuck in one spot.

"What?" I questioned.

She bit her lip again and ran her hand down her body. Her eyes trailed me up and down. "Can you leave the grill in?"

I threw my head back and nodded. This girl was unbelievable. I slid my grill back on my teeth.

"I'ma put on protection but I'ma tell you this na', it's gon' hurt, a'ight?" She nodded as she lifted up and crawled towards me. I grabbed her legs and pulled her to the edge of the bed. Licking my lips, I pushed down on the bed and pulled her panties down. Kissing her thighs once or twice, I blew air on her moistened clit, making her body shake as I trailed kisses up her stomach. Milah played in my hair as her back arched. She unsnapped her bra and gave me a sight to see, as she flung the bra to the floor.

I know some might say we're moving fast and ask why we're even having sex after what she told me? But it's more than just a sexual attraction with Milah. She made me feel wanted, and it was the same on her end too. I couldn't explain. She just made me feel whole. I've had many girlfriends but she was something special.

Her moans snapped me back into place as I ran my hand down her pearl. I didn't want to keep her waiting. I wanted to give her what she lost so long ago. Lifting up from the bed, I watched as she bit her lip. I cracked the condom open and slid it on. She lay there looking so innocent. It made me want to stop, on some G-shit.

"Milah? You sure this what you want? I can stop and you can wait, *we* can wait. For real. I'm not like those other dudes. You sure you ready for all I'm 'bout to give you?" Milah nodded half-heartedly. "Nah, I need you to speak to me, baby," I said with my eyebrows knitted together.

Her voice was so pure and sultry, "Yes, Cairo, I am. I'm ready for you, baby. I want you."

I nodded, putting one hand by her head as I grabbed my manhood, pressed both of my knees against her thighs, and pushed it in her softly.

I stared her straight in the eyes. Milah let a loud cry escape her lips that made me snap my eyes open at her. "You good, baby? I can stop if you can't take it. I don't wanna see you hurt."

She blinked and took a deep breath, nodded, and closed her eyes, trying to get her breath right. I nodded and pushed it in more. Her cries and moans mixed made me so internally weak. I went as slow as possible. Her small hands gripped my arms as I towered over her small, thick frame. The faces she was making was doing something to me. I'd thrusted once, cautiously. I didn't want to hurt her. She was so tight it made my manhood hurt a little.

"Milah? You know I love you, right? I don't ever wanna hurt you like this again." Little tears formed in her eyes and I wiped them away.

"Yes, okay, Cairo ."

I kissed her lips, making wet noises. Her hands grabbed the back of my neck and then my ass. Making me chuckle, this would be the only time I'd allow her to do that mess. But, I ain't say nothing cause she was just adjusting to my size. Slowly, her cries turned into soft moans. Until, I heard a *pop!*

"Ahhh! Cairo," Milah cried out loud, making me cover her mouth.

"Shh, baby, relax. Just take some deep breaths. You feel *so* good girl." I thrusted again but deeper this time, making a deep gasp erupt from her throat.

"Cairo! What the? God, you're too deep baby," Milah managed to get out through shallow breaths.

I paused as her sweet area squeezed around me. "I know. How it feel, baby?" I said, as I started stroking her again.

Milah sucked in her bottom lip as her body finally moved with mine. "It-it feels so good!" This shit was like agonizing perfection and pleasure. I was trying so hard not to lose myself. I buried my face into her neck as I kept that same rhythmic pace, that same movement that had Milah going over the edge. I was feeling her adjust more and more, as the wetness between her legs grew larger.

"You feelin' daddy, baby?"

Her voice broke as I spoke nastily into her ear. Milah tried to speak. As my long deep strokes smacked her spot, a deep satisfaction of moans escaped her throat.

"Ohh, Pri—" I gave her a deep and fast pump, making her dig her nails into my back as I looked into her deep hazel eyes.

"You know that ain't my name, ma." Her eyes closed tight, as my body weighed on her. Milah's legs wrapped around my waist tightly. Her moans got louder, so I kissed her to keep them down. I didn't need anyone in our business.

"Keep it down, baby. Now, what's my name?"

Her eyes were still tightly closed as I stared down at her. "Dad-d—"

I gave her a deep and slow stroke, pulling out and going back in it quickly. "Open them pretty eyes and look at me when you say it. Now, what is it?" I kissed her lips, feeling her shaking under me.

Her eyes fluttered open as her wet area pulsed and squeezed around my member tighter and the wetness grew like a waterfall. "Da-da-daddy!"

I started to pick up the pace, feeling her contract and pulsate around my dick faster than before. "You love the way I'm giving it to you, baby?" I whispered. Her body shook, but she didn't answer me. "Huh? Talk to me, Shawty?" Milah was losing herself. She was about to bust and hard according to the way she was digging her nails in my back.

"Oh, my gosh, Cairo, yes, you givin' it to me!"

I was hitting every spot she had. Then, she said those three words, those three gotdamn words. "Ah! I love you, Cairo ! Please, don't stop!"

My eyes were stuck on her as she was cummin' all on my man-hood. "You love me, Milah?" I kept going at a fast pace.

Milah's hands fell from my back onto the bed. Grabbing her wrist with one hand, I grabbed her right thigh and raised it up high, as I went much deeper and faster. My breaths quickened as her area gushed under me. "Oh, my goodness! Yes! I love you!"

Was this the sex talking? Or did she mean it? Then, I knew it was real when she said, "Cairo, I love you for being my first! I love you, so much!" Tears flowed out of her eyes and I wouldn't let up. She was sounding so good to me. I was about to let go, nut all inside the condom before I pulled out and shook my head.

"W-what's the matter? Why did you stop, daddy?" Milah wrapped her legs around me, trying to pull me back down.

"Because. Shit, girl, I'm falling in love with you and I can't!" She grabbed my face and kissed me. I tried to pull away but she wasn't having it.

Her teeth nipped at my bottom lip. "I don't care no more, Cairo. I want you and only you." She looked at me with lust, or was it love? I tried to move her hands but she wasn't having it. "You saying that 'cause I just gave you the best dick of your life. We can't be and you know it, Milah."

She kissed on my neck and somehow she flipped me over, ending up in my lap. I don't even know when I got on my back to begin with. Milah gripped my hands while leaning down to kiss me. "Shut up, Cairo. I don't care. I don't care about Ken, and I don't care about my father. All I care about is you!"

She straddled me and sat right on my manhood, making sure it got right in her center. Her hand grabbed my dick and started massaging me. I didn't even feel her take the condom off me. Making me groan, I pulled her up a little 'cause I would bust a nut any moment inside of her. Milah smirked and slammed down on my dick, making me go inside her. Gripping her hips tightly, I looked up at her with a raised eyebrow.

"Girl! Don't do that shit, yo'. Is you tryn amake me cum inside you?" She started giggling and moved off it, moaning a bit. When I flipped my head back, she sat on it again and started bouncing. "Fuck it!" I flipped her over, got behind her, and quickly started hittin' it from the back.

"Wait, Cairo, I'm sorry for playin'!"

I hummed and kept going, feeling it coming on strong.

"Say you love a nigga again." I slapped her ass and she cried out. I made her lie on her stomach as I laid on top of her, while holding onto her hands. "Play with me like that again and I'ma have yo' little ass tossed up! Ya' feel me?" She screamed my name and yelled yes. I lifted up, giving her a few more strokes before I pulled out. She looked at me with a surprised look. "Don't look at me like dat." She licked her lips, lifted up from the bed, and got down to where my dick was.

My eyes were low as I eyed her. "Nah', man. Betta get'cha ass up. That's for grown women to be doin' and you new to da' game." She rolled her eyes, opened her mouth, and sucked it in her mouth.

"Fuck!" was all I could muster to say. Why her ass didn't listen? Why? And she was doing wonders with dat' mouth and tongue. I'd never ask her to do this to me. Milah insisted.

After all we did, she fell asleep on my chest. She said she loved me, but could she live up to what she'd said? I looked down at her and kissed her forehead. "Happy Valentine's Day, baby. I love you too."

CHAPTER 13

Damaged Souls

Cairo Black

Looking out the window, I shook my head, turned from the window, and mumbled under my breath. That was about two in a half weeks ago and I hadn't heard from her. I felt so used. I knew my dick game was strong, but damn. Ever since that night we had sex, it had been different. I knew we should haven't done it. But, she was so tempting and Milah wanted it. I just wanted to make her feel good. Me being the good guy, I fell into her 'I love you' act. I hadn't even talked to her nor seen her. So, I decided to stop thinking about it and try to find out what was up. I got up from my bed, grabbed my phone, and my keys.

"Aye, bro. I'll be back in a few," I told Rome.

"A'ight, home skillet biscuit." He replied in usual corny fashion.

I laughed and shook my head. I had to close the door and look at him for a moment. "Man, that is so old. You need to let Raven Baxter go, dude. You know what she said on *The View* tho'? Don't look at me like that. I had to watch it for a project. That girl crazy. I feel for Watermelondrea!" He burst out laughing and fanned me off.

"I still think she fine, so I don't care if she is a lesbian. I'll turn that ass out and she'll most definitely love the dick again." I was crying from laughing so hard. I fanned him off like he did me and gave him the deuces. He did the same and I left.

After walking out of the student building, I jogged over to my Jeep, hopped in, and pulled off. I listened to Kendrick Lamar's *LOYALTY* as I drove less than a mile to the dorm. The short ride was smooth. I had been too lazy to walk, and why walk two blocks when I could just drive?

When I got there, I shut off my car and prepared for what I was going to say to her when I saw her. I had some choice words for her. Hopping out the truck, I made sure it was locked. I stuffed my hands deep in my pockets and walked up to her building.

When I got up to the third floor, I knocked on the door softly. Hearing music from the other side, I knocked again, this time a little harder. The door unlocked and opened to a giggling Bliss. When she turned around to face me, her smile vanished.

"Damn, I can't get a hey, hello, hi, nothin', huh?"

She nodded and let me in while pushing her short hair out of her face. "Uh, hey, Cairo." She'd said my name rather loudly so I knew something was up.

"Yeah, cut the act. Where my girl at?" I immediately stopped when she came from the other side of the room with Ken in tow. "The fuck goin' on, Bliss? Milah, what the fuck is this?" I questioned, as I stepped in front of Bliss.

Milah threw her hands up. "It's nothin' like that. Ken just came to talk, that's all. To clear some things up, Cairo."

I laughed in her face. "You can't be serious, right? You been avoiding me, haven't talked to me and shit this whole week, and you got this nigga in your dorm room? And you talkin' to *him* and not *me*?" She sighed and waved her hands in the air, trying to calm me down.

Shaking my head, I said, "What's up, man? I'm not about to be played. What is it, or *who* is it you want, Milah?" Ken leaned against the wall, not saying a damn thing.

"Me and Ken were just talking about things, okay? Nothin' more, nothin' less, so just leave it the hell alone," she explained.

"Nah', I won't leave it alone! You tryna' get some comfort from *this* nigga when I was the one who was there for ya' ass?"

"I'm sorry. Uh, I think I'ma just go, Milah. Remember what we talked about," Ken commented. She nodded, and he went on his merry way.

I looked at the door as it closed, then back at her. "Remember what? What you gotta tell him that you can't tell me?" Milah took an exasperated breath as her head moved left to right quickly. She reached up and rubbed her forehead though there was nothing on it. She turned and walked away from the door and took fast strides back to her bed. She plopped down and didn't say another word.

"Answer me!" I yelled.

Finally, her eyes find their way to me. The look she was giving me was cold and hard. "It was just sex, chill out, Cairo."

I paused and squinted my eyes as if I couldn't see her. "Come again? I know I didn't hear you clearly," I said, pressing my finger to my ear for emphasis. With a straight face, her gaze was unflinching—she didn't waiver, blink, or crack a smile.

"I *said* it was just sex, that's all. My father will be down here soon to check up on me, so just leave me alone for now." She tried to get up, but I grabbed her by her arm.

"*For now*? So, you still using me? Is that what it is? Huh, Kamilah?" She looked at my hand on her arm as if she hadn't heard anything I'd said or asked.

"Let me go, Cairo. I'm not about to have this conversation with you. This isn't about you, it's about me." I still didn't let her go. I was fuming. My fingertips squeezed harder, not on purpose though. My anger was becoming intense.

"Fuck all dat', I yelled causing Bliss and Milah both to jump nervously. You know what I gave you, what you gave me, and you know how I make you feel. So now you scared? Is that what it is? You scared your daddy gon' find out about us, huh? You scared to tell him who you really are? How you really are. I told you, I don't care about that! Yes, I know how I feel. You can't even be a woman about it. You must not love me!"

She looked at me as if I was someone else and stared blankly until she spoke. "Just leave me alone, Cain!" I looked at her like who in the hell was Cain. . . And then, it came to me. He was the dude who had been molesting her for most of her life.

Bliss grabbed her shoulders, then grabbed her face gesturing her to look at her straightforward. "Milah, baby, breath, okay? Just breath. That's not Cain, Milah," Bliss said soothingly. Her tone was somewhat motherly. "Milah? Kamilah! Where's your stuff? Fuck! Don't black out on me now," she said in a panicked voice. I'm sorry, Cairo. I've never seen her get like this. I think you should—"

I threw my hands in the air, cussin' at the entire situation. "Just go? Okay, I know. Just call me when she better, a'ight?"

Bliss sighed and nodded her head in agreement. Milah sat on the bed not saying a word and just staring into oblivion as Bliss was sitting next to her while rubbing Milah's shoulders. She appeared to be in a state of shock. I didn't know what was really going on with Kamilah. The one thing I did know, now more than ever, was I had to find out or get over shawty, and quick. I shook my head and made my exit.

As I was walking to my truck, my phone began to vibrate in my pocket. I stuffed my hand inside it and pulled out my smartphone. I looked at the caller ID and it was my momma. I smiled because I needed to talk to her, get her good and loving advice. I unlocked the door while answering the call.

"Hey, Momma. How's it going?" I asked, with a smile on my face. When I heard her soft sniffles come through the other end, my mood immediately changed. "Ma, what's wrong? You okay?" I asked, as I sat still in the truck.

"Um... well, I don't know how you're going to take this, but it's about your father," she said. Her tone was raspy and let me know she'd been crying.

I frowned and tried to figure out why she was calling about my father. I hadn't seen or talked to him since me and my brothers' high school graduation.

"What about him?" Even though my father wasn't our lives, I still had love for him. My mom cleared her throat before she finally told me what was up. "Come on, Ma. Tell me what's up and why you cryin'?"

She sniffled again and sighed deeply. "Your father nearly overdosed last night. The drugs ain't what ended his life though," she said somberly, "he committed suicide, baby," she managed to say. He's gone, Cairo. I'm so sorry you had to hear the news over the phone like this," momma said, through shortened breaths.

My heart sank. I knew my father was addicted to drugs and in need of help. But I didn't know it was *that* bad. He'd left to get his head on straight, to get his music career jump started. My father was supposed to let the drugs go and think about his children for once. When I last saw him, God, I hadn't even seen the signs. I thought he was better, but I guess I was dead wrong.

Clearing my throat to mask my pain, I said, "Wait? What, h-he can't be dead, Ma. I know I said I hated him but I didn't mean it! Don't tell me my daddy dead!" I felt tears slip down my eyes as I gripped the steering wheel tight.

"I'm sorry, baby. I really am. I already called your brothers. I want you to be strong. And, your father wanted you to know something." she paused, and my sniffles filled the silence. I wiped my nose, trying not to cry. "He wanted you to know that he was sorry for leaving you boys and he said he was so proud of you, Rome, and. . ." She started to break down before she rushed me off the phone. My mom never wanted us to hear or see her down.

My head hung low as I tossed my phone in the passenger seat. The longer I sat there, the more the tears flowed freely.

A knock on my window snapped me out of my thoughts and sorrows. I looked to my left and stared at Milah with watery eyes. She pointed at the lock and I unlocked the door. She opened the door and looked at me.

"Uh, I saw you sittin' out here. Are you okay, Cairo?" Quickly turning my face, I roughly wiped my eyes, sniffing hard as I grunted.

I looked at her. I was mixed with so many emotions. "Do I look fine, Milah?"

Kamilah was taken back by my tone. She sighed and shook her head no. She pulled the car door open. She pulled me into a hug and all I could do was cry. It was the first time I'd ever cried in front of a girl, period. Her phone rang and she looked down at it. She sighed from frustration and anger as she pulled away from the embrace. I could feel my brows as they furrowed together. Finally putting the pieces together, for a hot second I thought the moment was just about us, but I was wrong again.

"It's my dad. Can you hold on a minute, Cairo? Let me take this and I—" Holding up my hands, I pushed her back away from the car. I couldn't take this shit right now. I just kept my hands held high up for her to just stop talking. "Just take the damn call, alright? That's all you care about anyway. That's all I'll ever be is your little love affair. I'm out." I spoke with such distaste for the entire situation. I slammed my door in her face and left her there, calling after me to come back. I didn't know how to feel about the situation. I couldn't believe my father had left this earth. He'd left without so much as good-bye. I didn't know where I was going, but I had to get away. He's gone and he's never comin' back. A father that was sick with an addiction, loved his kids, wife, and music was never coming back.

The hurtful lyrics replayed in my head over and over again:

For everything I wanted and was told I couldn't get it. And with that I had to face it that my daddy was addicted... damn. That's right it wasn't easy growin' up, Mama was exposin' us to life as she knew it...

Kamilah Smith

I stood and watched as Cairo peeled out of the dorm parking lot. He was crying, infuriated, and crushed. I didn't understand why he had grown this upset, and he appeared to be more frustrated. Maybe he was right. Maybe I hadn't given us a chance. All I ever did was think of myself, he could've been going through some heavy stuff. And here I was worrying about my father. Looking down at the vibrating phone. I answered his call, and as bad as it seemed, I listened to my horrible father talk.

"Hello, Papa," I said through the phone, as I made my way back to my room. I couldn't help but look back a few times, just to see if Cairo was coming back. He wasn't. My mind was off its rocker.

I heard my father yell through the phone. "We have a lot to talk about, I'll need for you to run your mom's boutique on that side of town. Other than that what the hell have you been up to? I didn't help bring you into this world for you to disobey me! Our family has traditions and you'll follow then. Ken, that sweet boy, he called me." I paused and took the phone away from my ear, as if he was lying. Why would Ken, of all men, call my father?

"He what! Why the fuck did he do that?" I said, louder than I intended. I knew he was about to have a conundrum about that.

"Who are you talking to? Don't think because you're eighteen that you're grown, you can get your ass whooped, Kamilah Angel Smith," my father said, in his thick accent. I rolled my eyes. He had to say my damn government like that. My relationship with my father was bittersweet, the daddy's little girl he thought I was long gone when I turned eight.

"I understand and I'm sorry, Papa. But why did he call you? There is no point in that."

He sighed. "He called because he said you had an *episode*. You haven't been running your mouth have you? Are you taking your medication?" he asked, his tone stern and deep. It made me shiver and I wanted to cry.

"Yes, I've been taking my medication. I didn't have an episode, Papa. I'm fine, really. I haven't said a thing." My father was silent. I knew he didn't believe me because he believed his own brother.

"Just know, I control you. If you say anything like you've said at home to discredit my family's name, there will be consequences Kamilah. And, I mean that this time. To the fullest. You do anything or say anything, I swear, you'll be cut off. You get me? If that boy calls me again, me and you are going to have a big ass problem. Okay?" I sniffed and said okay.

"Alright, so get your shit together. That will be your husband soon, and I don't want to hear shit else about it. Oh, and your Uncle said hello. He misses his beautiful niece." I wanted to scream and cry. "He'd like to talk to you." That's when I had to stop him.

"Uh-uh-uh, Papa, w-we're, b-breaking up." I hung up the phone fast and got to the dorm room. I slid down the wall and tried hard to breath.

"Just breathe! Breathe!" I chanted to myself, as I slowly began to hyperventilate.

Bliss ran to my side, trying to get me to relax. "You okay, boo? We can't have you blacking out again."

I shook my head no. As the tears flowed harder, memories came back of Uncle Cain. She came over to me and stood by me, trying to make me feel better. But, there was no way I could feel better about this. I hated both of them, and I knew I'd never escape this nightmare. I'd never be as strong as Pyramids. I'd be as weak as the aging Pyramids and crumble every hour of the day like I had been.

Monet Dragun

130

CHAPTER 14

Tears On My Windowpane

Cairo Black

The day was February 20th, 2017, the day my daddy died. The rain was coming down hard. I kept my hand on the wheel. Thinking of what my mom had just told me hours ago almost made me hit rock-bottom. I didn't go back to the dorm, I didn't eat, I didn't even go to any of my classes. I had missed practice and hadn't felt like doing anything. All I did was drive. Everyone was blowing up my phone, but I didn't even bother to look at it. I kept my head straight as I drove down the dark road.

Then, my mind just drifted off to him:

"Son, I'm sorry I wasn't in ya' life like I was supposed to be. But, your dad ain't right, Son. He's sick. You gotta understand that, okay? Your pops ain't stable to be 'round. I want you to take care of your brothers, you understand me, Keith?" He nodded as he placed his strong muscular hands on Keith's shoulders.

"I understand, Pops. I'm older now. I know what's the matta. Are you ever coming back?" He looked up at momma and she had tears in her eyes. She couldn't stand to see this or see the man she loved sick, and leaving. He cleared his throat and looked down.

"I love y'all. I-I'll get betta for y'all, and I promise I'll be back. I have to go now, okay? Dad gotta get right." We all nodded. Rome and I ran into him and hugged him so tightly.

"Don't go! Please, don't," my brother and I cried. He hugged us back tightly and let us go. *"You're supposed to be the man of the house and take care of us!"* I remembered myself shouting.

"Stop that you hear me? I have to go, boys. I just have to. It's not good for me to be here right now. Be good, okay. Keep y'all head in those books and basketball, like I taught y'all. I don't want y'all to be no rolling stone like me, you unda'stand, Cairo and Rome? You too, Keith. Watch over them and do everything for your momma 'cause you the man of the house na'. And, Stacey, I love you. I love you so much, baby."

He picked up his hat, guitar case, and suitcase, and left on a dark rainy night, ten years ago.

That was the last time I'd seen him until my graduation. Now, today, he's left this earth without a good-bye. I slammed my hands against the steering wheel and kept driving. I didn't know where I was, but I had to clear my mind. Tears flowed, and for some reason, I slammed my foot on the brakes. Coming to a rough stop, I looked down at my lap as all my emotions came out of me at once.

You just gotta keep going without me, Son, I heard his deep voice say in my head. I looked out the front of the Jeep's window, looking into the night sky. There were no clouds, no nothing. I sighed to myself as I wiped my tears away. I hit the gas pedal and made a U-turn, headed back to the dorms. I was very unstable, and there was no one to comfort me except my brother.

***

As I got out of my Jeep, not caring if I got wet from the rain, I slowly walked to my building. I opened the door and went up the steps. When I got up there, I keyed myself in and wiped my wet face off with my hand. My brother was lying on the bed, looking up at the ceiling. I pulled off my shirt and pants and sat on my bed. I picked up my phone and called up my main man, Malone. I needed a blunt on a serious note. I know I wasn't supposed to be smoking because it was against the rules. But, hell, how I was feeling, I needed to light it up so all my pain could go away for the time being. His phone rang and rang before he finally picked up. I took a breath as I heard his voice.

"'Sup, Giraffe?" I mentally groaned. I wasn't in the mood for this.

"Nigga just bring the pack. I got the money." He didn't protest. He just said okay and let me know what time he'd be coming by.

"You know you can't be smokin'. Ro." Rome said with major concern.

I didn't even look at my brother. "So? I don't give a fuck. I need a stress reliever."

He sighed and sat up in his bed while rubbing his head. "That ain't gon' bring him back, Ro. The man was sick. Even before we were born." I kind of laughed a little. "Are you listening to me? He was my pops too, ya' know?"

I shot up from where I was sitting. "He left us! He picked heroin over us! Our fuckin' dad couldn't overdose on drugs so he offed himself instead! He left mom and Keith to take care of us! He chose that shit over us and had other fuckin' kids! Then, he left *our* mom to struggle! Why? Why us?" Rome got up and embraced me a brotherly hug. We held onto one another for dear life. Even though he was tryna be strong for me, I knew he was hurting too. We had lived the same heartaches. We were brothers with the same mother and father. Most importantly, we were twins. I was him and he was me. We had felt each other's pain our entire life, and today was no different.

"I know, man, I know."

It took everything out of me not to break down again. "He gone man and he ain't never comin' back. We didn't even get to say good-bye," my brother said, repeating my exat words. Now, he was in tears, and all we either of us could do to ease the pain was let it out. "We just gotta keep pushin, bro. That's all we can do," I told him. It was my turn to be his strength just as he'd been mine moments prior.

The wound heals, but it never does. That's 'cause you're at war with love. You're at war with love, yeah. These battle scars don't look like they're fading. Don't look like they're ever going away. They ain't never gonna change. These battles never let a wound ruin me.

Kamilah Smith

The flashbacks came on strong as I lay down. There was no stopping the harsh realities I'd lived in. My mind was forever corrupt, no changing it, no rearranging it. My life was forever messed up.

Alright, my sweet love. You know the drill: lay down and open your legs, baby girl. Oh, you are so sweet. Just like I remembered," Cain said but paused as I stared blankly up at the ceiling. My mind was pure black, as his grimy hands touched my skin. My palms were sweaty as my fists balled up. I lay there stiff as a board, as his two-hundred-pound body towered over me. I didn't blink. I couldn't blink. Shhh, you make any noise and the damage will be much worse."

I shot up out of my sleep when my alarm clock went off. I was soaking wet with sweat. I had tears in my eyes. I sighed and swung my legs over the edge of the bed. Bliss' bed was already made. I groaned at the time because she had already left me to go to her classes. I rubbed the little sleep out of my eyes and got out of the bed.

I grabbed my robe and beauty products, and walked out of my dorm room, down to the showers. I needed a hot one. My body was so stiff and tense. When I got in there it was empty, and I was happy because I'd have some peace and quiet. I put my stuff in the little lockup area and went in to take my shower. After taking off my robe, I hung it on the hook and closed the curtain. I let the hot water spray on my body as it ran down my face and hair. I closed my eyes slightly and started to drift a bit.

My mind was slowly easing into a peaceful mindset until it turned bad. His face popped into my head. The things he did to me caused me to quiver, as if the water raining down on me was ice cold. I quickly opened my eyes and grabbed the soap to lather up my washcloth. Vigorously, I washed and scrubbed my body. I wanted to wash every bit of filth of *him* off of me. I felt dirty just thinking about what the hell he'd done to me. *I could kill that man*, I thought. My father never believed me, and he never tried to save me. He kept me quiet, and of course, my mother went along with him. The only reason she was so quiet around him was because of what he'd done to her. But one day, all of them were going to pay. *All* of them.

Rinsing the rest of the soap off my body, I turned the water off. I got out of the shower and slipped on my shower slippers. Feeling a bit refreshed now that I'd taken care of my hygiene, I went back to my room.

I was going to call my mom because there were things I needed to get off my chest. Walking down the hall, the closer I got to my room, the more worried I became about how I would address the issues. Upon getting to my door, I noticed it was slightly ajar. I frowned because I knew I had closed this door. I was certain I had.

As I got closer, I could hear a male's soft cries and laughs. I opened the door and realized I had never locked it like I thought I had. I held my towel tighter around my waist. I stepped inside to the familiar voice and closed the door behind me. He looked helpless and sad.

"Cairo? Are you okay? When did you get here?"

The way he had sped off the last time I'd seen him, I thought he was never going to talk to me again, especially after what I'd said. But, here we were, both vulnerable, in need of a friend.

He smiled a crooked smile and pulled the pint size bottle from behind him and brought it to his lips. I wasn't surprised because the pungent smell of the whiskey had connected with my nose as soon as I'd entered.

"I-I'm just fine, if you say, I mean, if I must say." He started laughing and I quickly walked over to him and snatched the bottle from him. "You can't be drinking! You'll lose your basketball career and scholarship, Cairo. What's going on with you? Talk to me." He gawked at me with puffy, dilated, red eyes. He was crying. Something serious? "Talk to me?"

"He gone and he ain-ain't comin' back, Milah. Ya' feel me. He left us again for good this time. He killed himself! I want my dad, Milah. I just want my dad." He broke down in my arms. I had never seen him like this.

Looking at him, I knew how he felt. Although he was very much alive physically, I had lost my dad a long time ago. "Your father wouldn't want this. I'm sorry that happened, and I'm so sorry about the way I treated you. You didn't deserve that. I just wanna let you know I'm really ending it with Ken."

Glaring at me through glassy eyes, he pushed me away. "Don't lie to me," he shouted, "all you been doin' is using me, Milah. That's what everybody do. They lie to me and then they leave me! You don't love me so don't lie to me," he slurred.

I sighed and pulled my hair into a ponytail. "I'm not lying. I'm just broken, and you need to sober up. You have classes. I do love you, okay? I really do, I just don't know what to do." I pleaded.

"Oh, yeah? P-prove it."

I looked at him somewhat taken aback. "What? How am I supposed to prove it? Really, Cairo, you're drunk." I tried to walk away but he grabbed my arm. "Don't grab me," I said, raising my tone with each word.

He gazed at me with a cold stare. "Prove it. Prove you love me. You can't even prove it!"

I looked down at my feet. "I can't do that. I just can't."

He laughed and sucked his teeth. He pulled me closer to him and kissed the top of my head. "That's all I needed to hear. See ya' around, Milah. I-I'm done, we're over."

My mouth fell open as he walked to my door. My heart said stop him, but my head said let him go. "Wait!"

He shrugged and looked at me. "What? Damnit, what the hell do you want from me? Huh? To beg you, to trust you? To love you? Well, I did all of that. I already lost one loved one. Losing another won't be as hard. Good-bye, Milah. I'm not what you're looking for. You want somebody prestige and rich and I'm not that guy. I'll see ya'." He waved and walked out of my dorm room, closing my door softly.

I screamed at the top of my lungs and threw the glass liquor bottle at the door. "How could I let you go? How could I be so stupid? I love you too," I said aloud.

I grabbed my medicine off the dresser and looked at the bottle. Take two daily, was what the label read. I wasn't about to take it today though 'cause I clearly didn't need it. I flopped on my bed and let the tears fall. I had to fix this before he found someone worthy of him. I couldn't have that because I loved Cairo Black.

Give me a run for my money. There is nobody, no one to outrun me. So give me a run for my money. Sipping bubbly, feeling lovely, living lovely. Just love me, I wanna be with you, ayy, I wanna be with you ayy, I wanna be with you, ayy,

CHAPTER 15

Deserve Me

Cairo Black

You know what I'm thinkin'. See it in your eyes. You hate that you want me. Hate it when you cry. You're scared to be lonely. 'Specially in the night. I'm scared that I'll miss you. Happens every time. I don't want this feelin'. I can't afford love. I try to find reason to pull us apart. It ain't workin' 'cause you're perfect and I know that you're worth it. I can't walk away, oh! Even though we're going through it, and it makes you feel alone. Just know that I would die for you. Baby I would die for you, yeah. The Weekend's *Die for you* blasted as my wide eyes stayed alert from all my hurt.

The music played loud in my earbuds as I lay there with my eyes wide opened. I hadn't got no sleep all night. My head was pounding from the liquor and all I could remember was what me and Kamilah fought over. I was truly in love with the girl. But, it was clear she didn't feel the same. It was weighing heavily on my mind. After hearing what happened to my father, it just made it even worse. I didn't know what else to do. I picked up my phone and decided to call up my big brother, Keith. I needed him. I needed to vent and talk.

His phone rang and rang. I leaned up and ran my hand down my face. I didn't know what to do. I wish he would just pick up the phone right about now. I couldn't just sit around and mope all my life. I had to move on. The phone went straight to voicemail, so I hung up but before I sat the phone on the side of me, I hit him with a quick text.

Key my hitta': Hit me bk bruh. I need to talk to u. Sent- 4:23 am

It kind of made me worried that he wasn't picking up his phone. It irked me because I knew what he did for a living. It was not a day or night that I didn't worry about my brother's wellbeing. I had already lost my pops and I didn't want to lose him too. I was stunned from my mind and tried to think of something more positive. I had to focus on my academics, and basketball. I sat the phone down and sat there with my elbows on my knees. I stared down at the floor. I couldn't keep sitting around like this. I had a life to live.

I got up from where I was sitting and slipped on my hoodie. I slipped on my black KD's and walked out of the dorm room. I needed to go out on a jog to ease my mind a bit. It was going to prepare me for the rest of the day, hopefully. I ran a mile, trying to sweat away all the pain and hurt. I just wanted her to love me and I wanted all this pain to leave my body. But, I knew it was never that easy.

***

After my nice run I had prepared for class. My brother walked into the room and closed the door behind him. Rome had a growth spurt and was now a few inches taller than me. He rubbed the towel on his head, drying his curls. I still couldn't believe he had the barber chop his braids off. I refused to get my braids cut off.

Sighing, I put my pride on pause and said, "Bruh, I'm sorry for snapping on you." I could admit my wrong doings.

He looked at me and gave me a half smile. "We twins. I knew you didn't mean nothin' by it, Yung. One of us was going to go off. We lost our pops so what else could we to do 'bout it?"

I nodded in agreement and put on my belt. After that, I slipped on my joggers. I just wanted to be chill and comfortable today. "Thanks, bruh. Uh? Did the coach have a fit about me missing practice?"

He shrugged. "You know, he had his usual cuss and fuss 'cause his star freshman player wasn't there. But he understood the situation." He looked at me sideways and rolled his eyes.

"He probably was, 'cause I wasn't there either. I couldn't be there at the time."

I nodded, knowing the feeling. "Well, let's go before he has a fit and pops a damn vein, ya' know."

He laughed at little, slipped on his shirt, and grabbed his book bag and phone. I grabbed mine and slid it on my shoulder. He slipped on his white *Vans*, and I just had to as well.

"Damnnnn, Daniel! Bringing them white Vans back!" He cut his eyes at me and flipped me off which caused me to laugh hard as hell. It felt good too 'cause it had been a minute.

"You mad or nah? Huh, Rome drop?"

He groaned. "Fuck you! You think you funny? Well, that shit was funny. Kinda brightened up my day."

I dapped him up. As we left the room en route to practice. After all our jokes were out the way, I brought up the Milah situation. As we walked down the steps and out of the building, I was continuing to tell Rome about what happened between me and her.

"She said that? Yo', she wrong for that, man. My brother all that and a bag of damn Lays chips and she say some shit like that? She really must have some bad shit going on in her life."

I nodded and fixed my hat on my head.

"You shoulda never had sex with her. She was using you, dawg," Rome continued.

I shrugged. "Shut up. I mean, why? She told me everything. What more can I do to prove to the girl I ain't gon' hurry."

He stopped me and patted me on my chest, gesturing me to look ahead. I rolled my eyes and smacked my lips when I saw who was in front of me.

"Hello, Cairo," Brianna said smoothly, as if she didn't know I didn't like her ass. Man, I hated her boogie crusty ass.

"Move, man. I ain't got time for you. Fuck!" I looked back and there was Kamilah. I really wanted to say one thing, but Brianna really was pushing it,

"And Kamilah, why you wearing that shit? You look like a hooker," Brianna told Milah, followed by a snicker.

Milah stayed put, but Brianna stepped in front of me and looked me up and down like I wouldn't knock her ass out. She was lucky my momma had raised me better than that.

"You should really keep a leash on your girl." Brianna said.

I stepped in her face and she backed up a little, scared. It was time for me to change and let these hoes know they couldn't run over my damn kindness. *Kill these hoes with kindness*, I thought.

"Like I said, *Bitch*! Move outta my damn way. If you don't want to get cussed out, I suggest you step yo' nasty ass aside. You know damn well you gotta man but you steady bustin' your pussy wide open for every nigga you see! I know you wanna drop down on your knees when you see me, huh? See, that's that hoe-shit."

Brianna didn't have a comeback and she was looking so stupid, all she do was walk away.

Rome smiled with a goofy look on his face. "Bout time you checked her ass!" I shook my head and we continued walking to our classes.

When we got there, I saw Milah. She seemed so sad, it made my heart ache.

Bliss walked up to us and gave Rome a hug. "How you feelin', babes?"

He shrugged. "I'm doing betta, but seein' ya' beautiful face just made me feel a little betta." She smiled and kissed him. I gagged as if I was disgusted.

Just as I was about to walk into my class, I noticed Milah talking to Ken, but she was crying. I could tell they were arguing. I sighed and fought with myself not to go over to them and see if she was okay.

"Shut up, Milah. You were the one insisting on playing these games and look what happened. I had to lie to your pops now look. I'm sorry, but I can't do it no more. If you wanna expose me, go ahead and do it, I don't care. I'm tired of hiding. I'm sorry it had to go this way. You just need to tell your father the truth. I am really sorry, Kamilah."

Ken reached out to hug Milah but she rejected him and slapped him. She slapped him so hard, I felt the shit.

"I've been helping you out all this time, Ken. My father is the only reason you got the scholarship, nigga! Get out my muthafuckin' face right now, Ken! I hate you!" Milah yelled. Everyone in the halls had turned their attention on her and Ken. Ken didn't bother saying anything else, instead, he walked away.

Milah continued to cry and still hadn't noticed me. I chucked up my feelings and went over to see if she was okay. I wasn't the one who'd been acting like an asshole, she was.

I walked up behind her and tapped her on her shoulder.

"Go away, Ken, damn you!" she said, not realizing it was me.

I sighed while rubbing my chin hairs before I spoke. "I'm not Ken."

She turned around and stared at me as she wiped away her tears. "I thought you were done with me?" she asked.

I kept quiet for a moment. I ran my thumb down her cheek, then under her eye softly. "I was, baby. I heard what you said outside your room before I left. What is Cairo Black without his Kamilah?"

***

Nicki Minaj's *I Lied* played through my Spotify app on my TV:
Even though I said I didn't love you, I lied I lied. Even though I said I didn't need you, I lied... I lied. To keep you from breaking my heart, ooh. To

keep you from breaking my heart, ooh. Even though I said don't touch me, I lied, I lied. I can't fall for you, can't give my all to you. Can't let you think that I'ma let the game stall for you. Gotta protect me, you gotta sweat me... to keep you from breaking my heart. Sincerely, Love. Dot my I's forgive his dear soul, and love again.

"Say you lied like the once Iconic Nicki Minaj sang."

I looked at him and missed his big brown eyes. I deserved if he didn't want me, but my eyes widened at what he said next. "I was, Baby... I heard what you said outside your room before I left. What is Cairo Black without his, Kamilah?" Cairo said, holding my wrist softly.

I swayed from side to side, trying not to look up at him. He was so beautiful. I saw Brianna walking our way, so I pulled him close to me and kissed him. When she saw us kissing, she walked away in a fast pace. I pulled away from him and he wiped the lipstick off his bottom lip.

"Cairo, you don't want me, man. I'm just damaged goods. I have to take drugs just to keep myself from having nightmares. Why would you want me? Just go get with Brianna.

His eyes were glued on me. Cairo nodded his as his hand dropped from my wrist. "You don't get it. Listen. I didn't come over here for this. I'm not ya' play toy. When you get it together and tell me what you want and need, you can holla' at me." He planted a kiss on my forehead and walked to his class that was about to start. I was so ashamed of myself right now.

"Wait, Cairo!" Bliss shouted. He walked over to Bliss, and they were talking.

I had to do better to get better. As I was about to walk into the class with my head low, my name was called over the intercom.

"Ms. Smith! Please make your way to the grounds. She is excused from all classes today. Your father is here," the office administrator bellowed through the loudspeaker.

I could feel the lump growing in my throat and I turned my gaze toward Bliss. I mouthed the words *help me*. I could tell she was sad for me because she knew the relationship I had with my father. Whatever she said didn't help because the way Cairo looked at me. I looked away quickly. I took my phone out and began to walk to my dorm. I quickly called my mother. The phone rang three times before she answered.

"H-hello?" her raspy voice answered.

"Mama, papa is here! What am I supposed to do?"

She cleared her throat. "I can't say. Your uncle is here right now."
My heart dropped. I prayed he didn't touch her. "He didn't touch
you, did he?" She kept silent.

"Ma, I swear I'm going to get us both out of this." She said okay
before telling me good-bye and hanging up. I hissed and shoved my
phone in my pocket. I walked up to my dorm. While looking down fid-
dling with my keys, I accidently bumped into someone.

"Sorry, I—" My eyes trailed up from the man's Versace loafers, to
his Versace pants.

"Hello, my sweet, baby girl."

I nearly wanted to cry. "Hi, Papa. What are doing here?"

He pulled me into a hug, and I didn't want a damn hug from him. "I
had to pay my baby a visit. Now what is this between you and my son-
in-law? Anything you need to tell me?"

My heart quickened as I tried to regulate my breathing, "W-we
broke up, and I'm glad we did."

His eyes looked as if they had shifted into something more sinister. "Come on, right now. Right fucking now! How dare you break off
an arranged marriage and disgrace our family!" He grabbed my wrist,
and I pulled away from him.

I shook my head furiously. "No! I'm tired of being abused, molested, raped, and forced into a young marriage! You don't love me,
Papa! You let that man your own brother do this to me! I'm messed up
because of him!" My sudden revelation enraged my father and I could
see the fire in his eyes. "It's the truth, Father! You didn't want to believe
me," I shouted. "You never wanted to believe your own daughter," I
screamed.

My father grabbed my arm roughly. "You're lying! He would never
do that! You're just hot in the damn drawers! How fucking dare you
keep disgracing us like this. My patience is wearing thin with you," he
said.

I looked at him and tears ran from my eyes. "I hate you. Now, let
me go. You know he's sick. You know it!" He tugged again, and I
tugged back.

"Sir, I think you need to let her go," I heard his raspy country voice
say, as Cairo walked up beside me and grabbed my waist softly.

Then, another towering sweet voice spoke up. "Yes, Mr. Smith. Let
her go. Milah doesn't deserve this," Bliss said, trying to calm me down.

He smiled and let me go. "You do this, and you're cut off, dead to your mother and me. I can't believe you'd lie like this, Kamilah!"

I wiped my tears and looked at him like a strong woman and not a broke broken little girl. "My name is Milah, and I don't need your help. I can get a job and support myself. I'm a dancer, Father, and I what I do. I want to love who I wanna love, and your so-called son-in-law is *gay!* There it is, Dad! The full-on truth. I hate you for taking your trifling-rapist brother's side instead of your own flesh and blood, instead of believing your only daughter!"

He raised his hand to slap me, but Cairo grabbed his wrist and shoved him down. "With all respect, sir, your daughter is a pure angel. She doesn't deserve to be treated this way. You really wanna lose your only daughter? Let's go, Milah."

He stared down at my father, and my father looked up at him with a death glare. The tears gushed down my face nonstop, and my emotions had finally reached a breaking point. I eyed my father, realizing whatever relationship we had was long gone.

"Kamilah! Don't you walk away from me," my father shouted, "Kamilah!"

Shaking my head, I felt as if my whole world was collapsing. Just as my pyramid was crumbling down, it had all but crashed.

"You okay?" Cairo probed.

I shook my head. "Just take me back to class."

He looked at me but didn't protest. His big hands ran down my cool arms. It felt good to get the weight off my shoulder, but deep inside, I knew my terror was far from over.

Cairo 's hand ran across my wet face. "I'm sorry, I really am." He wiped my tears as if he knew what I was thinking.

"I'm sorry, I lied."

He nodded and kissed the top of my head.

Cairo scoffed because now he knew the whole situation. He hugged me tightly with his arm draped around my shoulders. "I still love you just the way you are. Okay? Just try and relax yourself."

I looked up at him and he pulled me into his chest and hugged me tighter. I had to right my wrongs.

CHAPTER 16

What Is Love?

Kamilah Smith

The professor stood in front of the Philosophy class giving his usual class lecture. I took notes and made sure everything was for word. "If you've ever been through a struggle there's nothing like having your loyalty and faithfulness tested. Living and going through the streets of New York when you're young, there's nothing you can't do. Dreams are high and so is your ego for dead presidents and lusty women. I was a Casanova who didn't give a damn about a woman's heart or feelings.

Then, when I got into my mid-twenties, I met Raine Michaels, and all that changed. She was the sexiest jawn." The whole class erupted in laughter. The professor chuckled himself, then cleared his throat. "I mean, the sexiest *woman* you could ever see. And, when they say love at first sight, I felt that. She changed my life for the better and I ended my player ways. Now, class, tell me what love is to you? Have you ever been so in love you lost sight of everything? Did you feel as though that woman or man of your dreams was the only one you would ever be with? Raise your hand if you have." A few students raised their hands, including me.

"Okay, so some of you know. But who knows what love actually is?" Our professor called on the light-skinned girl with long black hair. She was a beautiful Elvira. Her New York accent was strong and different. "Isn't love the way you feel about someone? How you show intimacy, attachment, commitment, and passion towards someone?" she said with confidence.

He nodded and the professor studied her. "Yes. That's particularly correct, but some parts are missing. Love in its own definition is different types of love. Love is or isn't the same for different types of relationships? Even as far back as the ancient Greeks, people have struggled with the nature of love. Poets have written about love, perhaps as long as poets have been writing. Psychologists may lack the eloquence of poets, but through empirical research, we can study the nature of love systematically. We can observe people in different situations, interview them about their life experiences, and develop questionnaires to investigate people's attitudes and behaviors. This way, definitions of love are drawn not only from personal opinion but from scientific investigations," he said, quoting from the 2016 version of *The Handy Psychology Handbook*. Coincidentally, I'd been reading the exact same book which is probably why I loved his course so much.

Some of the students were in awe with this statement. Some didn't believe it, some were even laughing. This was a daily for our class of different hours. But, the young lady who had boldly answered his question was the only true one who was intrigued, as was I. So, I decided to raise my hand and answer it correctly.

He pointed to me as he rotated his head some. "What's your name again? Sorry, I'm getting old and I don't want to pronounce it wrong. My students hate that," Professor Miller spoke, as I adjusted my glasses.

I pointed to myself. "Me?" I asked.

"Who is he talking to?" another female said, smartly across the lecture room.

I turned around and was about to tell her off. But Professor Miller stopped it before it even started. "Now, hold on. It will not be any of that in my class. But, since you have so much to say, continue, please."

"My name is, Milah."

"Well, Milah? We are going to come back to you. Now, you," he said to the girl in the back, "the one who wants to be rude in my lecture. Your name and how are factor analyses used in the study of love?" he questioned as he walked around his podium with his hands behind his back.

She looked at him with an un-studious look. She began to fidget and grow nervous. "My name is, Lynne," she said with a smart tone.

"Lynne? How are the factor analysis used in the study of love?"

"I don't know," she mumbled.

"Come on, Lynne. Don't be so unsure of yourself."

I knew she didn't know the answer when she became agitated and snappy. The professor knew as well.

Then, she snapped again, "God, I said I don't know the answer!"

The professor chuckled and shook his head as he pulled one hand from behind his back and ran his hand down his face to cover his shameful look. "Well, don't point out others if you can't point out yourself. Class use this as a lesson. If you can't hold your own, don't say anything at all. Now, back to my question. Milah, you said you knew the answer. Please, enlighten us?"

I looked up from my notebook and placed my pen down on the desktop. "And to answer the question that Lynne didn't. Factor analysis used to study love is one entity, or is it made up of many different parts? If I may quote, as noted by Lisa J. Cohen, "One way to explore the structure of love is through factor analysis. This is an important factor technique that shows how different items group together. It is used to investigate if a single idea is made up of separate sub-categories. Researchers create questionnaires based on a series of items, words, or scenarios related to love. They then ask research participants to rate their love relationships using these questionnaires, to pinpoint how humans react in their state of mind." This is the excerpt from the textbook I know more about this because someday I wasn't to experience true love" (2016). The entire class looked at me, as did Professor Miller.

Even though I knew the answer I still couldn't figure out what it was to love someone.

"Wow! Now class *that* is the exact answer I was looking for. Each and every one of you has experienced this. It seems as if Miss Kamilah here has experienced more love than most. Excellent answer, Miss Kamilah. Very excellent. Now, since we have dived into our subject of Psychology for the next few weeks, I want each of you to write a 700 pages essay on one life event, one tragic event, and one relationship that reflects directly to love. This essay will be due within three weeks. So, February 24th will be your due date. I expect for you to right that down now or circle it on your assessment sheet. Like I said in the beginning of this semester, that sheet will be your lifeline — if you lose it, you're out of luck. Because I won't be giving out anymore printouts, alright?"

"Okay," I said.

The teacher nodded as he walked back behind his podium and pulled up the next PowerPoint.

"Everyone take out your notebooks or tablets. I'd love for you all to pay attention. I will not be repeating myself."

I raised my hand, but he pointed to someone behind me. I looked backwards at the guy, he spoke up as he cleared his throat, "Yes, sir. But, will we be learning about Aristotle?" He nodded at Raymond's question.

"Nice question, now since—"

"Name is Raymond, Professor", he said, stating his name again, just to clear the air and spark the professors mind.

"Thank you, now since Raymond has brought that up. Let's start on the first slide of the notes." Dimming the lights with the remote, Professor Miller began to talk about the famous Aristotle and his belief and work on ancient Greek philosophy. It was crazy because he'd have to do this same presentation for the next five periods.

Soon, class was over, and I closed my notepad, turned off my recorder, and slipped my phone into my bag. I began to do some of my work while waiting for the bell to ring. My phone vibrated a few times and I knew someone was calling me.

The professor looked at me with an unusual expression. He called out my name, causing me to look around.

"Oh, gosh. I don't know where my mind is," I said, as I finally noticed the entire classroom was empty.

"Oh no, you're fine. My class doesn't come in for a few more minutes." I nodded.

Professor Miller was one of the coolest professors here. My phone chimed once again. I just ignored it because it was probably just Bliss. She always got out of classes before me. How? I didn't know. She was such a teacher's pet so it was easy for her to get out of class early. She wasn't doing anything wrong, she was going to the dance studio to learn more moves, for more reasons than one. She wanted Brianna off the team and fast, or at least get her demoted off being the team captain. If Bliss was able to do that, then all the ladies would vote for a new captain, and Bliss was striving for that position.

"If you have to go, go Kamilah. You are a hardworking student," he said.

I nodded and picked up my bag, making sure to open it to put in my papers. I slung my bag over my shoulder and made my way across the lecture hall chairs. I jogged down the steps and to the door. When I got outside of the classroom, I pulled out my phone and saw three missed calls from my Mama. I sighed in a little bit of frustration, knowing that it wasn't Bliss. Thankful that this was my last class, I walked down the sidewalk to my dorm and dialed my mom's number. The phone rang and rang, until her sweet voice boomed through the phone.

"Hello, my darling." Her voice spoke kind of raspy. Like, she just had been crying.

"Mama? You okay? I'm just getting back to my dorm." It was quiet for a second. "Hello, you did call me? What's the matter? Why are you crying?" I pressed as I walked into the dorm.

"It's nothing, honey, really. How is school?" Now, she was trying to get the issue off her.

"Mom, please, I know you. Tell me why you're crying. I'm begging you to tell me. Is he still there now?" There was a pause.

"No. H-he left as soon as your father called me ranting about you. Something is really off between your father and uncle. He's really upset because of you, his culture, and his brother." I didn't give a damn if he was upset. "And, I hate that he's cut you off. He is so—"

"Mama, stop! What did Cain do, please tell me? There is more than what you've told me about him. The man is sick, Mama!" She sighed. I got to my dorm room and let myself in. I walked in and closed and locked my door behind me. I could hear her sniffling over the phone. I ran my hand through my thick blond hair. I hated hearing her cry. I hated when she was sad. It brought me down. My mom was a part of me and I was a part of her.

"He said if I wouldn't have sex with him he'd continue to hurt you. I'll do anything for you but I can't do this anymore, You, your father, this life, I just can't. Baby, I'm going to move away for a while. I need too. I don't know where I'm going, but I'm going. Now I know what happened to Miranda."

I sat down on my bed and listened to my mom and she brought up a woman's name I'd never heard of. "I need a break. I let that evil man hurt you. I let your father be in denial, do all this to control your life and, Milah, I'm so sorry. I really am, I never could protect you. I should have done what I was supposed to years ago." I had to stop my mom because now I was crying. Now, I was trying to figure out everything.

"I swear, all of this will be over. He's going to get his. Mama, you didn't do anything. You've always protected me, and I love you so much. Don't say things like that, please. Please, tell me who Miranda is."

She sniffed once, before she started to talk again. "I never said anything about Miranda. Who is that? I hope you're not mad at me," she said. "I don't want to leave you to face this alone."

"You just said something about a woman named Miranda. Who is she? And I could never be mad at you, Mom. I love you and I love that you're trying to better yourself. I won't be mad if you leave dad. You need to. You need to focus on you."

We talked for a few more minutes until I heard her packing up things.

"Milah, my love, I don't know of her. I can't talk about her. I'm leaving now. If your father calls and asked if you talked to me today or seen me at the boutique just tell him yes, okay? I will call you when I get to my destination. I love you, my Milah bear."

I sniffed, letting what she said go for now. I kept it clean and shook my head. "I love you too, Mommy." The phone line went dead. I just looked at the phone. I closed it off and just sat there thinking.

At least my mom got away from all the turmoil just as I was trying to do. There was more I had to do. I had to have my uncle, I mean, he was no damn relation to me. I had to put him away. If my dad didn't believe me, he was going to see the truth.

At least I had my mom, she was the only blood related to believe me

Sharon Smith: Earlier that morning…

Beep... Beep... Beep...
Things weren't adding up, and soon enough these things had to be explained. My body was so tired and didn't want to get out of the damn bed. My arm slumped over the bed as I searched for my alarm clock. It kept going off as my fingers fumbled to hit the button. The loud vibrating made my ears ring. I figured my husband would go off, but I quickly remembered he wouldn't be home anytime soon since he was away on business. Now it was honestly giving me a headache better yet a migraine. My fingers touched the plastic material, finally hitting the button. Sighing in relief, I slung my tired cold arm over my sleep-crusted eyes as I tried desperately to adjust.

I was actually a morning person. I had been going through it with my inconsiderate husband. We hadn't been on great terms as of lately, to say the least. Then, on top of that, Cain, that damn Cain was pressing me. I just needed him to back off so I could actually figure the situation out. No doubt in my mind that I loved my daughter to death, but I had my secrets. Secrets I could not explain to my dear Kamilah. Things were already spiraling, what more could go wrong? There was no more counting on my ten fingers, how many times I had fought for my daughter. Way more than Asim had ever done.

Asim Smith, was brutal but loving. I had fallen for this man when I was just a teen back in France. I thought it was love. With his father being an oil tycoon from Cairo, Egypt. He was wealthy and heartless. But, then again, having a daughter did not change his ways. I was still shocked and appalled that he didn't believe his own flesh and blood. Family ties were a big thing in both of our families. I was in an arranged marriage with Asim when I was young but I didn't love him until the day we found out about my pregnancy. Soon, I did learn to love him. These thoughts made me want to sleep the day away.

My nose flared and wrinkled up as the smell of food made my body tense up. Our cook was not to be here for a few hours. Quickly, I pulled my forearm from my face and listened to my surroundings carefully.

My light brown face frowned when I heard some clanking. Leaning up from my five hundred tread count pillow and medium firm mattress, I slung the covers off my body and darted out of the bed. I walked over to our safe, put in the code, and it quickly popped open. I reached inside, snatched the gun, and switched the safety lock to off. I didn't care who the hell it was and why they were in my family's damn mansion in the first place. I made sure it was loaded, just to be on the safe side. I walked over to the door, opened it, peeked out, and listened.

Who the hell does this person think they are to be in my damn house? Plus, cooking my damn food? I thought. My side of the family didn't even fool with me, and I didn't fool with them.

I slowly walked down the steps and pressed my entire back against the wall as I slowly rounded the corner. My face frowned when Cain was standing in my damn kitchen shirtless. His dark scars covered his exotic white skin.

"Who the hell does he think he is?" I said to myself, then got loud as a bull. "The hell you doing here, Cain?" I said loud with authority. My full body came around the corner with the gun in hand while patting it against my bare thigh.

I only had on a purple lace crop tank and matching tanga panties. Cain spun around and clutched his chest as if he was scared. He began to laugh as his tongue ran across his teeth. My face was blood shot straight with no type of emotion.

"Damn, Shar! You really did scare the shit out of me, dead ass. What's the gun for? Got a nigga heart beating extra hard, shit!" Cain said with a deep laughter. I laughed lowly with no amusement.

Looking off to the side, I poked the inside of my cheek before saying, "Why are you even here? Just because Asim, *your brother*, who just happens to be my husband, isn't here don't mean you can make yourself at home free balling your ass through my house. I don't want to see your disgusting, perverted ass face," I said in a disgusted tone.

"Oh, baby, I just wanted to make you breakfast. After the bomb sex, you deserve a treat," Cain said, with a bright smile.

I was still disinterested and violated. "Sex? Please, we never had sex, Cain. You are delusional. Why don't you go and make breakfast for the bitch you were really fucking last night? Because, frankly, I don't want you here," I said sternly.

Cain's face dropped. "What you talking about, Sharon? When you left, all I did was finish up paperwork and went to my little abode that's that. Don't make me mad, you wouldn't want that, Sharon," Cain threatened.

I shook my head. "I have a voicemail from you and the bitch fucking. Do you want to hear it?" He stiffened. "Exactly. Now? Do you want to continue to lie? I'm damn tired of putting up with you. You did terrible acts to my daughter and think you can get away with it. Then, you try to have sex with me. Why? Why? Why do I do it? Because *I* generally have love for you. But, lately, that shit has been out the damn window. I'm through with you and the secrets I've been hiding. I've learned that you can't change no damn body. And if you want to go out and bone these broads, then go right ahead. Just don't so-call claim me then go out and fuck them hoes. I'm tired of being mistreated by your lunatic ass."

Cain stood there shook for a moment. He popped his neck from side to side and turned off the stove.

"I told you what I do, who I am, and what I'm about. But, I just can't tie myself down to one woman, Sharon. Sharon? Don't fucking walk away from me."

I turned back to him. "What? Or what? You'll kill me like you did my best friend, Miranda! Do you know a damn detective came to the fucking mansion? I should've had the damn nerve to put fucking nine shots in your damn chest! Wanna know why? Because whatever your ass is doing again and not telling me will jeopardize me and *my* family!

You sell drugs, that's cool Cain? Do you kill people? Yeah, you do that too! But one thing you will not do is touch Kamilah ever again! You can't have her or me," I yelled, tapping the gun with a mug on my face. To be straight forward I was sick of him, very damn tired of everything and everyone.

Cain's eye started to twitch as he spoke. "Who the fuck do you think you are, broad? You've been running your fucking mouth? What detective? Let me find out your ass talking to the police again, Sharon. I'll snap your fucking neck! Better yet, I'll snap Kamilah's. You only had her for the fucking money! You don't love her like you say, and you never loved Asim," Cain yelled back.

I was frightened to the core, but I wouldn't dare show it.

I shook it off and gave him the same tone back. "You tellin' people that this is your fucking address and you know it's a damn lie! If you get in any fucking trouble, they'll be coming for me, for my family! I love my fucking daughter. Did you love your child when you killed Miranda?" I raged on and on and began to explode in my native tongue.

Cain charged at me and wrapped his hands around my neck, squeezing inch by inch with his long fingers.

"Chill out, and put that fucking gun down, I'm not the one, Sharon!" I scoffed to the tone of his voice. I was scared, but there was no way in hell I, Sharon Smith, would let him see it.

"Cain, we are fucking done and better not go anywhere near her or you'll be the one dead," I said, meaning every word.

He tightened his grip and let out a deep chuckle. "Yo' ass can't leave me. You never could. You say that all the time and you know what happens." He leaned my body forwards as he leaned against the countertop. Pulling me on his chest, he looked me directly in the eyes. "Your ass comes running back every time," he said, smirking, "and you hop on this dick without a damn word. Like the bitch you are. *My bitch,*" he added. "You act all hard, but I see right through you. You're just a scared little thang. Just like Miranda and your little sweet daughter." His face was cold. A look I'd never seen before, but still, I didn't care at all.

I began trying to match his crazy. I laughed just as deviously as he'd done, and I cocked my rose-gold colored gun— courtesy of my loving husband.

"I'm your bitch, huh? I can care less about you, the same way you don't give a damn about me. You could be as dead as a stank ass rat for all I care. I'd suggest you get out of my house before you leave with bullet holes in your ass."

Cain looked at me and I looked at him, neither of us evoking fear. His strong hand was still wrapped around my throat.

He spoke up again. "Am I supposed to be frightened?" he asked, with an unearthly face.

"I don't expect your vile ass to be," I said with a stone-cold face.

He sighed and finally released my neck. Then, he rubbed his hands together. "I expect you to be at work soon, and that's all I gotta say."

I didn't blink and neither did he. I lowered my .40 caliber gun and he backed off. His face was uncertain, and I knew nothing good could come from this. I walked into the full kitchen area and looked at the food he'd cooked.

"Fake ass didn't even cook that food! Left the Denny's boxes in the garbage," I ranted.

My damp feet stuck to the floor as I walked out of the kitchen and up the steps. My body had a mind of its on as I walked into our bedroom and closed the door slightly. I tossed the gun on the bed when I heard the downstairs door slam. I sighed once more and stood in my big window. I waited for him to walk to the car. My eyebrows knitted together while my face completely frowned. When I didn't see him, I felt a sharp pain in my chest.

I was calling the Detective on his ass for all the bullshit he'd put me through. I need to see about my baby, Kamilah first though. *Where is my phone?* I wondered. I turned around to go get the cellular and Cain was right there. The look on his face was devilish. I gasped as he grabbed me harshly and slammed me down on the bed.

"Look who's scared now. Is this what I have to do to get you to love me, Sharon? Why? Why do you continue do me this way, why Miranda?" Cain taunted me in a sexy deep tone. I was so sexually turned on, I became scared. This was the main event that had sparked the war. I may have loved Cain but this was beyond twisted.

Kamilah Smith

After my talk with my mom, I had to blow of some sort of steam. I played Cain Bieber's *Sorry*. As bad as people didn't like him, I know they loved him now because I was in love with this song. As the beat came in, I pulled my hair into a ponytail and pulled up my leggings a little. Looking at myself in the big mirrors, his voice boomed through the speakers. Twisting my back slowly, I winded my shoulders and hips to the beat. Jumping up, I popped my shoulders. I started popping and rolling my hips to the music just like the dancers in the music video, but with my own flavor to my moves. I was hitting all the right points, twirling and popping my bottom to the beat.

As I was getting more and more into the dance, the music suddenly cut off. I snapped my head towards the stereo and rolled my eyes at the guy before me.

"What do you want?" I asked and took a sip of my water.

He stuffed his hands into his pockets. "I wanted to say sorry."

I shrugged. "For what? I don't need your sorry or your damn sob story."

He took off his glasses, and I sort of gasped. "Who did that to you?" I asked, trying not to laugh at him, but failed.

"Your boyfriend," he groaned.

I shook my head. "Well, he isn't my boyfriend. And, wow. How good did you piss him off enough to get a black eye, Ken? You need some ice?"

He huffed. "I went off at the mouth, duh. I ain't know your man was that strong, and the next thing I know his fist connected with my eye. I wanted to apologize for what I did and said, Milah. I hope we can move on. "

I held my hand up and combed my fingers through my hair. "No, now can I finish dancing?"

He willingly obliged and left the workout room.

The music came back on but restarted. I restarted my whole routine and was cutting up, until the damn music paused and played. Doing it three times, I looked into the mirror and stared at Cairo. I turned around and pushed my hair behind my ear. "Hi."

He pulled up a chair and sat down.

I frowned and positioned my eyebrows together. "What?" I said, trailing off.

"Finish your routine while I'm right here, gon' head, Milah." He slowly smiled and I folded my arms across my chest.

"I'm not in the mood for your games," I spoke with a stressed voice.

"Well, let's talk then. We need to lay some shit down."

I bit the inside of my cheek and eased down onto the floor. Cairo nodded and did the same. "Uh, okay? Well, let's talk then." He quickly grabbed me by the waist, making me straddle him. I slightly gasped as his fingertips rubbed across my soft flesh, sending chills down my spine.

"Yeah, let's talk."

Cairo Black

I fixed my hat and glasses while we both stared at one another. I began to play with my chin hairs as she sat in my lap and stared at me. I pulled her in softly and kissed her, then winked. She smiled and looked away, doing anything to keep from making eye contact with me. Fixing her sports bra, I sat back and waited for a moment. I looked up and down her body as I rested, back on my elbows.

"Let's talk," she said, looking at me.

"Well, first of all, why was your dad grabbing on you like that? I know he like a billionaire and all but damn."

She sighed and started to play with her nails. "Because I stood up to him. I officially ended it with Ken. Plus, I told my dad I wanted to love who I wanted to love. And I wasn't about to take his bullshit any longer." I nodded in agreement. "I had told him that he didn't believe me about what his brother did to me. He didn't even believe his own daughter."

Milah tensed up and looked away from me. "So? What your mom say? I'm still on the fence about her."

She looked at me and shook her head. "Wait? No, what? I don't want to talk about that. She brought up this woman named Miranda. I have a feeling that this mystery woman is how all the pain with Cain started. My father has been covering up for him so many years. I can't even fathom some of the hunts his brother has done. But my mom knew and acted as if she didn't. She's getting better and that's all to it. I'm done with living a lie. I care about you and I mean that. I'm tired of our college affair and I want to be with you but I want you to trust me. We have to trust each other. I hated that I've had to lie my whole life. I have to work on myself and for myself."

"Don't cry," I said, noticing the tears in Milah's eyes. "Really, shit gon' get better, Milah." I leaned up off my elbows and opened my arms for her to hug me. She hugged me tight as the tears flowed. To see her vulnerability made me feel like it was finally a break in our relationship.

Then, she mumbled, "My mama left him and I'm so glad because that bastard raped her too. But with all this hitting me so fast like this, I don't know what to believe anymore. I can't believe my papa because he didn't try to stop any of this. He won't even believe us. He'll believe his own brother over his wife and daughter."

I held her close as she cried her eyes out. I grabbed her face and looked at her while I spoke, "He needs to let time fix this. Not you. Your father needs to let the truth set him free. When he sees how his brother really is, he'll come running back to y'all. And if your mother knows something deep that she's not telling you, you need to let that go too. Please? Don't let your father go. I already lost mine. I don't want you to lose yours."

She lifted herself from my shoulder and looked at me. "You think he'll ever see the truth?"

I nodded. "If my dad could, so can yours. Let's just hope it won't be too late. Just by the way he acts, it seems as if someone is in his ear." I wiped her eyes and kissed her cheek.

"I honestly think you're right. I don't want you to leave me alone. I can't see you with anyone else. I'll get myself together, I really will."

I grabbed her face and kissed her lips softly. I laughed as her face blushed. "Just chill. We gon' be together. I was drunk when I said that. My emotions were all over the place. Yes, I have anger issues but that just drew me over the edge. I was wrong as well. I know how to control myself but I was just heartbroken. A nigga was shook."

She just sat in my lap and leaned her head into my shoulder.

"Yeah, your breath was smelling like some damn boiled bologna." I smacked my lips and acted like I was gon' let her fall.

"Stop! I was playing." All of a sudden, she let me go and got up. "Now, can I finish my routine?"

I nodded and shrugged. "Gon' head." I smiled. My phone vibrated and it was my brother. Opening the message, I laughed at his contact name.

Twinbooger: Bro! I'm dying, lawd! Sent- 6:56

I began to panic as I started to type in my message.

Me: What's up with u? U need to go to the hospital? 6:58

I looked up as the music filled my ears. Her routine was so sultry then Milah was twerking hella' hard to the beat. Then, she slowed down again as she winded her hips like she was a true Jamaican. My phone vibrated again, and I looked at it.

Twinbooger: I can't breathe! Man, she takin' my breath away right now. Her head hella fire. Sent 6:59

I threw my head back and sent my message. I wasn't trying to take my eyes off her, but my brother was buggin'. He played too much and it almost pissed me off.

Me: Fuck u. Bro, u such an asshole! I'ma kick ya ass when I get back to the dorm. U just blew me! Bye, cause u nasty bro. Sent 7:01

I tucked my phone back inside my pocket, not bothering to text him back when my phone buzzed once more. I shook my head as the phone vibrated again and again. I groaned and took out my phone to see who it was and why they were playing.

Key my hitta: Sent y'all some money. And I'm a'ight. Don't be stressed ova' ya big bro. Dad put me in charge and I'ma always be here, peace. Hit me back lata'. Sent 7:05

Key my hitta: love u noodle head, and chicken head too. Sent 7:06

I smiled, and I guess Milah saw it because she came over to me and sat in my lap. "Who you texting?" she asked, out of breath.

My eyes traveled up to her glistening body. I began to lick my lips before I spoke, "The fam. But, shawty you killin' it. Damn, what'cha doin'?" Her hands were traveling up to my hotspot and it felt good.

"Because I want you back and I want you to be my man. On everything, I want you to be mine." Milah kissed my neck but I knew we had to take things slow.

"Nah', we not gon' go through this again." I shook my head. "We gon' take this shit slow,. shawty. I feel you 'bout us but we ain't finna do that same shit again. We gon' get this shit right 'cause we ain't 'bout to fuck shit up, okay?" She just nodded.

"We need all the trust so no sex til we right."

She nodded but touched me anyway. "Can I at least kiss you like this?" Her lips kissed my lips as her tongue grazed my bottom lip then slipped inside my mouth. She had her slick ways.

I pulled back with a smirk. "Maybe, if you be good." She smiled. We began to kiss again, but what we didn't know was that someone was spying on us. Shit was about to get real ugly but we were finding out what love really was.

CHAPTER 17

Are You A Real One?

Cairo Black

Big Sean's *Bounce Back* blasted through my earbuds as I rapped the lyrics lowly:

Last night took an L, but tonight I bounce back. Wake up every morning, by the night, I count stacks. Knew that ass was real when I hit, it bounce back. (You ain't getting checks) Last night took an L, but tonight I bounce back. Boy, I been broke as hell, cashed a check and bounced back. D town LAX, every week I bounce back.

I laid in my bed, waking up feeling fresh. I yawned and rubbed my hand down my bare stomach and chest as I pulled the cover off me. My brother laid in his bed. That boy slept wilder than a bear. I shook my head and grabbed my phone, checking to see who texted or called me. I had a few texts from Key, Milah, and my coach. My phone began to chime off the hook. Other than that, I had likes and comments from some people I didn't even know. I shrugged it off as I began to scroll up the notifications bar, until I started to see the pictures I was tagged in. They were the pics from last night of me and Milah in the studio.

I frowned my eyebrows. I clicked on the Instagram post and went to that person's page. The unknown person had quick snaps of me and Milah kissing and even a little more than that. "Who the? Who did this shit? Oh my fuckin' God." I pretty much hollered. Rome hopped up out of his sleep, looking around the room. His eyes were slightly low as his chest heaved up and down.

"What? Huh? Who hurt?"

I looked at him and just shook my head. "Ain't nobody hurt! Someone was spying on me and Milah. I know that much. They took damn pics of us that are very intimate." I slung the covers off me and got up from the bed. He looked at me while rubbing his eyes, trying to comprehend what I'd said. Scowling, I looked at him sideways. "Man, go back to sleep with all that crust 'round ya' mouth."

He flicked me off, grabbed his pillow, and turned over. I grabbed one of my shirts and slipped it on. It was just too damn early, but I had to go talk to Milah.

I know she couldn't have done it. One, she had her phone, and two, she hardly even wanted anyone to know about us for now. There was no way it was Milah, she wouldn't do that. As it hit me, I stopped dead in my tracks. I knew exactly who the hell it was. I grabbed my toothbrush, along with my washcloth, and left the room. Without telling Rome where I was going off to, I closed the door kind of hard. I could hear my brother on the other side of the room saying something.

"Where you goin' mane?! Runnin' to get some of yo' girl punani?" I shook my head at him and walked down to the bathrooms. When I got there, I did my hygiene and ruffled a few of my curls. As soon as I got done with all of that, I left out of dormitory and hopped into my Jeep and drove over to her and Bliss' dorm.

When I got there, it felt a little off. It felt as if something was wrong. I got out of my truck and locked it. I slipped on my hat and went up to her dormitory. I was getting weird looks from some of the girls. I just knew it was from that damn Instagram picture. I jogged up the steps to only hear arguing. I ran up the steps faster and got to the door. I knocked and knocked, hearing the females argue louder. I grabbed the doorknob only for it to be unlocked.

"Mane, she gotta stop having her door unlocked." I shook my head as I pushed the door open. Milah and Bliss were arguing with Brianna. All I could say was, "What the hell just happened?" Fists were about to be thrown until I intervened.

"Aye!" I yelled. They all looked at me, giving me the death stares.

Milah began to point, as Brianna stood there with her arms crossed over her chest.

"Cairo, this stupid bitch was spying on us! She's the one that took those damn pictures and posted them!" Milah screamed.

Bliss chimed in as well. "Right, and this hoe gone record me and Rome. Get this bitch before I cut her! I'll be slicing a bitch like I'm a butcher! She got me fucked up!" she yelled. Brianna just stood there unbothered.

"So, you did post that shit?" I was totally wrong. I thought it was Ken 'cause I had given him a black eye. *Great going, Cairo* . I mentally face palmed myself but was brought back to reality when the argument really got heated.

"Don't ever in your damn life do some sneaky ass shit like that hoe! You trying to get me kicked out of school and the dance team hoe!" Milah screamed.

"Back up out my face. I ain't did shit and you can't prove shit! But what I can prove is that this Smurf-ass bitch is a full-blown hoe who got exposed. She's trying to steal my spot as team captain," Brianna challenged back.

"Who you calling a *Smurf*? Hoe, I will Molly wop your ass around this damn room! Keep fuckin' around with me. You know what? I'm through talkin'. I'm about that action, scary hoe." Milah laughed lowly as she kicked off her shoes then pulled her curly hair into a bun. She was about to throw them hands until I stepped in again.

I pushed them both back as Brianna swung first but hit me instead by mistake. "Aye! Bliss, step back Ali. You too, Tyson." They both smacked their lips.

"Now, Brianna, I'ma be real damn nice. Did you post this shit? You really trying hard to break us up 'cause you love a nigga, huh? Because ya' ass finna get beat and I really should let her stomp yo' shady ass out." She crossed her arms against her chest like she didn't give a damn.

"I ain't saying a damn thing. There isn't a person in this room who is going to put their hands on me! You'll pick that little crack head ass blonde chick over me? Fuck is that! She don't even want you." I laughed a little as I held Milah back. She was a short little pint who would drop kick her without caring. She was little, but tough.

"Listen, and listen real good. I don't want you, okay? Yo' shit whack, your breath stank, ya' shit loose, and we all know you got ass shots on account of yo' boyfriend's money. We all know he got yo' donkey elephant-ass teeth fixed. We all know he got your tits done when yo' ass was fuckin' with me. I was dumb enough to fuck with you before I even knew all of this. So bitch, you ain't shit but a fake ass raggedy-thot doll with no morals what so ever. Milah has class but your trif' ass, that's all you do is show your ass! And I'm sick of you tryna break us up.

I don't want you. I made one mistake gettin' with you. I'll never do that shit ever again in life. So, delete that shit! 'Cause I swear if my girl and her friend reputation get fucked up, yo' believe you me, I'm comin' after yo' ass. Oh, and for your information, I took the liberty of calling your boyfriend. I spilled all your dusty ass tea. So, you should be gettin' a call real quick."

She narrowed her eyes at me. Bliss cracked up even harder as she pressed stop on her iPhone.

"Yep hoe, got all that on video," Bliss said, with confidence as she waved her phone in the air. The time on the screen ticked and ticked. All eyes were on Brianna now as she was bright as a tomato.

Brianna gasped slightly, then corrected herself. "Fuck you and yo' bitches!"

Before I could snatch hold of her, they both socked her in the mouth. A few hits was what her ass needed. After they had made bruises and blood splatter over her shirt, I finally broke it up.

Pushing them back I snatched her up, tears were running down her cheeks. I laughed slightly before saying, "Give me your phone or I will tell administration about what you did. Yo' ass can get kicked out of school for this shit." Brianna huffed and puffed as she wiped the corner of blood off her lip.

"Keep crying, you big ass baby. And, give me the damn phone or they'll forcefully take it from you. We all know you don't want that heat."

She took it out of her pocket and I snatched it. Opening her phone, I was surprised she didn't have a password on it. I deleted every photo out of her gallery, back up iCloud, emails, and social media. Then, I threw the phone at her, making her fumble for it.

"Now, get the hell out of here. I swear if I see you around here again, Brianna, I'll do worse than what they already did to your sorry ass. And, that's a promise."

She brushed past all of us.

Kamilah started to laugh deeply. "Did she just brush me? Hell nah'."

I grabbed Kamilah and pulled her into me. Kissing the side of her face I said, "Calm down, Tyson."

Milah mugged me. Then, she asked with a silly face, "Why I gotta be Tyson?"

I began to laugh. "Because your voice sounds like his," I said, imitating his and her voice in one. "And I knew you woulda' bit her damn ear off." She slapped my chest, and I laughed.

"Whatever," was all she could say.

"Now, we gon' have to get shit right 'cause I can't be having people thinkin' bad 'bout you."

She nodded and kissed my cheek. "I'll fix it. I promise," she said into my ear, then kissed it. And that's when I figured out Milah was a real one.

Kamilah Smith

Dipping low into my splits, I pointed as Bliss yelled, "Don't let no bitch steal your pride, money, nor your man!" She cheered, as I finished my routine. After practice, me and Bliss had spilt ways. We were on a real mission to get that crazy hoe Brianna off as team captain. We were so close because she was going to have the whole team looking like hoes with the way she choreographed the routines.

Displacing her from my mind, I went over to Cairo 's dorm room. I still hadn't gotten any messages or calls from my mom. I truly missed her even though I wasn't with her. My phone vibrated and it was her calling. I looked at my notification. It was a voicemail from my papa. I rolled my eyes and placed the phone to my ear, listening to it.

"Kamilah, please talk to me, my love. Where did your mother go? Please call me back. We need to talk."

I cut it off and deleted it. If he didn't believe me, then I wouldn't be talking to him for a long while, probably never. There was no *forgiving this sick shit. Too much damage was already done.* Hell no, he let his own blood destroy my childhood and life. I would not forgive the evil within that man until he was dead incarcerated for his pedophile activities.

One of the guys opened the door for me, and I smiled as I walked in and up the steps. These guys were so sloppy, gross, and goofs. As they saw me walking down the hall, they either chanted Cairo 's name or some other mess. I just rolled my eyes and knocked on his door.

"C'mon in!" I smiled and opened the door and locked it behind me, as he'd told me to do.

"Hey, Cairo Noodles." He cut his eyes at me, and all I could do was laugh.

"That ain't funny man. But, was'sup though?"

I shrugged and sat next to him. "Nothing. I just wanted to chill with you. I just came from practice." He looked at me and tilted his lips to the side. "What?" I questioned.

"Yeah. I can tell. Did you even care to take a shower?" He laughed but I found nothing funny. I balled my hand up into a fist and raised it high as if I was gonna hit him. "I take it back! A'ight," he yelled out playfully. "You better not hit me, man. But, you want a nigga to rub your damn feet to make you feel better, huh? That's why you here, you ain't slick. Every time you come from dance practice you always want me to do that shit, funky ass feet." I popped him anyway and we both laughed. He patted on the bed gesturing me to sit. I smiled, kicked off my shoes, and dove in his bed like a little kid.

"Please?" I pleaded with puppy eyes.

He rolled his eyes and grabbed my legs before putting them in his lap. "Man, a'ight. This the last damn time," he said, smiling.

"Okay, baby. I knew it wouldn't be the last time because he'd said it so many times before. I smirked.

He cut his eyes at me and squeezed my foot.

"Ow! Okay, okay!" I shouted.

He continued to rub my feet so softly. He grabbed some oil and sent me into heaven. As he was doing that, I started to play *Angry Birds 2* on his phone.

"Aye, while you doing that, I want to know everything about you, mama," he said. He wanted to know everything that he could possibly know about me too. But as we were enjoying our time together his phone rang in my hands.

"Hold on, this Milah," I said, before placing the phone to his ear. Then, everything turned from playful to serious.

"What you mean? Where was he? Aw nah, you lyin'," Cairo said, in response to the caller's words.

I was so confused at what was going on.

Cairo pulled the phone from my hand. "Man, oh man! You gotta be playin' a joke on me He tough as rocks, and he's all my momma got right now," he said into the phone.

He shot up from his spot and swung my legs in the process, which almost caused me to fall.

"How many times, man? Who did it?" Cairo yelled in a furious tone, as he paced the carpeted floor.

I began to fiddle with my fingers as I eyed him anxiously. "Is everything alright?" I asked. He didn't answer me. So, I just stayed quiet as I listened to him on the phone.

"Who did it? Do you know?" He got silent then he finally ended the call.

Cairo began to yell and mumble before throwing his phone on the bed. He was l scaring me shitless.

166

"Babe, y-you okay?" I questioned in a low voice.

He snapped his head at me. "Do I look okay? Do I," Cairo shouted, making me jump.

He just hung his head low and that's when I noticed the tears. "Really, Cairo, just calm down. Is everything alright?" He shook his head no. "What is it, talk to me."

"It's-it's my brother. I don't know how to feel right now." Cairo said and paused. He stood in front of the bed with a dazed look on his face.

I took a guess and my heart caved. His pain was my pain and my pain was his. "Is it Rome?" He shook his head no. My heartbeat slowed down as I took a slow breath.

"Nah', my brother, Keith. They said he was shot. I don't know what to do, man. I just don't-don't know what to do."

I held him, rubbing his head. I tried to get him to calm down but it was too much to handle right now.

"He gon' be alright, okay? Just have faith, baby."

He stayed silent. His phone started ringing again and he looked at it before picking it up. "H-hello?" He held his hand over his mouth as more tears fell down his eyes. I hated seeing him like this. Cairo would always shut down when anything bad went down, and I didn't favor that at all. He was all for his family and nothing could break that bond, nothing. And I knew I couldn't mess up this second chance with him. He needed me and I needed him. Pulling him into a hug, I held onto him as I kissed his sweet face. We lay down together and I talked him into a deep sleep.

This time, won't you save me. This time, won't you save me.
Baby, I can feel myself givin' up, givin' up...

***

I sat outside of the therapist's office, and for the first time ever, I was early. Usually, I wouldn't be early and I was always angry about going. I had been going to the Moana Harvey Therapy office for six years now. It was torture for me, and it had been fifteen ago years since the first time my parents had made me go to a shrink. For that very reason, I did thank them. For some reason, deep inside my broken heart, I couldn't forgive them for not protecting her. That was one thing I'd never forgive or forget.

167

That day flashed in my head on more occasions than one. I thought I'd be getting better, but just when I was getting better, it would only get worse.

I finally got out of my car and made my way inside the place I hated most. I sat in that waiting room like I did two days out of the week. Sitting with one leg crossed over the other, I picked at my week-old acrylic nails that desperately needed a fill in. After that talk with Cairo, I knew I had to get myself right for him and this relationship.

I began to pop my gum as I listened to Summer Walker's *'Over It'* mixtape. I was so into the title track song, I didn't hear Moana's receptionist, Marji, call my name. I continued to pop my gum not even paying attention. I didn't realize she'd walked up to me and tapped my shoulder lightly. When I felt her touch me, it caused me to divert my eyes from the screen. I looked up with a smile and pulled my ear buds out.

"Hi, Marji. Sorry, I was listening to this new song. Is she ready for me?"

Marji nodded. "Yes, she is. You can go in now." Giving her a faint smile, I stood up with phone in hand and grabbed my *Michael Kors* purse. Placing it on my shoulder, I walked to the door and continued to the back room. I took a slow deep breath as always, just to keep my nerves in check. I would do it each visit before going into room three, Moana's office.

Opening the door, I was immediately greeted with a pleasant hello from Moana. "Hello, Ms. Smith, have a seat. How are you doing on this fine evening?" she inquired, as I took a seat in the all too familiar cream chair.

Crossing my legs, I pulled my purse off the edge of my shoulder before replying to Mrs. Harvey.

"I'm doing better than usual, Moana. And, you?" I said, as she crossed her legs then leaned forward in her chair, towards me.

"I'm doing well. Now, shall we get started?" I nodded and grabbed a Kleenex out of the box, privately spitting the gum out and tossing it in the trash. Moana pulled out her notes before turning on her recorder.

She cleared her throat. "I want to go over something you told me last week. Your life story starting off so tragically filled with abuse and rape since you were eight. It stuck with me and I wanted you to get past this, I could see the hurt in your eyes," she said, looking at me over her reader glasses.

I began to rub the back of my neck and sighed. "Okay, where do you want me to start?" I asked Moana softly.

"Well, first off, you told me you still don't forgive your parents, but you haven't told them why to give yourself for closure, and this is new from you, Milah. So, I want you to explain that to me," she said, leaning up a little and looking at me with a soft smile.

I took a moment before speaking. Then, I closed my eyes for a second and began talking. "My birthday isn't the only time he's touched me. This is one of the many incidents of my abuse that really broke my spirit beside the first time when I was eight. This time of so many really hit hard it was so vicious that I nearly committed suicide. Anyway, I don't forgive them because I didn't want to go down south in the first place, they never believed me. But, mom and dad insisted that I go with family and have a nice vacation. Since I didn't get out much, I agreed. I remembered the family reunion being amazing, but it became all dark when I went out with some of my cousins." I paused.

"Was he on the trip too?"

"Of course, he was. I was close with my cousins, so I thought I'd be safe. Out of all the begging I did for him not to come, they insisted we needed an adult to watch over us. No one ever listened to me because he was the cool uncle. Why couldn't they just listen to me for once? They didn't see him for the evil person he actually was, everywhere I went he was always there." I paused and began to fidget with my fingers, causing Moana to look back up at me from her notepad. She'd seen the look on my face and quickly passed the Kleenex box to me.

Moana did the breathing method with me and then said, "Just relax, you're safe. It's okay to talk about this, just breath."

I nodded and dapped my eyes quickly so my mascara wouldn't run. I took a slow inhale, and exhaled it out, "Okay, I'm good. Should I finish?"

"Yes, Milah."

Nodding, I began to play with the Kleenex as I began to talk again. "We had gone out to this expensive resort that had a lovely waterpark. Everything was so fun, and I was having a great time. The best time in a long and for the first time I was being a kid again. I wore a cute one-piece swimsuit; I remember it vaguely it was my favorite piece that my granny sent me from Paris. It was blue like the big sea – saltwater but fresh. It had these pretty flowers all over it. I was always self-conscious about my body, but my big cousin had talked me into wearing it. Even though I had a cover up on, I still felt self-conscious. I remember, we were walking from the pool to some of the water rides. Cain was conniving I still don't know what it is about me that made him so infatuated with me. I know he never did this to any other girls; I was the only one. When no one was paying attention, he would always look at me in a certain way, but I didn't understand it. The man was my uncle, and in all those years, I still couldn't understand it until that day.

I told my mom how he would look at me, but she just brushed it under the rug and tell me to stop telling lies. From then on, it began to feel more awkward. When she and my other older cousin, who was just a year older than me, went off to get food, they left me and Uncle Cain at the poolside. I wasn't in the mood anymore and I wanted to go up to the hotel room. For all the reasons, I didn't trust him at all, he said he'd never touch me again, sadly I believed it. Even though he was family, I had learned of the story, *Cain and Able,* in bible study and Sunday school. I knew he was a bad name, his name said it all. Cain was trying to converse with me. Yes, he was nice, but his eyes, they were always bright and eerie. I remember his eyes always being focused on my chest, but he'd play it off, then he'd look me up and down, almost in a lustful way." I paused and wiped my nose. I took another short breath before continuing. "When they brought the food back, I was more than relieved. He made my skin crawl. I remember he was sitting next to me and my cousin. I should've known not to sit near him, but I was just ready to eat the food and go to the hotel.

That was the biggest mistake of my life. But, this wasn't the first time he's done this. I could remember feeling woozy after drinking my beverage. I didn't even know it, but he had slipped something into my drink. I kept telling Robin that I wasn't feeling good and I was ready to go. My cousins kept calling me a kill joy and weird, so Cain volunteered to take me back up to the room. Everything was spinning and there was no way I could say no. When we got to the room, he took advantage of me like he had done when I was eight. I screamed 'no' so much, but no one came for me. My family didn't come to save me, and he *was* my family! He did anything and everything to me. It felt like hours of torture. Since I was older he could do whatever he wanted now! Cain was a grown man who to pleasure in what he did to me that day and over the years. That day I laid in a lot of my own blood. That's why I won't forgive my parents. I never wanted to go there knowing he would be there. They weren't even with me! They just shipped me off there." Before I could even fathom it, she was at the point of tears.

"Milah, it's okay to cry. That was not your fault. Your parents have to come to terms with the truth, it's not their fault. This is lot to take in. They had no clue that would happen to you," Moana said, trying to console me. But, I wasn't having it.

"What? Not their fault! I told them and they didn't even believe me! If they would've believed me and kept him away from me, it wouldn't have happened! I was raped more than once, Moana! I was just a child, a teenager, a young adult! Not one member of my family saved me! Not even my own father. And they're my blood, they're supposed to protect their loved ones. So don't tell me it was no one's fault! If they would have believed me when I was eight years old, when my innocence was first taken from me, he'd be rotting in jail!" Moana was taken aback by me. She never thought I would have such an outburst about what happened to me so long ago.

"Your PTSD is acting up again, Milah. It's starting to get worse." I couldn't hide it from her, I felt so defeated. I sighed, with complete hopelessness. Moana jotted down a note on her pad. "We may have to put you back on your medication."

I began to sniff. "I don't want to go back on those meds, Moana. My life is such a wreck. I'm in college. I can't be going through this. Those pills make me fill so empty and depressed."

"No, it's not, honey. You have a wonderful life, you're in school, and you amazing people in your life. Your life is not a wreck. Okay? We are going to pull you out of this, I promise. You'll only feel that way for a short time"

I was unsure but nodded anyway. "Okay, Moana. Thank you." Moana gave me a smile and reached out as she grasped my hand.

"Remember, don't let that overtake you. You're stronger than that, but I think that's enough for today. Same time on Thursday, okay?"

"Okay," I said, only partially agreeing.

"One more thing. Talk to your parents. Especially your father. That's your trigger. You need to forgive them, alright, Milah?" I nodded once more and gave Moana the best smile my emotions could muster up.

"I'll try, but I won't make any promises."

Moana laughed a bit. "That answer is good enough for me. It's progress."

I got up from my seat, as Moana called out through the intercom. She handed me the prescription note. Saying our goodbyes, I headed out of the office. Folding the white paper in half, I slipped it inside my opened purse.

When I got out of the building and made it to my car, I had to take a breather. *"Pull yourself together, Milah. You can do this."* Even though I told this line to myself more than once every day, I didn't believe one word that came out of my mouth.

***

It was around three in the afternoon. I had joined my mom's boutique in the *Phipps Plaza,* weeks upon weeks ago to satisfy my father. Sitting behind the counter, I continued to flip through the pages when I heard the bell being chimed from the front door of the store.

"Hello, girly!" Bliss' voice boomed through the store as she came in. I smiled as she strutted in with her Versace bag on her shoulder. Her Louis Vuitton heels clicked against the hard floor. Bliss' parents treated her well and spoiled their only daughter to the limits she was like like me. And, Bliss deserved as such, she had three brothers, so there was no limits to getting what she asked for. I was kind of happy to see my friend, but I shook my head at the purse and heels she sported. Bliss was my girl, but mama was over the top. Bliss was like my sister so I didn't mind. I was used to this side of her. She looked at the new shipments that I'd recently put on the shelves, walls, and tables. In all actuality, I loved my job. I had only been working here for a few weeks.

"Girl, whatever you need. You know I got," I said, as Bliss walked over to the counter and gave me a warm hug. I wasn't in much of a hugging mood or any good mood for that matter. That therapy session really threw me off. But, I let Bliss slide, didn't want her knowing I had been truly sad all day.

"Slow business day, huh?" she asked.

I nodded as she looked at the new jewelry I had placed out. "Yes, Eden is in the back unboxing the other new shipments. I hate when our days are like this, girl," I said, causing her to nod.

"Well, I'll have to get to work soon. Mom got me that internship at *Cosmopolitan Magazine* but the hours at the hospital are wowing me.

I'm caught in between the two girl. I just had to stop by to get that new outfit I had on hold," Bliss said with a smile.

"You know I got you, girl." I walked to the cabinet behind the register and pulled out the outfit. I had it nicely wrapped up and placed it on the counter. Bliss pulled her wallet out of her designer purse. I kindly rang up her stuff up and said. "That'll be $79.81."

She swiped her Visa debit card. As I typed something into the computer, her receipt came out of the machine. I waited till the recipient stopped so I could pull it off. "Would you like your receipt in the bag or with you, Bliss?" I asked as I did every day.

"In the bag, I'm going to wear this outfit on my date with Rome tonight. I'm loving the hours I'm experiencing at the hospital for credits, but then again I want this full-time job at the Mag. But, I need a break and I need to be with my baby. I feel as if I'm neglecting him. I think I'm in love. Rome treats me so special. Just his height, body build, and voice brings so much sexual tension." Bliss, spoke.

"Girl, you acting like I'm not talking to his twin. Y'all been together since the beginning of the semester. I'm so proud of you."

I secretly wanted to be in a relationship. But, it wasn't a secret any longer. Cairo and I were really working on ourselves. I didn't want our life situations to hold us back anymore.

Bliss said, "Almost a year. Have you told Cairo how you feel, *again*? Y'all need to stop the run-around and just go out on a date and make it official."

I handed Bliss her bag and she grabbed it.

"I know. I did that. I don't think I'm ready to go that far yet. I just, I just don't know, B." My face changed some.

"What the hell? You deserve to be happy, Milah. Y'all both do. To be honest, y'all both need one another. Don't let what happened to you destroy you, Milah. Talk to him, keep talking to him. Don't let what y'all going through tear you two apart," Bliss said with an angered expression.

"Bliss, I know what you mean. I'll figure everything out. I'll tell you how it goes, you already know I will."

Bliss mumbled a, "Mhm." The bell at the door chimed, and a group of women came in. "I'll talk to you later for sure, I have to get going."

I waved at her and she did the same. She walked past the girls, as they shopped. I walked from behind the counter as Eden came from the back room. Diana was folding up the new clothes. I simply sighed lowly to myself as the soft music played in the boutique. I really needed to figure certain things out with Cairo. But, ultimately, I needed to figure out aspects of my life. Even though my parents let me go from the bird's nest, I still felt trapped. I really hoped my phone had buzzed in the other room since there was an important email I had been waiting for. I'd been waiting since the day my mother brought up the name Miranda.

I just hoped I'd be better inside and out after finding out the truth.

CHAPTER 18

Wild Thoughts

Cairo Black

Nobody knows what I go through. Wish you could put yourself inside my shoes. You got friends that ain't friends no more. They don't understand the life I chose. See, the money and the fame, it can hurt everything you love. Got some people that depend on me and I can't give up. They don't know what I'm going through. They don't know what I'm going through. . .

The song lyrics of August Alsina blasted in the stadium. As my head raced with thoughts of winning while I was on the basketball court. "He banks left, he banks right! Look at him, Josh! He does a crossover. As they close in on him, he passes it to his brother, Rome. They get in the cut. Oh, they might be trying to trap them. He does and spin." The announcers and crowd were so anxious. They only had 10.5 minutes left in the game and they were down three points.

"The question is? Can they do it, John?" I was sweating bullets. This wasn't the best game I'd played, and I knew why. I looked back at the coach and called for a time out. The Ref blew the whistle, and I passed the ball to him. We all jogged over towards him. Someone passed me a towel and a cup of Gatorade. I was way too nervous. I was too worried, and I still hadn't seen him. Me or Rome.

"Come on, men! We got this, a'ight! Don't look at the time. Play with your hearts, not your brains! Go out there and bring this game home! Now, Rome. I'ma need for you to stay in the outside pocket and pass it to Cairo. We need that three-pointer. All I can say is defense! Okay, don't let them get through because they'll all surround, and we can't afford any fouls." We all nodded and did our break. I dapped up my brother, as we did out little handshake. "We got this."

The Ref inbounded the ball to Rome, and I swear I was seeing double and shit. I shook it off and stayed focus. He bounced it a couple of times using his pivot foot, then he bounced the ball to me. I caught it, as they started to charge towards me. I side stepped, went forward to my jump shot and it was like everything went in slow motion.

"Is it going to make it? He was farther from the three-point line! And, it's all net, baby!" The crowd went crazy as the timer went off. Now that we won the game, we had some other business to handle.

One Day Later...

"Man, I don't want to see him hurt Ro. You know I may be hard, but I'm sensitive. I hate it, but it's true. Our family means everything to me," he said, looking at me as we sat in the truck.

"I know, man. I feel the same way. It's like my heart don't beat the same, now that I know he may not be okay." He closed his eyes and nodded.

"Ready?" I nodded, and we both got out of the truck. We were just alike because we shoved our hands into our pockets and walked, kind of long if you asked me. We walked into the hospital and walked up to the receptionist desk. "Hi, I'm, we're here to see Me—"

"Excuse me, hun. I'm a little busy," she said in a real country accent. She tapped her long nails on the desk and I wondered how the hell she got the job. She had the obscene weave and she kind of looked like a cross between Wanda from *In Living Color* and Shanaenae from *Martin*. I was really irritated, and she had the nerve to be cackling on the phone.

"Excuse me, lady. Miss? Please, we need to see our brother," Rome and I said at the same time.

She looked up, looked us up and down like we were trash. "Hold on, look, I said hold on! Now, take that ghetto shit somewhere and go sit down," she said, shooing me off with her god-awful nails.

"Listen here, wicked witch of the gotdamn south! We need to see our brother, now! Can we sign in before I get unruly in this piece?" She rolled her eyes. "You black and act like you wanna be white but fucking got this damn shit in yo' head and them false ass nails. Bitch, if you don't tell me where my brother is!" She rolled her eyes and scoffed at me, as she mumbled something. But, Rome and I heard it.

"I can't stand New Orleans ghetto ass negros." I was about to ring her damn neck when her boss came around the desk and started yelling at her. He was black, and I was glad she got her ass checked.

He pointed his finger in her face as he spoke in anger, "Don't ever talk your own kind like that. This was your last chance. Get up and go to the back now!" She got up with a slum glum look in her face, and all I could do was laugh.

"Sorry for the inconvenience. But, your brother is in room 1012." I nodded, and Rome and I sighed our visitor passes that he had given us. My palms were shaking, and I was so nervous. Our big bro would never get hurt. But, we were wrong. As we finally got up to the room, Rome and I both pushed the door open.

"Hey, Ma." She shot up from her seat and ran over to us, giving us a big squeeze.

"How is he?" Rome question. She wiped her eyes as she looked over at him.

"He's trying to pull through. They shot him six times. Six damn times! He wasn't doing nothing. He wasn't selling or any of that. He was just going out to get me some food and they tried to rob him. He didn't have any money because he sent it all to the both of you and payed my bills. Plus, he's been taking care of Layla. That boy is a saint! He didn't deserve this." I held my momma as Rome walked over to Key, taking his hands in his.

"It's okay, Mama. He gon' pull through. You know that."

"I already lost the love of my life to these streets. What else can I lose? I can't lose my son, Cairo. I can't lose none of ya'." My mom broke down in my arms. We had to call our aunt to come get her because it was just too much for her. I sat across from Key, who was still heavily sedated.

"Bro. You gotta tell me who did this to you? You got to." I hung my head low and just prayed. Something started to vibrate. It wasn't my phone or Rome's. I looked around and found his bloody phone. I looked at the text that was coming in and was kind of shocked. "Aye, Rome, look at this?" He came over to me, and I showed him the text.

"So, they trying to say they shot the wrong person?" I looked at my brother and just shook my head. I was putting the pieces together.

"Yeah, they were looking for Keith Sr, our pops." I sat the phone down in the bed and put my head in my hands.

"So, that crackhead father of ours almost got his own son dead! What the fuck else can go wrong! That ain't my dad! It just ain't." I looked over at Key, as his chest heaved up and down.

The heart monitor beeped as the regulator pumped up and down. "You gotta' fight this, man. You got family and a baby on the way that needs you. Come on, bruh." I grabbed his hand and squeezed it, only to feel a little pressure back.

"In time." His eyelids flashed open just as quickly as they closed. Shaking my head, I leaned back in my chair.

"He gon' make it. I know it," Rome said, looking up at me.

"Yeah, he got too much to live for to go na'." That was the truth, but our own father was the one who brought this pain on us, once again.

Sharon Smith

Days Prior...

I tore myself from the window when I saw Cain pull off. Walking into the bathroom to wash the sex off my body yet again, I had to get prepared for my day. I was going to work at my boutique, but also had other plans to negotiate. Business had to be handled, some things just had to come first and end the mutiny once and for all. I had to go see Vincent and figure out some things. I was always with Cain when my dear husband was away. Unfortunately, I told my daughter the lie that I was only doing this because of the protection for her.

But, it was deeper than that situation. After we'd have sex and he got what he wanted, Cain never told me anything again. I was just another pretty face. I may have lied to my daughter about my whereabouts, but in my mind, it was for the best. Vincent, my informant, knew everything and everyone. If he knew anything about Cain, I needed to find out something, and coming from Vincent, it was valid. Cain couldn't be putting my efforts and my own dark secrets in danger. I wasn't about to go to jail for some man, a man who was a brother to my all-powerful rich husband. It just wasn't happening.

***

My long legs shined under the streetlight as I got out of my black Mercedes. My second car, my second baby. My tall red bottoms heels clicked against the black asphalt as I walked up to the door. I didn't have to tell Vincent when I was coming. All I had to do, was show up. We were cool like that. I knocked on the door twice and the door swung open. A man in an all-black tux with a gun looked down at me.

"You must be Shar?"

I nodded. He stepped aside as my long legs lead me in. My black stretch skirt clung to all my curves, as I sashayed away from the man. I could feel his beady eyes on my luscious body, and I definitely didn't approve of that.

"You must be new, first day?" she said, turning around and catching him looking at me like a piece of juicy meat. The man cleared his throat as he closed the door.

"Yes. Uh, yes I am," he said, trailing off.

I spoke up firm and pointed my long stiletto nail. "Well, listen up. I don't play the staring game okay, hunny? If you knew who my husband was you'd keep those eyes elsewhere before they get cut out. I'm a grown ass woman who deserves respect, so if you don't wanna get hurt and get this fucking Red Bottom in your eye, I'd suggest you keep your *eyes* in their place? Got it!" He nodded franticly, and I smirked. "Other than that? You'll be cool with me, baby boy." He smiled half-heartedly and looked off, as I walked away. I made my way to the back of Vincent's business and walked into his open office,

"Shar! I swear, you like fam but can't you ever give me a heads up," he said, laughing deeply.

"Nope!" I said, popping the *p*. I sat down in the chair as my hands smoothed out the skirt my slim thick body sported. Then, I crossed my leg over the other, looking at him as he wrote some stuff down.

"But, what's going on?" Vincent questioned.

"I need help. I need a contract kill out. A set-up basically."

"I've given you all the help I can give. You're like my sister and all. I turned you into what you are now. Do you know how soft you were when you came to see me? Now, look at you, hard as stone. But I'm outta the game, got a brand new job, life, and wife. I'm legit now baby." He confessed.

I looked at him while smoothing some more dark red lipstick on my full lips. "Yeah, yeah. I know that. But, this is really fucking important."

"Can't get your hands dirty, Boujee? What's the deal, Ma?" He pondered.

I closed the lip stick, kept a straight look, a serious tone when I spoke, "You know, Smith, Cain Smith?"

He laughed as his eyes flickered. "How could I not? That Cracker Jack mix breed ass nigga? He softer than wheat toast." Vincent laughed out loud, but I did not.

"How well do you know him?" I asked.

"I've known that boy, his *entire* family, since he was little. Now? You asking me a lot, to kill a rich father and son. Which is your brother-in-law. I started his crazy ass in the game, I should've thought twice. But, it is what it is. I ain't tell you because you was head over heels with his brother, Asim. I wanted you to trip and fall on your own. But, why you want me to kill him?" Vincent probed, I was a little stunned at his confession.

"I don't need *you* to kill him, no, that's too easy. I need you to get him to kill a man named, *Keith*, which will spark a fire. Which will set the little cutie off, someone more devious will murder him. Cain kills the man he thinks he snitched on him then he'll come after the girl. But wait? *So*, you knew he killed someone?"

Vincent looked up at me. "Why? That's a long story I'll never speak on again." He said with a shrug.

"Because a damn Detective from an *old* case came to see me. You know how lowkey I am, you know his past can't be dug up." He nodded in agreement.

"I told you the Smith's wasn't right. Don't have him bring trouble to your hustle. And stay away from the Detective. What's his name again?"

"Detective Raheem, and it's not a he, it's a *she*." I said, then I thought back to myself, *she was fine, very fine.*

"What? You're lying! No, first name?" he asked.

"Vincent, she didn't say all that," I protested.

He squinted his eyes at me. "Don't go talking to this woman, for real."

I sighed deeply while closing my eyes, "I'm not," I said as my eyes opened to look at him. "I don't fuck with the Feds or police nor *women*." He hummed an okay and passed me a piece of paper.

"My next assignment, huh?" He nodded. "Important affiliated person, huh?"

Vincent nodded again before he spoke, "Yep. He has started a business off of doing no-good things. Such as: taking in kids and using them for money. But, that's none of my business. I just want the job done so he won't have anything else to say. You feel me? I gave you this job because you actually stand for something. The reason this is your job is because he has millions of dollars that he didn't make the right way. I want you to break him down in every way. Use your pistol if you have to. He's not worthy of even living. I know I'm not a good person. But, he's ten times worst, like Cain."

I didn't bother to ask anymore or any less. I just grabbed the info and got up. "Got it. Now, I have to get to work, okay? Remember what I asked for. Get it done, please."

Vincent nodded and shooed me out of the office. I walked out of his office without another word. I had things to deal with and more things to plot out. One thing didn't stand out to me though, Vincent had his very own motives as well. Dark ones. Evil ones. That he thought I had no idea about.

Kamilah Smith

Instructing the girls to do the next move in the sequence of our dance routine, I said, "Okay, girls... let's get in formation." We started to do the steps, but Miss wishy washy wanted to come over and turn off Beyoncé's *Formation*. She stood there tapping her foot, looking all tough.

"This is not what I scheduled for us to practice!" she yelled, making some of the girls laugh. "What the hell is so funny?" Brianna stomped.

"Having a little temper tantrum, huh? Oh, it's okay fake-Rihanna. We all know you fucked and paid your way to get here! You did not earn it like we all did."

Her face dropped. She was finally exposed for the fake whore she was. "I earned this spot!"

We all cut her off. "Shut up! You're off the team and we got all the votes to do so. You're a disgrace to your loving team," one of the girls said, speaking up for all of us.

"And, who will be the captain 'cause y'all ain't shit without me!"

They all laughed and dabbed her off.

"We picked Bliss as the head captain and Milah as the Co-captain."

Her jaw dropped, and Bliss kindly closed it.

"Don't want any flies to go in. 'Cause we all know what been *in* your mouth." She screamed and stormed off.

"Now that she's taken care of, let's get back to practice ladies," Bliss said.

I smiled at her and we did our routine for the completion to the Beyoncé song. Glad we got that hussy off the team. As practice finally died down, we all grabbed our things and went off to our dorms.

"Milah, I'm going to Rome's dorm. You'll be okay by yourself?"

I nodded. She gave me a nice tight hug and we parted ways. I walked over to my car and fished my keys out of my bag. My phone buzzed and I sighed to myself, knowing it was Cairo. I held my keys as I opened my phone. I looked at the message as my smile faded. It read:

Uncle dearest: U shouldn't walk in the dark by yourself. sent 8:15

I looked around and no one was there. I stuffed my iPhone into my pocket and tried to open my car door. I felt someone or something behind me.

"You been telling people your business, you fucking told your mom something. Did she go off to the damn police and snitch?"

I turned around to my uncle in the flesh. I was staring straight at the devil. He had this deathly smirk on his face as he stepped closer.

"I'm dreaming, I've got to be dreaming!"

He shook his head no and touched my arm. "No, not at all. Answer my fucking questions. Now you been talking to your papa, huh?"

I shook my head no, as the deep fear ran through my body. "No-no, I haven't," I lied, but I knew he saw right through me.

"Yes, you have now you say anything, and I swear I'll kill you. I'll kill your ass dead. Get in the car! Now!" He yelled.

"No! You're not going to hurt me again. I know about Miranda too! Get the fuck away from me, for good!" I knee him in the crouch and tried to get into my car. "Enough is enough!" I turned around and kicked him more and more.

He yelled, "You don't know shit about Miranda! Get the fuck back here bitch!" Cain yelled as he laughed, "I will find you, make you miserable, and kill you! No one will find your rotten body!" He coughed up blood as he cackled.

I began to kick and stomp him without mercy. "You wanna pray on defenseless women! Not anymore you won't! You stupid sick bastard!" With each word, I kicked him in the balls. "Ever touch me or my mom again and I swear, I'll be the one killing you." I gave him one last kick and opened my door, quickly putting in the key and pulling off.

I quickly sped off to Rome and Cairo 's dorm. When I got there, I ran into the room, knocking on their door hard. I had tears in my eyes, and I was scared out of my mind. All I could hear was moaning and what not. The music was too loud for Rome and Bliss to hear me.

"Hey, Milah, uh, if you're looking for Cairo, he's in the lounging area." I nodded at one of their friends and went to the room.

It was quiet and no one was in there but him. He was sitting there in the big couch by himself. I opened the door and walked over to him. "Cairo?"

He turned around and his face quickly got serious when he saw mine. "What's the matter?"

I just broke down. "He tried to hurt me, Cairo but I fought back and came here."

He held me close to him. "Who? Your dad or uncle?" I started to cry hard, and he knew who it was. "I'ma kill his ass! Where he at na'?"

I pulled him back down and just hugged him. "Don't leave me, please."

He held my face and kissed me. "I ain't gon' leave you. I'm sorry I wasn't there." He kissed my lips again and we just sat there as he tried to sooth me. "I think you need to take some self-defense classes." I just laid in his chest, not saying a word. "Milah?"

I sniffed and looked at him. "Yes?"

He looked at me and sighed. "What is it?" I questioned.

"Do-do you want to be my girlfriend? I can't stand it any longer. And I can't stand you getting hurt." I crawled into his lap and just nuzzled my head into his neck, kissing it a little. "Uh? Is that a yes?"

I giggled a little. "Yes… it is." He kissed my forehead and made me feel safe. I wanted to feel safe 24/7.

"We will be taking this slow, okay?"

I nodded into his neck.

"That's a good thing. Because Rome be blowing Bliss' back out. No wonder she be limping during practice." We both started laughing. My phone vibrated. I looked at it only for it to be my father.

"Cairo, you gotta help me expose my uncle. I want my dad to see him for who he really is."

He nodded, agreeing with me. "And, how are we going to do that?"

I ran my hands through my hair. "I have an idea. I'm not the only girl he raped and abused." Cairo looked at me with a saddened and confused expression.

He knew I was serious by the devious look on my face. This was my only chance to prove my dad wrong and send Cain to jail. So I sat back as I placed the earbuds in my ear and blasted Frank Ocean's *Pyramids* and sang along to the lyrics. "*Set the cheetahs on the loose. There's a thief out on the move. Underneath our legion's view. They have taken Cleopatra, Cleopatra.*"

CHAPTER 19

The Plan

Kamilah Smith

After my ordeal with my psycho uncle, Cain, and the beautiful question Cairo had finally asked me, I decided to go back to my dorm room with him. In all honesty, I didn't feel safe without him. How did my uncle, I mean the *devil*, get on the campus anyway? There had to be something going on. I didn't want to keep thinking about all this negative energy, I just wanted to have a peaceful night. But by the way my mind kept wandering back to him, I just kept feeling worse. I guess I was staring off into space because I didn't hear a word Cairo had said.

"You okay? Ain't nobody gon' hurt you," he said, rubbing my back, as we walked towards my room. "If he even come this way, I'ma hurt his ass. Bee'lee dat, baby."

"Truth is. I'm not okay because he tried to hurt me again. My mom left, my dad is crazy and—"

He pulled me into a tight hug and kissed my head. "Everything will get better. I promise." He opened the door to his room and let me walk in first.

"How do you know?" I asked, taking a seat on his bed and pouting. He looked down at me and couldn't help but snicker at my face. "Why are you laughing?" I asked, and folded my arms across my chest.

"If you could see your face right now. You look like a big ass baby, Milah. You need to relax and try not to stress. Really, that man ain't gon' ever hurt you again, okay?"

I sighed and agreed with him. "Okay, Cairo. Well, can we lay down? I'm pretty tired."

He nodded, and I got up to take off my clothes. After doing that, I went over to his drawer and pulled out an oversized T-shirt. When I slipped it on, it smelled exactly like him.

I smiled, as I sat on the edge of the bed to put my hair in a messy bun. Cairo, on the other hand, kept his eyes locked on his phone screen.

"Is everything okay?" I questioned him. I got into the nice sized bed and laid next to him while he sat on the bed.

"Uh, everything is okay. My momma just texted me and told me my brother's okay and he's awake now." He ran his hand down his face. I placed my foot on him and he gently grabbed my leg and began to rub it. He was still on his phone.

"That's good to hear. I'm glad he's okay. He seems like he's a good influence in your life."

He looked over at me and smiled. "Yeah, he is. My mind was wrecked. I don't know what I woulda done if he ain't wake up."

I could tell his brother was the man figure in his life, and hearing him say that confirmed it. I t listened to him tell me how much of an impact his brother had in his life after his dad left. I wished I had a brother or sister. Maybe I wouldn't have gone through all this pain in my life. But, things happen.

"I wish I had someone like your brothers." He looked at me. He could still see my pain. While he talked, my phone vibrated. He was nice enough to hand it to me.

"Thanks," I told him.

He nodded and put down his own phone and crawled in the bed next to me. He laid next to me and put his arm over his eyes.

I checked my messages to see who had texted me. I rubbed my eyebrow as I went through them. Then I saw the unknown number again:

Unknown: I'll be watching u. that little stunt u pulled just fucked ur life up. Just like Miranda, I'll do u even worse. But no one will find ur remains. Sent 12:45

I closed my eyes and prayed silently. I was glad Cairo hadn't seen me. I didn't want him to see this. I didn't want him to lose his scholarship over me and the terrible situation I was in. This torment had to end. I locked my phone and placed it on the dresser. Small, quiet tears fell down my eyes. "Babe get some rest. I hear you awake over there," Cairo said, and put his arms around me.

Biting my lip, I mustered up the courage to reply. "I'm going to sleep now," I said, as he squeezed me softly.

"I love you, and I promise ain't shit bad gon' happen to you. He'll never touch you again, I swear."

I didn't say a word. I just turned on my side and silently cried myself to sleep. I was contemplating on how to get away with murder. And that plan to get him locked up was out the window. I was tired of being the victim.

***

The next day, later in the evening, my mind was on my work, but I couldn't stop thinking about all the texts I was getting throughout the day. I still didn't know how he got into this campus and who could've possibly helped him. As I was sitting in the study room, someone had come and tapped my shoulder. I looked up to see Bliss with a cheesing grin on her face.

"Hey, why so glum chum?" I stared at her and rolled my eyes. I ignored her and continued to do my work.

"You mad at me? Why?"

"Because the devil himself tried to rape me on the campus, but I fought back. I came to the dorm and you were too busy fucking Rome. When I needed you, you weren't there." I picked up my books and was about to leave before she grabbed my arm.

"I'm so sorry! I really am.

"Shh!" We both looked over at the teacher and nodded.

"I didn't know, I-I'm so sorry. Girl, you're my best-friend. I'd never want anything bad to happen to you."

I nodded, as she pulled me into a hug. "I know and I'm sorry for snapping. It's just, he's been texting me these horrific texts. He's watching me, B." I passed her my phone and she made a shocked face.

"Did you tell Cairo?" I shook my head no. "Why?" she probed.

I grabbed her arm, dragging her to a part of the room where no one could hear us. I began to pace back and forth. She just looked at me crazily.

"What's up, girl? Talk to me. You're all jittery and shit. You smoking that pipe?" I looked at her with a dead ass serious look. She raised her hands in defense.

"I'm going to kill him. I can't take this anymore. I was going to set him up but after all these texts, he's going to try and do that to me first."

She just looked at me like I was out of my mind. "You're serious? You can't be?" I nodded. She began to laugh, and I wished I'd never told her.

"I shouldn't have said a word about this. I don't want you in this. I'll do this on my own. I love you, Bliss, but I can't take this anymore."

"But, it's not murder if it's called self-defense." She pulled me into a hug and a few tears slipped down my cheek. "I'd never leave you in the dust." We were playing wicked games.

***

As the text messages I received got deadlier and harsher, I knew this had to end, this deadly cycle had to cease. I still couldn't find out who told my business in the first place. For instance, I had asked Ken, and as tough as he wanted to be, he would never tell my abuser to come here and do something like that to me. I sat in my room and my leg bounced uncomfortably. I didn't know if I could or couldn't do what I'd planned. Bliss stood across the room, thinking and waiting, biting her nails like she was hungry and anxious.

The phone vibrated and we both shot up to check it. "You check?" I said.

"No, you check it," Bliss stammered. I rolled my eyes and picked up the phone. I read the text and knew our twisted plan would go well. They made sure they had everything they needed.

"Is the gun loaded?" Bliss questioned.

I pulled the revolver out, flipped the chamber, looked at Bliss and nodded. "Remember, there's two warning shots in the barrel. If he doesn't stop before that, that means it was self-defense after those two shots. It's over." Bliss nodded and we left out of the room.

"Cairo doesn't know where you're going, right?" I took a deep breath and nodded.

"He doesn't know and neither does Rome, right?" I asked Bliss in return.

"Right."

We pulled on our hoods and walked down to the car. This was going to be the hardest thing I'd ever attempted to do. But it had to come to an end, someone was *not* going to make it home tonight. It all falls down from here.

CHAPTER 20

Murder on My Mind

Kamilah Smith

We sat waiting, waiting for the right time for him to leave his office building. He had just sent me a message saying he was going to come and 'pay me a little visit tonight'. But, I refused to be a victim any longer. Tonight was going to end my terror from this monster.

Bliss held my hand as we watched him pull off into the darkness. "You sure you want to do this?"

I looked at her as I started up the car. Taking a deep breath, I looked through the windshield as I trailed his car.

"Kamilah? You there?" she asked, in a shaky tone.

"Yes. Yes. Bliss, I need to do this, I *have* to do it. That man is smart. I know he has big time lawyers because he runs that damn mob on the west side. They can get him off, and he won't even do jail time. My own dad won't even believe me, so what's the point? He gets the chance to rape me again, maybe even kill me, and he gets off Scot-free? Hell no! It's time I fight back and do what I should've done a long time ago, *stand up for myself.* Tonight, it all ends, it ends tonight Bliss," I said, turning the corner and keeping my speed, as I tried to keep the damn tears from falling.

"So, how are we supposed to tell the cops?" she asked. I knew she was trying to back out.

"Bliss, you don't have to do anything. You don't have to see anything. I'm going to be the one pulling the trigger. You've been covering up my ass and messes for too long. There's no way you can clean this up. I read up on all I had to, and I've got an alibi. This is all self-defense. I have all his threats and everything. The bruises that never went away, the scars that never healed internally, and all the trauma that would take years to overcome, I'm evidence of all that shit he put through. My witness will be my mom. You'll just be my person of reason. You knew where I was all day, plus I was with *you*. You don't have to be at our dorm room because he's unpredictable. If anything happened to you or anyone else I loved, I don't know what I'd do—."

"Wait, pull over! Listen," she said, interrupting me, "you're my best-friend. You're my sister for Christ's sake, and I'm yours. And I said I'm here for you, *through thick and thin*. We ride or dies forever, Milah. You're right. This has to end, *now*."

I smiled at her and she leaned over and gave me a tight hug. She nodded at me and I started up the car again. I pulled off and headed back to the college. My mind was reeling, and I didn't know if I could pull the trigger if and when it came down to it. I didn't know what else I was in for. My phone vibrated and Bliss picked it up and typed in my password.

"He sent you a text and it's pretty bad." I sighed and asked her to read it to me. "Just know, I know where you stay. I know your every move, lil bitch. You're always mine. Remember I have a tight hold on you. And, after I'm done with you, your mom is next. By the way, she might be having *my* baby."

As Bliss read off the message, I began to get angrier. I hit the gas pedal and took the back road, the short cut to the college. If he thought he was going to get away with this, his death was going to come to him real early. In a few more moments, it was about to go down.

***

When we walked into the dorm apartments, it felt so eerie. I didn't know what to feel at this moment. I clutched my bag as the gun sat tucked in the back of my jeans. Bliss walked alongside me and she was quiet, and I was too. We walked onto our floor and walked towards our room. She entered first and I wished at that moment I could stop her.

"Ew, the matching twins." I turned around to an annoying voice.

"Bitch shut the fuck up. I'm not in the mood for your bullshit! You got me," I snapped at her. I guess she saw the fire in my eyes and backed up a bit. But I saw something in her that was even worse than her level.

"You should really watch who you're talking to." She laughed a bit and turned around, switching away. My hand reached for my gun but my sweet soul held me back. I flicked her off and turned to go into my room. I walked in and closed the door behind me. I turned on my light and heard mumbling. I looked over at Bliss' side of the room and dropped everything in my hands. He stood over there with Bliss pinned in his grasp.

"Let her go!" I said, getting frantic. I stepped forward and he pulled out a knife.

"You thought you could out master the *master* of deception. The fuck made you believe you could follow me and I not know! I thought I taught you better, baby girl. Ah-ah! Take another step and her blood will be all over this carpet. I know you don't want any more blood on your hands." He grinned.

"What do you mean? What do you want from me?"

He shushed me and waved the knife around. "Hmm, two girls in one. This is going to be a playful night. Now, strip. Do it now. And then I'll tell you why I should've killed your ass a *long* time ago."

I began to sweat and I didn't know if I could pull out the gun. He had a knife to her neck. I didn't know what I'd do if he was to kill Bliss right in front of me.

"I said strip!" He hollered. I flinched at his tone.

Frantically nodding, I began to take off my clothes. I looked at Bliss and she nodded at me. I didn't want her to get hurt. I couldn't let that happen. He pushed her forward and she stumbled next to me. He went behind his back and was about to pull out something, but before he could get the chance, I pulled out the gun, shaking in the process. Bliss looked at me and back at him. He looked up and started laughing like it was a joke.

"What are you going to do with that, huh? Shoot me?" Cain laughed darkly.

I cocked the gun, shaking even more. He stepped forward and I kept pointing it. "Don't come any closer or I'll shoot! I swear I will."

He laughed again, and before I could blink, he charged at me, tackling me to the ground.

Bliss tried to get him off me but he punched her in the face, knocking her out cold. "You think you tough! You were never tough. No one would ever believe a little hoe like you." He stuck his nasty tongue out and licked me down the side of my face and neck. I turned up my face in pure disgust.

"What kind of sick person are you? You're my family, *my uncle*, get off of me!" He slapped me, causing the gun to fall out of my hand. I tried to fight him off but I was too weak. I began to have a flashback. I began to call out my mom and dad's name, knowing they weren't going to save me, this time or any other time. His hands went in places he was never supposed to touch. I snapped back into reality and kneed and fought him off. I fought to grab the gun. I got the chance to kick him off me.

"You little bitch!" He grabbed at my panties. I kicked him in the face and he punched me repeatedly in mine.

Spitting out blood, I yelled, "You won't hurt me again!" As I yelled out my last fit of rage, I tried desperately to crawl over to the gun. He pulled me by my hair and I could feel it ripping out of my scalp from the root. I felt so damn hopeless but I wasn't about to let him do this to me or my friend. I threw my elbow back hard, feeling it connect with his nose and eye. This gave me the advantage to move forward. Just inches, *inches*, away from the gun. My hand touched the cold metal, so close to it. He pulled my head back again and I grabbed the gun and turned around, pulling the trigger, but nothing happened. All the gun did was click. My heartbeat began to quicken as I looked at the side of the pistol and realized I had never taken it off safety. Tears began to well in my eyes as the evil smirk crept on his lips.

"No, no, no!" Cain charged at me once again and wrapped his veining hand around my neck, squeezing it in the process. As he picked me up, I stared at the devil himself as the blood dripped from his nose.

He laughed before he spoke. "Bitch, you really thought you could kill me? Nah, never that, baby girl. Now I'm gonna fuck you up worse than I did you hoe-ass mama. You ready for the story of a lifetime?"

My eyes bulged open as wide as fifty-cent pieces as Cain squeezed me around my neck even tighter. My oxygen was beginning to get cut off, and it felt like my windpipe was being crushed. The tears flowed freely and mixed with the snot that ran from my nose. My eyes burned, and all I could think about was Bliss lying on the floor unconscious, and Cairo.

Cain looked deranged as he smiled in my face. Then with the speed of lightening, he cocked his hand back and knock me out cold.

CHAPTER 21

Love on the Grave

Cain Smith

Sparking my blunt, I placed it to my lips, quickly taking a drag as I inhaled the smoke. My eyes never left Kamilah, she resembled Miranda so much. She had been the love of my life at some point and time. But life never goes on the way you plan it. She was supposed to be my wife and have my babies. But my brother took that all from me once our father introduced Miranda as his wife-to-be. She was supposed to be mine! The day I killed her is the day I found out she was pregnant with his child, Kamilah. She was supposed to be my daughter.

I was the man in the middle, the man she lied to in order to keep her marriage with my brother safe. The lies she put in my head about leaving him and running off with me never came true. So now I'm here, waiting to finish ruining my brother's life byway of his sweet beautiful daughter. I didn't care if she was my niece. I never claimed her as my blood anyway. I smirked at the way she was tied up in the chair. It took me back 18 years prior when her whore mother was in this same situation. But unlike Miranda, I wasn't going to kill Kamilah. I was going to corrupt her to the brink of destruction.

I stood up, walked over to her, and dragged my hand across her full breasts, all the way up to her jaw, cupping it as I kneeled down in front of her. Slapping the side of her face, it was time for her to awaken from her slumber.

"Aye, wake the fuck up!" I yelled. Kamilah's eyes slowly opened as I smirked in her face. "So? How did you sleep?" I cackled.

"Fuck. My head," Kamilah wheezed as she finally laid her eyes on me. Then out of nowhere, she spat in my face. My smirk disappeared. I grabbed her tee shirt snatching it off her body and wiped the spit off my nose and lips.

"Oh, baby girl. I don't know why," I slapped her in the face, "you keep testing my patience. I keep telling myself to spare your life, but bitch you keep pushing me to slit you throat!" I screamed in her face, causing her to look the other way as she cried out. I stood up fixing myself as I popped my neck.

"Now, do you want to cooperate, baby girl?" She was quiet for a second, so I raised my arm and got my fist ready to break her jaw. Once she saw what was about to happen her little voice spoke up.

"Okay, please, Cain! I'm going to cooperate!" She pleaded with me. Satisfied with her answer, I continued to fix my collar.

"Good girl. Now, here's how we are going to play this game. I'm going to tell you the truth, something your fuck-ass daddy should've did a long time ago. But like the bitch he is, he wouldn't do that. See it was June 2002, a very damn hot and humid night. I'd just got done fucking Miranda, ooo-wee I put that good dick on her. You know, how I do you sometimes. Anyway, I knew some shit she thought I didn't so I had plans for that hoe. You hear me?"

Kamilah nodded in confusion, "I-I hear you," she said.

I continued. "Baby girl was badder than a muthafucka, had ass you could sit a bottle of Cognac on, and a bomb ass rack of titties that sat straight up. For her age, she was the shit, the finest thing of that time. Bitches these days wish they had a body like hers that was real. Don't even get me started on her facial features. She was everything, and like a fool I loved her." I paused as I cleared my throat and took another drag of my blunt.

Kamilah looked at me wondering where this story was going. But I was going to get there very soon.

"See Miranda thought she could out master me. Huh, the main reason she's dead till this day." I looked off and my mind traveled back to when I killed her.

I thought Blood was thicker, that was a lie. She was bruised and bloody from the top of her head all the way down to her feet. It was fucking sad too. She knew I was the Cain Smith, the mobster with no morals. As rich as I was it still couldn't mask my crazy. She wanted to resist my charm but she couldn't deny her love for me. We were supposed to get married but our religious beliefs wouldn't allow us to do that. I wanted her to leave my brother so bad, but she was in love with him. Just as she had told me, Miranda was in love with both of us— the two men she thought she could lie to.

"Fuck. How am I going to be able to get myself out of this one! Help!" I could hear her scream from the other side of the door.

She could scream at top of her lungs, hoping and praying someone would help her, but that was never gonna happen. I knew for a fact that being alone in the dark was only making her anxiety worse. Again, I had my reasons for doing her like this. She was forced to love my dear older brother when all along it had been me first. But she couldn't speak up like I did, the reason our father doesn't speak to me now. I thought the love of my life would never betray me, but that was a complete lie once I found out her secret.

So, I lured her over to the house with thoughts of a wonderful evening filled with wine, gourmet food, and mind blowing sex. But I was a wolf in sheep's clothing. I had used my cunning ways on Miranda, and she didn't even known it. I let her kiss on me like nothing had ever been wrong.

"What's wrong, babe?" she'd asked.

I sighed, and then that's when I snapped into my other personality. Grabbing Miranda, I dragged her by that silky hair, slapping her around. I had beaten her to the point of no recognition. Of course she couldn't fight back, being she was only five feet, one hundred twenty pounds.

"You gon' tell me the truth yet?" I yelled.

She was tight lipped and that only pissed me off more. If she didn't want to talk, I swore I'd beat the truth out of her. But just like me, she was strong. That was the best thing about her. The only way to end it would be for her to tell me what was real, not to continue protecting my brother. It was only breaking my heart more since she wouldn't. So she did everything to save him, having nowhere to run, nowhere to hide. She had no option but to be tied down like a dog awaiting to be put down. I wish, I just wish my life could be different. I trusted her, promised to never hurt her, but that was a lie. Once I felt betrayed, there was no going back or talking me off the ledge of killing her. I wanted to cry the pain away but what problem was that gonna cure?

I walked into the room as quiet as a mouse, watching her as she stared hopelessly into the blind fold.

"Please God... don't let me die today," I could hear her pray silently as she was sniffling.

I slammed the door making her panic, Flicking the light on, I was taking all the time I wanted, knowing the silence was killing her.

"Cain! What the fuck? I've been here for hours!" I then ripped the blind fold off her face with force making her head jerk back. Her eyes squint as the light beamed in her eyes. Once her vision came back, I was illuminated by the bright lights behind me, I was glowing, which intensified Miranda's fear. Squinting my eyes lowly as I stared at her, the

clothes I sported earlier were now discarded. And at that moment I wore nothing but black with gloves. It wasn't looking good for her right, but that was the monster she had brought out. That was the monster she had heard about all those years. But she choose not to believe it.

"Please, just let me go, Cain! We can work this out." She had nerve to beg as she looked at me through those puffy eyes. The whole situation had my mind in a wreck and the endless tears never stopped flowing. My expression turned wild as I tried to ignore the pain etched across my face as I stepped closer. Laughter erupted from me as I stared at my prey. I began to clap out of nowhere. It made Miranda jump. She knew this wasn't the Cain Smith she had said I love you to and lied to. I would never fall in love with another. I was a complete stranger.

"Very good act... here I was loving you all these years. And you thought you could do me like this! You stupid bitch!" I shouted as I grabbed her face and squeezed her cheeks with such force it made her wince. Once she tried to snatch her face from my hand, I pulled my pistol out and ran it down her face. Right then and there her body froze. She wouldn't dare move a muscle once that gun came into view.

"You wanna keep playing with me, huh? Is that what you wanna do. That'll make you die real quick!" The fire in my eyes had Miranda frightened as I pressed the cold steel of the gun against the temple of her forehead. Immediately, the tears streamed down her face and she closed her eyes in fear, panting breaths of hesitation escaping her throat.

I came into her view as I kissed the salty tears off her face. I knew they were burning the small cuts I'd left on her face when I beat it in.

"Act? What act? W-what, are you talking about? Cain, I love you. We've been together for so long, years! I cheated on my husband with no remorse for you. Why are you doing this? Please just answer me that, Cain, you know I was going to leave him, you're my one and only! I don't love him at all, and you know this!"

She tried to lie to me again. If she thought it was going to affect me, she was dead wrong. She knew I was no open box, so if she even thought she could figure out what was going through my head, she was wrong. I pulled the gun from the side of my head and ran the cold steel on the hot flesh of my face again, but that time, I went all the way down to her breasts.

Then, my other personality snapped out again, "Shut up, Miranda. You know what the fuck you did. Fuck! She thinks we're crazy, Cain.

Cain isn't crazy." She looked at me in utter fear. I pulled out a hunting knife from behind my back with my left hand. I looked at the gun and then back to the knife.

"Hmm, now? Which way should you die? By the knife slicing through your flesh or the gun blowing your brains out? Shit maybe even my bare hands? I could do all three. It's more fun that way. Well for me at least," I said, giving her a demonic look.

"Please, Cain! Think about what you're doing... think about us? The career you built, your family, and us!"

"I have no family." I roared, then softly said, "I don't even have you!!" I shouted with a velvety tone.

"You're hurting and scaring me... please stop this sinister game! You're acting crazy!" Miranda should not have called us crazy again.

I laughed slowly. "Oh, but dear, my dear Miranda, you weren't hurt when you were trying to get me locked up! Now were you, sweetheart? I saw you, rubbing him like we didn't have a pact! You can't deny it!" I smirked with a smile, but as quickly as it appeared on my face. It changed just that fast as I toyed with the gun.

"And, now, it's time for you to die. You broke my damn heart, you know. I won't go down for this. For all the money I've spent on you! And all the love I gave you, how could you do this to me? I got disowned for you, my family thinks I'm sick because of you, Miranda. You can't lie your way out of this one." I grinned.

"No, no please! I'd never do anything like that to you! Never in a million years would I dismay our relationship and love for one another. You're seeing things! You know I would never rat you out! You're hearing things! You've gone mad!" Miranda screamed once again, trying to break free from the bondage I had on her. But, it was no use; there was no escape from this real life nightmare.

She cried more as I watched her. I licked those dry and cracked lips that were beginning to bleed. Her head jolted back as I darted my face into hers. My expression was so sadistic, that my skin was touching hers as I taunted her.

"Ahhh! Please," she screamed.

"You can scream better than that, baby! Can't you? I know you can, you done it for me before! 'Cause ain't nobody coming to save you. You ran your fucking mouth too much! I get what I want, and I do what I want. Now, this is what I must do! I'd suggest you say your last prayer!

Might as well say bye-bye to the world, because you are done for!" I said with a darkened voice.

"Please, I love you so damn much. Cain don't do this! I never told anyone what you did, my love! Your horrid secrets always stayed with me! Just let me go and we can work this out! You're just sick please, you need your medicine!" she cried out, thinking about all the love I once gave her.

Slap!

I sent a bare, open-hand slap across her face, sending her head flying to the left. Miranda began to breathe deeply as she looked back at me. The blood trickled from her lip.

"You're such a beautiful liar! My brother ain't coming to save you. And, I ain't gon' pity you now either. It's over wit'. Any last words?" With that being said, I discarded all my love for her and cocked my gun. I pointed it at her head. "Say your last prayers or I will, bitch."

I walked around her once more and slid the knife down her cheek. Blood ran down her once beautiful face and she screamed in pain as it sliced down her tender flesh.

"Now, I lay me down to sleep... if I should die before I wake, I pray my Lord, my soul to take." I slid the knife under her neck and the cold steel of the gun pressed against her temple.

"You won't get away with this. This will be with you forever. Your family's money won't get you out of this one! I love you and my unborn child! That's something you'll never be able to take away from me."

When Miranda said that, my eyes welded with tears for the first time in and long time. I was unbearably heart broken and that's when I lost it. Stepping back a little, I pulled the trigger as she watched the spark flicker in the chamber of the gun.

POW!

My trigger finger went wild. I had shot her in the chest, as the smoke escaped from the chamber. I watched hopelessly as the blood ran like an overflowing river, down her chest. Her body slumped over as I watched in heartache as she began to gargle up blood while tears escaped her eyes. I grinned unsatisfied.

"I loved you, but I also hate you at the same time. Cain, you're going down for this... oh, Lord, how can I fix this one shit?" I sung to myself, as I wiped the bloody knife on the white cloth and tossed it on her dead face.

Finishing my story, Milah was in tears. I took my last puff of the blunt and exhaled the smoke. "That night ended with a gruesome scene. Your mother was on the brink of death. But lil bitch, you survived. And every damn day I look at you, I see her. I loved Miranda but don't get it twisted, I killed her as well. The moment they cut you out of her cold ass body is the day I regret ever letting her live that long."

Standing up I cupped her face and kissed her cheek.

"Thought you should know. Everyone around you told you endless lies. You were never supposed to be born into this world. Let me remind you: I let yo' ass live, hear me? This is the only chance you'll ever get at that, bitch. Now, I'm going to have my way with your little friend while you suffer and watch, then I'm gone." I smirked and pat her face twice as I stood up straight and unbuttoned my pants.

"Cain! Stop! Don't do that to her!"

I turned and looked her in the eyes as I hovered over her dear friend. "You tried to kill me, now I'm going to kill you internally like I've been doing all this years. After this, I'll let you make your little scene, let you tell your dad. Remember I got you like a puppet."

CHAPTER 22

No Pray for Love... is this the end?

Cairo Black

Placing the basketball on the floor, I plopped back on my bed, causing my head to hit the pillow. I was alone in my room. I didn't know where my brother had run off too, probably to go bone Bliss. Those two were at it all the damn time like rabbits and shit. I was surprised she wasn't knocked up yet. So, to occupy my time, I was catching up on some of my assignments. I was looking through my play book and doing homework. I hadn't talked to Milah all day and it seemed a little off. It wasn't like her not talk to me or harass me about coming to my dorm to see me. I hadn't paid it no mind because she had her life and I had mine. But I ain't gon' lie, I missed her, and I kept having this weird feeling that something was wrong.

You know how you keep getting a text or call and you think it's your Bae?

Yeah? I know: that's how I feel. I just keep thinking about her, again and again.

Then, that's me right now.

I know I sound a little feminine, but that's my girlfriend and she should be treated like a queen. I sat up against the wall and pulled my phone off the bedside table. I used my Touch ID and unlocked it. I went straight to my messages and was about to text her when a call came in.

Twinbooger is calling... Seri announced.

I rolled my eyes at his contact. Pressing the green answer button, I placed the phone to my ear and heard him breathing hard. I knew he was running.

"Talk to me?" I said, sitting up straight in the bed. That quick, my happy tone died down.

"Yo! Bro get down here to Milah's dorm now! Some shit just went down!"

I immediately shot up from my spot and started pulling on a Morris Brown shirt. "Why? What happened? Is she okay?" I asked, rambling on. I was scared out of my mind now.

"It's bad man, it's really bad."

I cursed under my breath and slipped on my *Nike Slides*. I talked to him for a few more minutes before I left the room.

"Fuck! I forgot my car keys." I doubled back and jogged back to my dorm. I keyed myself in and sprinted to my side of the bedroom. Looking for my keys, I was looking under my bed and everywhere. "Shit, where are they?" I asked, flipping everything over. I was had almost tore place up to find the damn keys. A squeaky, irritating, voice spoke up and I froze in place.

"Looking for these, Cairo?"

I popped my head up from underneath the bed and stared the damn demon bitch in her eyes. "What'chu doing here? And, why the fuck, and how the fuck did you get my keys?"

She shrugged and spun them around on her finger. I stared at her intensely. She laughed. "I want what's mine. Cairo, don't you get it? I'll do anything to get what's mine! We were made for each other. So what, I was with you and my boyfriend. Well, he's my ex-boyfriend now. Do you know how good I use to put it on you? Then, you started dating her!"

I looked at her like she was crazier than she actually was, which wasn't possible. "How did you know I was dating Milah? We ain't tell nobody."

She shrugged again and licked her lips before she spoke. Sashaying around me, she smirked a grim ass look toward me. "Don't worry, I have people who tell me things. Don't you get that? You ain't shit without me and you definitely not shit with her. Do you know how bad she bringing you down? The lies? The sex? The gay fake boyfriend? And now, a murderer? You really know how to pick 'em," she said. She laughed and flipped her hair. She stared at me like this was a game.

"Wait? What do you mean murderer? Brianna, you are nuts!"

She started laughing again and it made me look at her like she'd really lost her damn mind.

"That bitch tried to ruin me so I ruined her first. I made a few calls, said where she'd be and voila! Shit popped off like popcorn. So either she's dead or her uncle is. She should really try to whisper."

I walked towards her, fast. Startling her, I pushed her into the wall and snatched my keys. "Yo', you crazy bitch! Do you know what you've done! I oughta fuck yo' ass up!"

She smiled, but it didn't faze me like she thought she had. "Hit me and watch you and her career go down the drain."

I grabbed her arms and started shaking her, causing her to scream. I slapped her and threw her to the ground. "Stay away from us! I mean it!! You're going down for this!"

She lay on the floor, crying. I grabbed her by her wrists and yanked her up.

"Get the fuck out! Try me, bitch!"

She ran down the hall as I jogged in the other direction, going to my Jeep. I reached my truck and hopped in, quickly putting the key in the ignition. I started it up and pulled off spinning wheels.

I was speeding to get to her dorm. I couldn't believe this was why I hadn't heard from her all day. I ran all the stop signs, not giving two shits. Either Milah was dead or her uncle was. Either or, I was shocked it even had to go this far. As soon as I saw the sign and street for the ladies dorm, I hurriedly pulled on her block and watched the flashing red and blue lights. I stopped my truck and looked through the groups of people. When I spotted my brother, I quickly stopped my Jeep and turned it off. I hopped out and slammed the door.

I ran over to Rome and he was holding Bliss in his arms, rocking her back and forth, with a blanket wrapped around her. She was in pure shock, her body was slightly bloody and bruised. "Bruh, what the fuck is goin' on? Is she okay? Bliss are you okay?" I asked, as I ran up to them.

"Cairo, shit is bad. She killed him in self-defense. He tried to rape both of them, look what he did to Bliss! He raped her man and Milah shot him. Twice with warning shots then one to the chest which killed him." Bliss started wailing.

"Is she okay?" I asked, rubbing my hand down my face.

He shook his no. "Bliss is not okay… but ya girl she's right there. I don't know if the popo will let you talk to her."

I waved him off. "Fuck all that. I don't give a damn about 5-0. I pushed through the crowd and ducked under the yellow tape.

"Sir, you can't—"

I pushed him back in a rage. "That's my girlfriend, man!" I yelled in anger. He didn't say another word. I walked past him and skipped over to Milah. She didn't see me and she kept talking to one of the officers. I stayed in the background listening as she began to talk. Clearing her throat to keep from shaking. She was bruised and had someone else's blood on her. As she talked, I listened to every detail.

"He j-just bum-rushed us. He knocked my friend out. He was going to rape us but I fought back. It was a hard struggle. He said he'd kill my mom after he was finished with me. I don't know if it was for a ransom or what! That intruder wanted to hurt me that bad and I still don't know why," she said to the officer.

"I'm so sorry you had to go through this. Now, you said he had raped your friend then tried to do the same to you? But you got ahold of his gun and shot him?"

Milah nodded. "Y-yes. I can't believe something like this could happen. I tried so hard to protect her. She's like my sister! I had to do it myself." She paused, and I frowned my face up, looking confused.

This whole story don't sound right. I know she lying, I thought.

"So? You said this stranger was sending you threatening text messages? Why didn't you bring them to the police, Kamilah?".

I balled up my fists in anger as she spoke to her. She was right. Why didn't she tell me or the police? Milah tensed up and started biting her lip. She was lying. I knew Milah.

"Detective Raheem, I don't know. I'm not a bad person. I don't know why anyone would want to target us. We should be safer on our campus." She started to sob and that's when I walked over to her.

"Baby, it's okay. You don't have to suffer anymore." She nodded in my chest and I looked at the detective.

"And, who are you?" she asked.

"Her boyfriend, Cairo Black." She wrote it down and nodded. "And I think you need to go and find Brianna Haynes. She's the one who caused all of this. Milah could have been dead right now, look what happened to her friend. And it's all Brianna damn fault." She looked at me and knew I was serious by my facial expression.

"Are you sure?" I nodded and showed pictures of when she was spying on us.

"I'm very sure. She's a jealous ex who hates Kamilah and her friend Bliss. So, I'm sure of it." She nodded and patted Milah on the leg before leaving.

"I swore, I lost you! Why didn't you tell me, why Milah?" I said, enraged.

She just looked at me and sighed, wiping away her tears. She pulled me to the side and placed her hands on my face, as I gave her a once over. She had a busted lip, marks on her neck, and blood all over her.

The once loving eyes she used to stare at me with were now replaced with ice-cold daggers.

Her voice was steady as she spoke. "I planned this, all of this. I followed him and waited for him to make his move. I wanted him dead. I wanted him to suffer as I did. I felt empowered holding that gun and pulling that trigger. Even though he's dead, I still feel like he's out there, watching me. I know it sounds crazy. It was hard for me, so hard. I had to watch him destroy Bliss like he did me! You don't know the half of it, Cairo. I wasn't supposed to ever be born.

There's a lot of shit that my own father has been keeping from me. They let this man torture me for this long and they knew, they fucking knew he killed my real mother. I will find him and next time he won't walk away. He hurt my friend, Cairo! That's the last thing I never wanted to happen. He can hurt me a thousand times over, but Bliss no, hell no. He fucked with me for the last time. I've been knocked down off my throne for too long and if that bitch Brianna thinks this is over, she has a lifetime and the life after death to know that's not true. I'll never be knocked down again." I didn't like this new Milah. She was deadly, and I didn't know what she was truly capable of.

"You coulda died tonight! I love you but what you did was not smart. What you screaming, fuck your life? Do you have any idea how anyone else feels? You know people love you and you do this!"

She looked at me for a moment before she spoke. "Until all my pain is gone, my love will still be an *oasis*. Nonexistent."

I looked at her shocked as she wrapped her arms round me. I didn't know how to speak on what she'd just said, so I didn't. I just hugged her back. "I hope this doesn't hurt us. I'm here for you, no matter what. Okay?"

She nodded. I didn't know how to put all this together. It was just out of this world crazy.

Every King needs his Queen, right?

Asim Smith

Days prior, I sat in my in-home office and scrolled through the google searches on my Apple desktop computer, soft music playing in the background. I was desperate to find out where my brother Cain lived now. I had found out some terrifying news about my younger brother. Everything my daughter had said was true. I had been up night after night, learning more and more about my young brother's deep dark past.

I was paranoid and beyond unfocused on my family. I didn't want to think of that fatal night when Miranda was murdered in cold blood. All this time he knew exactly who to blame for her death. Every day I went to work, which was not the usual because it was my business and I was the boss. Inheritance was a big deal, inheriting stocks, bonds, and more from my rich mother and father, particularly my father. I didn't have to come in everyday, but he did. I was so focused on this one man I hadn't paid my two daughters or my unborn son any mind. And they noticed it.

Sharon missed me as her husband when she was hidden away in an apartment across town. She thought I didn't know but I had deep connections. However, she had pulled it together and came back home. It's like I was a stranger in our own home. When she had a problem, she would usually go to her father for advice, and for the past few days, he'd dismissed her to go ask her mom.

Eventually young Ebonique was going to come into the dark equation. Ebonique, was soon going to get hit even worse with dark secrets. I didn't want her to but everything comes to the light. I didn't take her to school, didn't tuck her in, didn't play catch, and she didn't favor dolls none, but I never played video games or tag with my own daughter either. I was hell bent on finding where Cain was so I could get *rid* of him. I went to every website, had paid someone to search for him on the dark web. I'd done everything to find him. I even typed in our family name but only my younger estranged sister and I popped up. I was stumped. I thought of people I could possibly call. People who knew my deepest, darkest secret. But before I could even do that, someone knocked on my door lightly. I had been in here all day and unfortunately I couldn't turn them away.

"Come in," I said, finally giving my eyes a break from the computer screen.

My daughter walked in and took a seat by my desk.

"Dad?" Ebonique said, in a stale voice. I looked at my young brother's daughter, and she looked at me.

"Yes, Ebonique?" She sighed and put her elbows on my desk, looking at me more. I sighed and rubbed the bridge of my nose.

"Dad, why have you been so distant? You didn't even make it to our game last night. And you hardly paint and color with Jack and I anymore," she said, speaking of her imaginary friend.

I looked at her sideways. "Jack isn't real. And yes, yes, I have been distant. Your game was last night?"

"Dad you were not there! And Jack is real! I looking for you and you weren't there. You've been messing up a lot of stuff and that's not right, Daddy!"

I sighed again. I didn't know that my work was overtaking my life so much. "I'm sorry, baby girl, it's just that I've been busy a lot."

She waved me off then tossed some pictures and other things I had missed out on onto the desk. "Think about that, Dad! I have a feeling it's something you're not telling me! You've never been like this. I hate it and I wish we never met."

She turned around quickly and exited my humble office. Ebonique was only eleven, fucking eleven.

I just sat there, trying to figure out what to do. I heard footsteps and knew it was my wife. Her heels clicked faster as she entered the office. She stood there with her arms folded across her chest, staring at me like she wanted to fight. So, yeah, I knew she was mad at me. I sat back in my chair and looked at Sharon as I toyed with my thick beard.

"So, you don't have shit to say, do you? You still ignore the fact that girl that is calling you dad. She's *not* your daughter! Your daughter is away at college, crumbling at the seams," Sharon said, giving one of those looks I absolutely hated with a passion.

"What do you want me to say? I couldn't believe my young brother had done some sick shit again! Damn, I've been working on it," I said, rubbing my temples at the same time.

What I didn't know was Ebonique had heard the yelling from her new room and tiptoed down the hall. Walking up to the cracked door, she eavesdropped.

Sharon laughed and wiped the corner of her eye. "You cannot be serious. I know she's not my daughter. Kamilah was raped by that man. Luckily enough, I had to have sex with that sick bastard to keep him satisfied. Thank God he didn't know about Ebonique! God knows what he would have done to that poor child! But why did it have to be my damn fight? Because you were never man enough to stand up to your baby bother! He killed her mother! What more could he take? You never in your life worked day in and day out like this! Missing family events, everything your kids do, so don't bullshit yourself! You ought to be ashamed of yourself. I don't know what's gotten into you but you need to cut it out! Your daughter and Ebonique are infuriated with you. And I hope you pray that Kamilah forgives you."

I was boiling so I just had to close my eyes and rub them. "Hunny, you've been doing what? You screwed my brother? Had sex with his twisted ass! It's just some things that I have to fix, okay? But I'll be damn if you go fucking my blood in the dark! Is that okay for me to do, you whore!"

She stood there, stunned at my tone.

"What is all this about, Asim? You cannot fix your deranged brother. And a *whore*? I've done more for this family than you ever have! So don't you ever in your life call me that! You can't change your past or whatever your trying to fix, okay! I've done everything to protect my damn daughter, what have *you* done, asshole? You know what? I am done with this conversation before you raise up my damn high blood pressure. And since you want to be in here all hours of the night, you can sleep your ass in here!"

Ebonique turned around and ran back to her room.

Sharon just turned around, storming out of the office as her heels clicked with anger. While exiting my office, she made sure to slam the door, causing me to sigh and slam my hands down on the desk. *He just can't stay alive.* There was no way Cain could live after what he'd just learned. It just couldn't be possible that he was still on this revenge.

I sat back in my seat while rubbing my beard. I thought of the night Cain had killed Miranda and almost killed his soon-to-be-born child, Ebonique. If Miranda would have taken Cain and not have slept with me, none of this would have ever happened. I spun around and looked up at the family portrait. All this could have been hers. But, instead, she stayed with Cain, but instead, I was in an arranged marriage to Sharon. And, of course, if he couldn't have her, no one would, not even Cain Smith.

I shook my head, spun around, and looked at the computer screen from my position, and leaned forward. Typing on my computer, an email chimed in and I opened it.

If you want Cain dead… send him off to the one person who is willing to kill him. Reply to confirm.

I looked at the message and stroked my beard once again. My troubles could be over for good. Cain would be reunited with Miranda, and my daughter's heart would finally be able to heal. I smirked and replied to the informant.

Cain was going to be dead, and my family name would be clear from his sin just like he should have done years ago. I should have killed Cain for what he did to Kamilah when I had the chance. I should have waited there a little longer, just watching him suffer from me taking his sweet daughter from him. But me killing him wasn't enough, it wasn't justice.

After I sent the email out, I sat back in the black, leather swivel chair and clasped my hands together while putting them against my smooth Egyptian face. My mind began to drift off. I wanted to ease things and leave my damn past in the past. But if he wanted to come back and cause hell, we could do that. Hell, I was just as cunning as Lucifer himself.

Kamilah didn't know she had a sister, well cousin, but that would have to be a secret for now. My phone buzzed as I looked at the caller ID. It was my dear father. Answering the call, my father's husky voice spoke into the phone in Arabic. I had broken the news to my father but my father was smarter than that and he knew just how his young son was.

Gahiji was surprised it took this long for me, his eldest son to figure it out. When I told him what had to be done, my father accepted what would come to his young son Cain and who had to do it. Everyone had to die soon enough.

As I said goodbye to my father, I sat the phone face down. Then, *BOOM*, it hit me, the flashback of when I came over to Miranda's house. We had been separated for some months at the time but ever since that night everything had been bad.

Cain walked out of the room, I could see his figure run through the long hallway on the top floor. I had heard screaming and rushed up the steps.

"Miranda! I know you are not fucking Cain! This is why we are separated now!"

I heard somebody quickly running down the steps and before I could get to the second flight, Cain was coming down. We stood there looking at one another.

"Cain, what the fuck? Where did all that blood come from? What have you done? What the fuck! You've gone way too far this time," I yelled, as I grabbed my brother by the collar.

Anger shot through my body as I looked at him with blood all over his clothing.

"I did what I was supposed to do a long time ago. If I couldn't have her, no one would, not even you, Asim!" Cain chuckled darkly. I pushed him back hard.

"You killed her! I'm not covering up for you this time! No, no, no! I'm sick of cleaning up after you, shit! You sick bastard!"

Cain laughed once again. "You wanted to steal my woman. She's still breathing though. Maybe if you get to her in time your baby won't die. And I know I'm sick. Aren't you your brother's keeper?" Cain said as I look at my brother coldly. "And she was pregnant so you really have to help me now, big brother."

I was breathing hard as I threw a punch towards my brother's face. Just another problem to cover up over his selflessness and undermining insanity. All I wanted to do was save my child.

I snapped out of my thoughts as my memory faded of that dreadful day. I ran my hand down my face trying to rid the image of Miranda's dead body. With my brother's death I thought all this would be over and all this bad blood would be gone for good. But I was entirely wrong. My daughter was causing this deadly web and my family's dark secrets were only going to make matters worse.

Cairo Black
The Following Week…

I had just got back from my game. We had lost a hundred and seven to ninety. Our streak was finally cut short. It was kind of hard, but you could lose on *any given Sunday*. To be very honest, I was still a little mad at Milah. Their dance team was away at the football game for support. But, I didn't let her see or know that. Me and my brother weren't talking because of the incident. I truly couldn't let her slip away. Sighing, I ran my hand down my face as I stood there for a moment, then began walking up and down the hallway, while trying to get my thoughts together. Then, I placed my hands on top of my head as I stopped walking. I had to keep fighting for Milah. Even though I had her physically, I didn't have her mentally. After her the suspect was wheeled away in a gurney, shit just didn't feel right, it was like she was a different person now. Even though Kamilah said she had killed him. Things still weren't adding up.

She was still so broken. I had walked to her room, just staring at her door while she was listening to Mary J. Blige's *Not Gon' Cry*. I raised my hand to knock but the music got louder. I took that as a sign and left. She didn't even open up to me and I wished she had. Kamilah was my heart, and I was gonna do anything and everything to show her I wasn't going anywhere. I walked into my dorm apartment building and texted my big brother who was full and well now.

I keyed myself into my room and smiled as she laid on my bed with my jersey on. "Sup, girl," I said, coming into the room and closing the door. She got up from the bed, pecked my lips and neck.

She slid her hands down my chest as she exhaled slowly. "Hey babe. I came to be your cheerleader tonight. I know you lost your game plus, on top of that, I couldn't be there. But you won in my eyes. You played great as always. I saw the video on Facebook. But, enough about that. Now, up daddy."

I did what she said. Milah kissed me again as I picked her up and kissed her back. Dropping everything, it got intense real fast.

Milah giggled as she threw her head back. "Ohh, I love you so much, Cairo! I'm nothing without your love!" she moaned out, as I snatched that shirt off with one hand. This wasn't the usual Kamilah. She was wild and I actually liked it. Plus, to make matters sexually worse, Milah ain't have a damn thing on under the jersey. We both placed kisses all on each other's necks. Smacking her ass hard, I threw her on the bed with plans of making love to her. She had this look in her eyes that made me tense inside. And let's just say, protection was not in the equation. I was going to extend our love. No one was gonna love her like me and no one was gonna love me like her.

CHAPTER 23

The last few months have been great for once. Things were like they should be, normal. When my mom and brother finally met her, it was the best day ever, to be honest. I wanted to settle down with Kamilah. Good thing we'd pulled it together and got ourselves on track. There were still secrets hidden away in the dark, things we couldn't bring to tell one another. So, enough of my thoughts...

What more can I say? Love is love, but our college affair hasn't ended just yet. This was my first, and never the last, experience with Kamilah Smith. Some things just have to last forever. We both have a long journey in life. Will we make it? Pray for us because I know I am.

So? What was this thing called again? Y'all still don't know? You know this thing I'm talking about? Not the love or distrust...

No? Let me tell you, let you in on a little secret. It's called *life*. We live it every day and I've been living it for nineteen damn years now, and so forth. It hasn't been all that grand, if I must say. I wish I had a Pyramid. I don't know why. I just wish I did. Wait, I know why. So, I could give it to the love of my life, Kamilah. Just to show her how much I love her for the queen that she is.

I know, I know. I sound crazy, right. But her name is really, Kamilah, is my rock and I'm not worthy of her. And, I'm basically the man she loves but we've been through hell and back. Let's just say I'm not like the other guys she'd talk to. I'm not rich and fancy like her past boyfriends. But, I'll be the best she ever had, and I won't be replaced.

Crazy, no. I'm crazy for her. And, with all that's gone down, will this all be an allusion? An oasis?

So? What is this thing called life again? I don't know. I wish I knew. Maybe we'll figure things out together. I just wished Milah saw what I saw. Me and her against the world. A Pharaoh and his Queen, I believed. But life didn't want it to be. And then, the next thing happened ...

To Be Continued...
I'm Nothing Without His Love 2
Coming Soon

Submission Guideline

Submit the first three chapters of your completed manuscript to <u>ldpsubmissions@gmail.com</u>, subject line: Your book's title. The manuscript must be in a .doc file and sent as an attachment. Document should be in Times New Roman, double spaced and in size 12 font. Also, provide your synopsis and full contact information. If sending multiple submissions, they must each be in a separate email.

Have a story but no way to send it electronically? You can still submit to LDP/Ca$h Presents. Send in the first three chapters, written or typed, of your completed manuscript to:

LDP: Submissions Dept
Po Box 870494
Mesquite, Tx 75187

DO NOT send original manuscript. Must be a duplicate.

Provide your synopsis and a cover letter containing your full contact information.

Thanks for considering LDP and Ca$h Presents.

Coming Soon from Lock Down Publications/Ca$h Presents

BOW DOWN TO MY GANGSTA
By **Ca$h**
TORN BETWEEN TWO
By **Coffee**
THE STREETS STAINED MY SOUL **II**
By **Marcellus Allen**
BLOOD OF A BOSS **VI**
SHADOWS OF THE GAME II
By **Askari**
LOYAL TO THE GAME **IV**
By **T.J. & Jelissa**
A DOPEBOY'S PRAYER **II**
By **Eddie "Wolf" Lee**
IF LOVING YOU IS WRONG... **III**
By **Jelissa**
TRUE SAVAGE **VII**
MIDNIGHT CARTEL II
DOPE BOY MAGIC III
By **Chris Green**
BLAST FOR ME **III**
DUFFLE BAG CARTEL **IV**
HEARTLESS GOON **IV**
A SAVAGE DOPEBOY II
By **Ghost**
A HUSTLER'S DECEIT III
KILL ZONE **II**
BAE BELONGS TO ME III
SOUL OF A MONSTER III
By **Aryanna**
THE COST OF LOYALTY **III**

By **Kweli**

CHAINED TO THE STREETS II

By **J-Blunt**

KING OF NEW YORK V

COKE KINGS IV

BORN HEARTLESS IV

By **T.J. Edwards**

GORILLAZ IN THE BAY V

De'Kari

THE STREETS ARE CALLING II

Duquie Wilson

KINGPIN KILLAZ IV

STREET KINGS III

PAID IN BLOOD III

CARTEL KILLAZ IV

Hood Rich

SINS OF A HUSTLA II

ASAD

TRIGGADALE III

Elijah R. Freeman

KINGZ OF THE GAME V

Playa Ray

SLAUGHTER GANG IV

RUTHLESS HEART II

By **Willie Slaughter**

THE HEART OF A SAVAGE II

By **Jibril Williams**

FUK SHYT II

By **Blakk Diamond**

THE DOPEMAN'S BODYGAURD II

By **Tranay Adams**

TRAP GOD II

By Troublesome
YAYO III
A SHOOTER'S AMBITION II
By S. Allen
GHOST MOB
Stilloan Robinson
KINGPIN DREAMS II
By Paper Boi Rari
CREAM
By Yolanda Moore
SON OF A DOPE FIEND II
By Renta
FOREVER GANGSTA II
By Adrian Dulan
LOYALTY AIN'T PROMISED
By Keith Williams
THE PRICE YOU PAY FOR LOVE II
By Destiny Skai
THE LIFE OF A HOOD STAR
By Rashia Wilson
TOE TAGZ II
By Ah'Million
CONFESSIONS OF A GANGSTA II
By Nicholas Lock
PAID IN KARMA II
By **Meesha**
I'M NOTHING WITHOUT HIS LOVE II
By Monet Dragun

Available Now

RESTRAINING ORDER **I & II**
By **CA$H & Coffee**
LOVE KNOWS NO BOUNDARIES **I II & III**
By **Coffee**
RAISED AS A GOON I, II, III & IV
BRED BY THE SLUMS I, II, III
BLAST FOR ME I & II
ROTTEN TO THE CORE I II III
A BRONX TALE I, II, III
DUFFEL BAG CARTEL I II III
HEARTLESS GOON
A SAVAGE DOPEBOY
HEARTLESS GOON I II III
DRUG LORDS I II III
By **Ghost**
LAY IT DOWN **I & II**
LAST OF A DYING BREED
BLOOD STAINS OF A SHOTTA I & II III
By **Jamaica**
LOYAL TO THE GAME
LOYAL TO THE GAME II
LOYAL TO THE GAME III
LIFE OF SIN I, II III
By **TJ & Jelissa**
BLOODY COMMAS I & II
SKI MASK CARTEL I II & III
KING OF NEW YORK I II,III IV
RISE TO POWER I II III
COKE KINGS I II III
BORN HEARTLESS I II III
By **T.J. Edwards**
IF LOVING HIM IS WRONG…I & II

LOVE ME EVEN WHEN IT HURTS I II III
By **Jelissa**
WHEN THE STREETS CLAP BACK I & II III
By **Jibril Williams**
A DISTINGUISHED THUG STOLE MY HEART I II & III
LOVE SHOULDN'T HURT I II III IV
RENEGADE BOYS I II III IV
PAID IN KARMA
By **Meesha**
A GANGSTER'S CODE I &, II III
A GANGSTER'S SYN I II III
THE SAVAGE LIFE I II III
CHAINED TO THE STREETS
By J-Blunt
PUSH IT TO THE LIMIT
By **Bre' Hayes**
BLOOD OF A BOSS **I, II, III, IV, V**
SHADOWS OF THE GAME
By **Askari**
THE STREETS BLEED MURDER **I, II & III**
THE HEART OF A GANGSTA I II& III
By **Jerry Jackson**
CUM FOR ME
CUM FOR ME 2
CUM FOR ME 3
CUM FOR ME 4
CUM FOR ME 5
An **LDP Erotica Collaboration**
BRIDE OF A HUSTLA **I II & II**
THE FETTI GIRLS **I, II& III**
CORRUPTED BY A GANGSTA I, II III, IV
BLINDED BY HIS LOVE

THE PRICE YOU PAY FOR LOVE

By **Destiny Skai**

WHEN A GOOD GIRL GOES BAD

By **Adrienne**

THE COST OF LOYALTY I II

By Kweli

A GANGSTER'S REVENGE **I II III & IV**

THE BOSS MAN'S DAUGHTERS

THE BOSS MAN'S DAUGHTERS II

THE BOSSMAN'S DAUGHTERS III

THE BOSSMAN'S DAUGHTERS IV

THE BOSS MAN'S DAUGHTERS **V**

A SAVAGE LOVE **I & II**

BAE BELONGS TO ME I II

A HUSTLER'S DECEIT I, II, III

WHAT BAD BITCHES DO I, II, III

SOUL OF A MONSTER I II

KILL ZONE

By **Aryanna**

A KINGPIN'S AMBITON

A KINGPIN'S AMBITION **II**

I MURDER FOR THE DOUGH

By **Ambitious**

TRUE SAVAGE

TRUE SAVAGE II

TRUE SAVAGE **III**

TRUE SAVAGE **IV**

TRUE SAVAGE **V**

TRUE SAVAGE **VI**

DOPE BOY MAGIC I, II

MIDNIGHT CARTEL

By **Chris Green**

A DOPEBOY'S PRAYER
By **Eddie "Wolf" Lee**
THE KING CARTEL **I, II & III**
By **Frank Gresham**
THESE NIGGAS AIN'T LOYAL **I, II & III**
By **Nikki Tee**
GANGSTA SHYT **I II &III**
By **CATO**
THE ULTIMATE BETRAYAL
By **Phoenix**
BOSS'N UP **I , II & III**
By **Royal Nicole**
I LOVE YOU TO DEATH
By Destiny J
I RIDE FOR MY HITTA
I STILL RIDE FOR MY HITTA
By **Misty Holt**
LOVE & CHASIN' PAPER
By **Qay Crockett**
TO DIE IN VAIN
SINS OF A HUSTLA
By **ASAD**
BROOKLYN HUSTLAZ
By **Boogsy Morina**
BROOKLYN ON LOCK I & II
By **Sonovia**
GANGSTA CITY
By **Teddy Duke**
A DRUG KING AND HIS DIAMOND I & II III
A DOPEMAN'S RICHES
HER MAN, MINE'S TOO I, II
CASH MONEY HO'S

By Nicole Goosby
TRAPHOUSE KING **I II & III**
KINGPIN KILLAZ I II III
STREET KINGS I II
PAID IN BLOOD **I II**
CARTEL KILLAZ I II III
By **Hood Rich**
LIPSTICK KILLAH **I, II, III**
CRIME OF PASSION I II & III
By **Mimi**
STEADY MOBBN' **I, II, III**
THE STREETS STAINED MY SOUL
By **Marcellus Allen**
WHO SHOT YA **I, II, III**
SON OF A DOPE FIEND
Renta
GORILLAZ IN THE BAY **I II III IV**
DE'KARI
TRIGGADALE I II
Elijah R. Freeman
GOD BLESS THE TRAPPERS I, II, III
THESE SCANDALOUS STREETS I, II, III
FEAR MY GANGSTA I, II, III
THESE STREETS DON'T LOVE NOBODY I, II
BURY ME A G I, II, III, IV, V
A GANGSTA'S EMPIRE I, II, III, IV
THE DOPEMAN'S BODYGAURD
Tranay Adams
THE STREETS ARE CALLING
Duquie Wilson
MARRIED TO A BOSS… I II III
By Destiny Skai & Chris Green

KINGZ OF THE GAME I II III IV
Playa Ray
SLAUGHTER GANG I II III
RUTHLESS HEART
By Willie Slaughter
THE HEART OF A SAVAGE
By Jibril Williams
FUK SHYT
By Blakk Diamond
DON'T F#CK WITH MY HEART I II
By Linnea
ADDICTED TO THE DRAMA I II III
By Jamila
YAYO I II
A SHOOTER'S AMBITION
By S. Allen
TRAP GOD
By Troublesome
FOREVER GANGSTA
By Adrian Dulan
TOE TAGZ
By Ah'Million
KINGPIN DREAMS
By Paper Boi Rari
CONFESSIONS OF A GANGSTA
By Nicholas Lock
I'M NOTHING WITHOUT HIS LOVE
By Monet Dragun

BOOKS BY LDP'S CEO, CA$H

TRUST IN NO MAN

TRUST IN NO MAN 2

TRUST IN NO MAN 3

BONDED BY BLOOD

SHORTY GOT A THUG

THUGS CRY

THUGS CRY 2

THUGS CRY 3

TRUST NO BITCH

TRUST NO BITCH 2

TRUST NO BITCH 3

TIL MY CASKET DROPS

RESTRAINING ORDER

RESTRAINING ORDER 2

IN LOVE WITH A CONVICT

Coming Soon

BONDED BY BLOOD 2

BOW DOWN TO MY GANGSTA